About the Author

Born in Hong Kong to expats from Liverpool (and something of a nomad ever since), Stephanie is based in London but manages her sanity by escaping to any kind of coast. Before returning to her first love of writing fiction, Stephanie spent many years pursuing alternative forms of storytelling, from stage to screen and media to marketing. Meanwhile, an enduring love affair with words has led her down many a wormhole on the written page.

Drawn to what connects rather than separates, Stephanie is fascinated by the spaces between absolutes and opposites, between science and spirituality, nature and culture. This lifelong curiosity – and occasional conflict – has been channelled into her debut novel, *Bone Lines,* and into short stories, poems and various works in progress. This includes ideas for the continuation of the *Children of Sarah* series, of which *Bone Lines* is the first story.

BONE LINES

BONE LINES

STEPHANIE BRETHERTON

This edition first published in 2018

Unbound

6th Floor Mutual House, 70 Conduit Street, London W1S 2GF

www.unbound.com

ISBN (eBook): 978-1-912618-49-1
ISBN (Paperback): 978-1-912618-48-4

Cover design by Mecob

Printed and bound in Great Britain by Clays Ltd, Elcograf S.p.A.

MIX
Paper from
responsible sources
FSC
FSC® C018072

For Holly, James, William and Juliette

Dear Reader,

The book you are holding came about in a rather different way to most others. It was funded directly by readers through a new website: Unbound.

Unbound is the creation of three writers. We started the company because we believed there had to be a better deal for both writers and readers. On the Unbound website, authors share the ideas for the books they want to write directly with readers. If enough of you support the book by pledging for it in advance, we produce a beautifully bound special subscribers' edition and distribute a regular edition and e-book wherever books are sold, in shops and online.

This new way of publishing is actually a very old idea (Samuel Johnson funded his dictionary this way). We're just using the internet to build each writer a network of patrons. Here, at the back of this book, you'll find the names of all the people who made it happen.

Publishing in this way means readers are no longer just passive consumers of the books they buy, and authors are free to write the books they really want. They get a much fairer return too – half the profits their books generate, rather than a tiny percentage of the cover price.

If you're not yet a subscriber, we hope that you'll want to join our publishing revolution and have your name listed in one of our books in the future. To get you started, here is a £5 discount on your first pledge. Just visit unbound.com, make your pledge and type SARAH18 in the promo code box when you check out.

Thank you for your support,

Dan, Justin and John
Founders, Unbound

Super Patrons

Hilary Alcock
Lucy Allen
Kim Baiden
John Ball
Anton Betaudier
Antonia Blackmore
Gabrielle Bretherton
Linda Bretherton
Wilbert Broeksmit
Alan Brooke
Matthew Byam Shaw
Colin Caffell
Louise Carroll
Melinda Chandler
Sian Coakley
Robert Cox
Tim Crouch
Lucina Cunjamalay
Katherine Dixon
John Dominic
Francesco Dori
Kate Drewitt
James Dryden
Rebecca Evelyn Barnes
Linda Flower
Mercedes Freedman
Kate Gemmell
Andrew Gemmell
Giles Goddard
Eamonn Griffin
Rufus Helm
Gabor Hevesi

Gábor Hevesi
Mimi Hwang
Dominique Jackson
Mike James
Elena Kaufman
Stephen Kinsella
Helene Kreysa
Allison & Sean Krivatch
Damon L. Wakes
Kevin Lane
Ann Karina Lassen
Karin Lilleberg
Jane Lomax
Adrienne Lyster
Mandy Marshall
Anthony McAulay
Juliet McDonald
Craig Melvin
John Mitchinson
Mary Monro
Naomi Moore
Lauren Mulville
David Nicholls
Kwaku Osei-Afrifa
Jan Page
Nasrin Parvaz
Sally Peterson
Juliet Pospielovsky
James Atkinson & Rebecca Pretty
James Raiher
Philip Reeve
Stephanie Ressort
Leslie Rice
Rachel Ritchie
Deborah Roberts
Helen Robertson

Janet Rutter
Dee Schouten
Keri Selig
Lucienne Smith
Simon Stanley
Jane Stewart
John Talbot
Brad Temple
Jay Watson
David Westhead
Julie Wills
Paul Woodgate
Moira Wooley
Timothy Wright

Now and Then

She has grown accustomed to the cold. The first astonishing snows fell on the forest canopy in her sixteenth summer, a few months after the sun had darkened and the dawn had drowned in dust. No one had seen such things. Now, as days and distance she cannot count have passed, the infant moves heavy in her belly and the snow is thick and set. It is days since she has eaten. The penetrating chill she has learned to bear, but the hunger never ceases to hurt.

This ghosted woodland has outlived all use. She must soon attempt the open wastes beyond its borders, but not empty-handed. She moves downwind to the last of her traps, whispering a worthless prayer to the Spirits that have abandoned her. Nothing.

Another stab of regret now for allowing the pregnant gazelle to skip her spear. She had lingered too long, feeling the life between them. Then, at her feet near the tangled trunk, scratch marks. She squats and digs, dragging splinters of stone and root under her cracked and bleeding nails, but it pays. The small creature that buried this hoard would suffer, if it had life enough to return here, but she would walk another day.

*

The odds were incalculable. How many different ways might the remains have been missed? Yet here they lie in a locked and chilled cabinet, waiting for their secrets to be revealed. As Eloise sets out to decode the genetic message they have left behind, she pictures the happy accident of their discovery. She imagines Max, the young Australian scientist climbing the ice cap on Mount Kenya, stopping to gulp the thin air before tumbling into a hidden crevasse.

She feels him falling, senses the shudder at the end of the sturdy rope that saves him, the slow unwinding of its spin, the dizziness followed by the relief. She shares his dawning curiosity, the momentary disbelief, the rising excitement. For as Max kicks out in search of a foothold deep within the crevasse, a small section of the

1

frozen wall crumbles away. What is exposed beneath is ancient and unyielding, but neither rock nor ice.

She wonders, could he have suspected the true value of his find at the time, perhaps through some deep instinct sharpened by adrenalin? Certainly the clever fellow had prevented any further damage at the site and before his companions had hauled him out had marked the position of the skull with a climbing bolt, tied for good measure with his red bandana. But what if Max had not been leading the group that day, or they had taken a different route by only metres, or the glacier had not been weakened by unnatural warmth? What if, in desperation, he had clambered out before he could take a closer look? Serendipity, for Eloise, could be no better described than by the bequest of these bones.

Regardless of the unique conditions that had unearthed them, here they are now at both the end and the beginning of their story and Eloise knows that she is privileged to be a part of it. It has been a struggle to get this far but finally, the elegance of a rare genetic alphabet is unravelling before her in bars and strips and gaps and repetitions. Together they compose the tale of a life, a single long-forgotten life, but it is more lovely to Eloise than Mozart. The breakthrough she has been anticipating for so long, a journey through the past delivering her so keenly into the present, and a gift she hopes will enrich understanding as much as it has her own life.

*

The agonies of labour have begun. She has carved a burrow in the dirt, lies on animal skins, breathes and squats and rolls and stifles her screams. She has seen what happens when the cries and scents of childbirth draw a predator. They are all so few now, hunter or hunted. The mating that created this crisis was tender but temporary and they had parted with little pain. To become attached was pointless – he was probably bone under snow by now. And yet, such a dangerous attachment is coming. She had felt this within weeks of failing to bleed. Whether the infant thrived within or withered, survived or succumbed, the bond has twisted tightly into her soul. She will live for it, die for it. Nothing will be the same.

1

Casting a casual glance in the mirror as she washed her hands and splashed some cool water on her face, Dr Eloise Kluft noticed the new strands of grey in her parting mingling with the blonde. Natural blonde. The Nordic blue eyes that had once, since emerging from childhood, seen pure love looking back into them, were now shot, tired and yellow. How time sneaks past us, she thought, how easily we become stuck in its footsteps, left behind in its rush to be somewhere else.

It was true that the overhead strip lighting of the ladies' room was far from kind. Nevertheless, she was drawn in by her own displeasure. Soon, this self-scrutiny inspired other questions. How did we concern ourselves with ageing, she wondered, or with our own physical identities, before we made mirrors? How did we measure or value such things?

Eloise let the cool water run over the thin skin of her wrists as she maintained her examination of the stranger in reflection. The exercise was partly dispassionate observation, partly to punish herself for not keeping up with her life. There were more frown lines than crow's feet, for sure, but what did that say? The little mole that her mother had loved to compare to an errant musical note was now subsiding into the fold between her nose and mouth. Once, she had been considered a beauty. Yes, she could allow herself that much without vanity. Maybe still, at forty-five, to those who could see beneath this prelude to decay. Ah, but what did any of that matter now?

Eloise knew that the gold and the blue and the translucent skin were recessive phenotypes, and that her eye colour was a weak mutation that was unlikely to survive for many more generations. Much as the way this particular branch of her patriarchal name might go, not surviving beyond her own lifetime. How often had she been forced to explain how her crisp English accent came with this Scandinavian ('No, no, not German') surname? Or indeed, how often had she been required to sound out phonetically the syllables of her first name, 'No, not Ail-oishe... no, not Ee-lice... no, no, don't

3

worry, but it's Ell-o-eeze (please). Yes, yes, like the song.' No wonder those closest to her had resorted to their own shortened variations. Elly, LoLo, Lou… she didn't mind, but always appreciated it when anyone made the effort to get it right.

Her phone began to vibrate in the deep pocket of her lab coat. She didn't bother to pull her wrists from the stream of cool water to check it. If the call was work-related then it would come to her extension from the switchboard. She had no qualms about taking personal calls at the Institute, especially during a coffee break, but these days the most likely greeting when answering her mobile was an automated sales pitch.

A few years ago she might have rushed to scan the screen as a reflex, *just in case*. Looking for those three simple letters, for the identification of her pain, for the faintest possibility of her heart's reprieve, but she tortured herself no more. The single syllable that now seemed to name her every regret had long since been redacted, from all digital memory at least.

How many rings was that now? Someone was keen. She was about to dip a wet hand into her pocket *(just in case)* when her phone gave up any hope of an answer and yielded to voicemail. Wiser and more resolute than its owner, perhaps? Whatever this call was about, it could wait. Eloise dried her hands and gave one last glance to the mirror, if only to double-check that, yes, she really was starting to show her age. *Oh well, never mind*, she thought, *merely another biological process to observe*. Back to work. Back to the comfort and the promise of the petri dish, the pipettes and the centrifuge… and tomorrow (tomorrow!) the delivery of such an opportunity, the beginning of a project that she could hardly believe was coming her way.

As soon as she'd heard the rumours of the discovery, Eloise had abandoned pride, let go her reserve and lobbied, cajoled, pitched and persuaded, determined that she must participate in this venture in some way, whatever the cost. Now both she, and the Institute whose reputation she was gambling with, would have to prove themselves. Could there be anything in this remarkable find that they would be able to read?

4

Eloise took her time to walk back to her laboratory, fantasising about relocating the work to the kind of wondrous new interiors enjoyed by the geneticists at the Natural History Museum. Her equipment was as good as any, her team top-notch (and the new grant was nothing less than a miracle) but despite its tired grandeur, this beloved old building would need to be gutted and refitted in order to compete with the sleek, seamless, light-draped luxury of the museum's facility, even if working there might make one as much of an exhibit as the curiosities next door.

Sometimes Eloise felt that she had come so far in life only to be returned to the design standards of her university days, stuck in a crumbling cloister, its classic innards updated only as recently and appealingly as the 70s or, if lucky perhaps, the 90s. The acres of synthetic finishes, the chipped and peeling laminate, the tone-upon-tone of grey – bar the occasional chromatic relief in sickly shades of salmon-pink or bird-poo green. The single exception was the sparkling new glass-boxed 'clean room' – a centrepiece addition to her laboratory for which Eloise offered daily gratitude to the Foundation – and without which they may have failed to meet the criteria for winning the new project.

The lab was as warm and sticky as she had left it, the archaic air-conditioning struggling to cope with weather that London, as usual, was poorly prepared for. But then, she lamented, weren't we always confounded by our capricious climate? Falling leaves, sudden snowstorms, swelling rivers, all bringing us to a standstill of impotent surprise.

It was amusing to see the Institute's staff in such an informal state of undress. Lab coats abandoned (though not by Eloise, who had standards to set), ties askew, sleeves rolled, sweaty necks mopped with rags of cloakroom towelling, file covers requisitioned as fans. One or two sensible souls had raided their holiday wardrobes and Rory, her young, long-haired lab assistant, was squeezed into a frayed pair of cut-down jeans, his aerated sandals frowned upon but ultimately forgiven by the hygiene (if not the fashion) police.

As she gave her team permission to leave early (maintenance needed more time on the ventilation) Eloise was not relishing the

Tube ride home, proximity to all that other perspiration was the last thing she needed. She decided to avoid the crush of a station change and to walk ahead to the nearest Northern Line stop for a more direct journey home. But then she kept on walking, hoping it would appease the hormonal switchblade that she could sense was straining to snap open.

Simple pleasures, these were always the solution. A cool shower, a classical CD on her prehistoric stereo and an hour outside in the hammock.

Once home and this plan of relaxation accomplished, she discovered that the long, light evening was doing little to lift the unusual heat, even under the refreshing shade of her favourite silver birch. Eloise had grown to love her garden but it was a joy that had come late to her in life. *God and gardening. They say that's all that's left to women of a certain age.* Eloise would be horrified if she ever found god – or, at least, the god of any blind, restrictive conformity. Surely that would be the first indication of dementia and she would know how to take care of that. Write herself a prescription, before she forgot how and when to administer it with final effect. Done and dusted.

Sipping her Sauvignon, relishing its sourness, she wondered how she had come to be so sour herself. It seemed that so much of what the world presented to her lately was cause for complaint (at worst) or a cynical reflex (at best) – even if good manners tended to restrict these to unspoken commentary. Eloise realised this was a corrosive quality that did little to enhance her happiness, or her sociability.

It was not always this way. Or was it? Was the bitter seed planted early, did it come to her with the hair colour and the curiosity and the ability to sprint for gold? No matter. There was always the work, always the vital demands of adding to the greater good. And tomorrow! The arrival of the most distinguished of VIPs, a thrilling new occupant for the clean room who would require the utmost of care. To strains of *The Pearl Fishers* swimming on the summer air, her spirits re-surfaced.

*

This unexpected valley, a dark and narrow rift through the plateau beyond the wastes, holds hidden life within its deepest soils. A handful of roots with nourishment enough. She has moved on again, despite the spasms that cripple her to a crouch every few hours, but the blood and water have stemmed and should leave no trail on the air. Whenever this tiny, miraculous creature swaddled against her chest attempts to cry, she turns her inward to suckle under the deerskin cape, and lightly smothers her, whether she is willing to feed or not. There must be no sound.

She pushes on in search of shelter in the valley, more for a sense of safety than in any expectation of true rest. Sleep is a stranger to her now. Before coming upon this strange slice into the land she had stopped only when she could walk no more. The plateau was too exposed. Had she dreamt all those glinting eyes the night before, watching her through the darkness, shining in the night mists? Why had they not attacked? Perhaps she had answered their staring with silent insistence and the pack had understood her need to live. Left her alone. She has never felt more alone.

The one who had lain with her was heading another way. She remembers how she'd tried to tell him, no, come with me. Why? his eyes had asked. She'd tried to explain, to draw in the snow the tribe she'd seen in a fever, a clan not yet torn apart by madness, still holding to their hearts, to their truth. They are far south and west, somewhere not dying, somewhere still living. But he was born to a tribe unknown to her and they shared few sounds in common. It seemed he had neither the understanding nor the faith to travel with her. How could she be surprised? Even the remainder of her own band had not believed her, this shadow over the earth had hidden too much. Taken too much. Fear had fully consumed them and they had refused to follow.

In the same mistaken way as the child's father, her lost and no doubt short-lived lover, her own kind had not trusted her. Oh, but they should have done, they should have come! The women of her line were legendary wayfinders, knowing how to count the un-shifting shapes of the earth, how to keep certain stars at their backs. How to smell and dig for water, how to find the lichens that had soaked up the morning dew, even in seasons and journeys without rain. Yet not one had believed her vision of a place free from the icy hunger, and the hatred it had brought. Not one had followed.

She is sorry there is no other to see the child's eyes now fully open, no other to watch her face begin to form. But sadness is an extra weight she has no use for.

Ahead, there is some hope of shelter under the arched roots of a twisting tree, once a giant, now a hollow corpse. Perhaps it had been the ancient guardian of this stubborn sliver of life, a place that refuses to follow its passage into memory? An act of defiance that she both recognises, and is thankful for.

Yes, there is a useful enough void within the base of its trunk. It is dank and musty inside, things crawl and wriggle here that may not prove the best company – even if some can be caught and eaten.

She will build a large fire a body's length outside the only opening she can climb through, then make a stone pit beneath another small opening to the sky and bring some smouldering charcoal within. That will work. The thick hide of her cloak will cushion against the knotted roots of the black and rotting earth. Her weapons will lie close to hand. She has made more pleasant shelter than this, but they will be warm here, and if not fully dry within its dampness, then at least not so exposed. She will make the best of it. There are some pungent leaves nearby that can be burned in offering to sweeten the smell of her new den.

Despite the grief that hangs like smoke above this lost and lonely cleft into the earth, despite their solitude, she allows a little hope. Leaving the new shelter a while to venture deeper into the valley she follows a trail of fresh scat to make a shamefully easy kill, and the foraging this way is more fruitful. She will feed long from this good fortune. Sinew from the young buck's carcass will make a strong sling for when the infant grows heavier. Before long she will need to shift the weight to be carried at her back, although the little one has travelled well so far, tucked under the winding strips of hide and fur that protect them both. The child has had no choice.

How often has she been tempted to stop and indulge this mysterious melting of her heart, to give her daughter whatever she wants, whatever she needs? But the long travels of her tribe had taught her all too well that newborns must soon understand the need for stillness and silence. The need to stifle their hunger, if they – if their families – were to survive while on the move or in the open. It was so with any creature at risk from any other; it was so with men and women. Those who were not strong enough were mourned as their mothers walked onward – and forgotten in time. Although, now that she has a child herself, she fails to understand how such a thing was ever possible.

But here, finally, is some safety. Yes, this seems the right place to stop and to rest, to allow the child to suckle more often and for as long as she needs. And, thankfully, she feeds more easily these days. At first she'd questioned how any woman before her had managed the task, or borne the discomfort. Perhaps she should have learned more about such things when she had the chance, but even in other, better times she had enjoyed few close friendships amongst her own sex. Her gifts had set her apart. The destiny that the elders had always impressed upon her had called her away from simple pleasures. How often had she dismissed any idle chatter, scorned any trivial concerns? There was always some deeper wisdom to acquire.

Now she wishes every other woman she has ever known to her side once more. To leave the child in another's care for only a few moments. For even one night. But as rare as it is to see signs of other people in these times, she has no trust for strangers. First tracking them, then hiding and watching until she can understand their ways and sense the condition of their souls. Since that brief, surprising, yet sweet time alone with the girl's father, there have been no others worth revealing her presence to.

She wonders how well the child will continue to fatten if the ache of hunger ever finds them again. How will she keep the little one alive if the milk refuses to flow? She has fought hard against the swallowing fear that every moment of motherhood brings. Had her own mother felt this way, as lucky as she was to rely on the comforts of her clan? There is no other knowledge for her to call upon now but what little she can recall, or what is granted in her deepest thoughts. She is thankful, at least, that the child is a girl. More likely to stay close and listen as she grows. Yes, this little one will be wise, like her mother.

Of that she is sure. In what other ways might the child resemble her? She watches to see.

And what of the father? What had her daughter gained from him? Yes, the eyes. Those shocking flecks of amber. Perhaps a touch of his sun-dusted hair, those burnt tones like a crab shell left in the fire. She had never seen such colouring in the men of her kind before, and he seemed to be like her in most other ways. Maybe she will have the gift of his speed? She hopes so, that would be a benefit. He was fast, faster than any she had ever seen, but he was not clever.

He had come from much closer to the rising sun, from where the dust and the dark and the dying was worse than even she had experienced. He was looking for something, heading north. Fool. There was nothing left there, only ash and ice. His wretched coughing, the flecks of blood in his spit, these could only worsen in the cold. He did not carry enough furs and he would need them there. She had given him one of her own, knowing she could replace it more easily than he. Together, she might have ensured his survival, but alone? He could not live like her.

And yet he was beautiful, oh, breathlessly so. The eyes. It was for those that she had not killed him. He had been easy to track. From the first startling footprint from the east. Fool. Her spear arm raised, she had been ready to strike first. But then... he turned.

2

As the dawn tumbled through her tall windows and nestled beside her in the empty spaces of her bed, Eloise awoke, long before her alarm. Even before the plaintive cries of Newton, the belly-bloated old cat that seemed to love her. Although she knew this was also the kind of 'love' that was spread liberally around the neighbourhood and to anyone who would feed him. Eloise also knew that this was a sad old cliché. Single woman with cat. *Oh well, never mind*, she comforted herself in her habitual fashion. She cared little for what anyone thought of her anymore (the sabotage of self-loathing notwithstanding) and she had, for the most part, made peace with her decisions. But perhaps the time had come to consider getting a dog?

Dogs had been the consistent company of her childhood. Her surrogate sisters and brothers, how could her parents have denied her? Often these had been strays adopted at some foreign archaeological dig, against all advice, against all reason and always with the warning that she (and the poor bewildered hound) would suffer through six months of quarantine to bring it back to England. But Eloise was nothing if not determined when it came to saving things – and it always felt more than worth the trouble in the end. Especially with Won Ton, the mangy but determined little mongrel rescued from a cage at the back of a restaurant in Kuala Lumpur one summer, while on their way home from a sweat-soaked dig in the Bujang Valley.

This love of animals had been painfully tested along the scientific path and some terrible compromises had been made, even if Eloise had always been persuaded of the 'greater good' and, wherever possible, had avoided *that* kind of research. She could not deny, however, that innocence had been lost – and she felt unworthy these days of all that trust. All that unquestioning love.

Even when Newton had come into her life and chosen to stay it had seemed like his decision more than her own. Was she ready for a trip to Battersea, for a tour of the adoption cages and the agony of choosing? Oh Lord, she asked herself, how on earth would Newton cope with a canine interloper? Probably by deserting her for good in favour of less treacherous neighbours. No. No dog, not yet. Better not. Not with the start of this exhilarating new endeavour. Eloise knew she would be unable to offer the kind of dedication that such genuine devotion deserved.

Was it so important to be loved, she wondered? Better to be respected and remembered, surely. To be of service. (If not always agreed with.) Certainly her work as part of the team that had unravelled the human genome had not always been well-received. The full picture had confirmed not only how closely humanity was related but also how recently connected by common ancestry, indicating a global population crash, or series of crashes, in particular between 70,000 and 80,000 years ago. No one cause for this was clear but geological and climatic volatility, or other natural crises, seemed to have reduced humanity to barely viable populations at times. It seemed incredible that *Homo sapiens* had succeeded as a species at all. And yet, it was these kinds of genetic 'bottleneck' and 'drift' events that had influenced both DNA and human destiny so profoundly.

At first, colleagues in China had not been best pleased with some of the revelations from the genome project, local orthodoxy preferring to believe they had evolved entirely separately, from a much older stock of humanity. But most had acknowledged a more recent shared heritage with stoicism, if not complete conviction. For apart from tiny traces of DNA from archaic hominins who'd made earlier explorations, it was clear that all modern humans owed the *majority* of their blueprint to those few *Homo sapiens* in Africa who'd survived such crises, before spreading out once more.

Yet controversy arose with each new piece of the archaeological puzzle. Eloise was given to despair on several occasions as fringe elements found excuses in the latest evidence to interpret or justify some cherished belief. And as for the die-hard racists, how could they ever accept that we all owed so much to a handful of African mothers? That we remained so similar, so brotherly bound and demonstrably equal in potential. The New Age fantasists, although well-intentioned at least, were little better in her estimation, with their hare-brained hallucinations about extra-terrestrial or angelic intervention.

To Eloise, the knowledge of our tightly knit kinship was priceless. Mere fractions of differentiation. She might be growing increasingly grumpy with each diminishing ovum, but she remained a humanitarian at heart. Obviously the fundamentalists, of any faith, were out of the equation before you could say Darwin (or Dawkins) but ultimately, with time and the opening up of minds, she hoped that this molecular siblinghood would bring only good. *Unity in diversity*, the Galapagoan bequest. Perhaps in only another generation or so?

Eloise peeled herself away from the creamy tangles of her bedlinen, keen to prepare for a momentous day. Newton, aware now that something had shifted in the mood of this large and well-loved but little-changing home, followed her around with an insistent curiosity.

*

This was a river, once. It had curved and turned, widened and narrowed, swelled and flowed, as all rivers do. Now the water has fallen and hardened into ice and the banks are cruelly steep, but she must cross here. There is no time to seek out a better place, soon it will be dark. It is too open on the shrivelled and stony land that has led upwards to this unwanted and unnatural cliff. The lower bank on the sheltered inner loop of the other side has deeper sand and still some scrub. It is the better place to rest.

She unwraps the skins from her feet, switches the papoose to her back and tightens it. Edges over. Stops, waits, closes her eyes and concentrates, then thinks her way down, wills her toes into footholds, fingers into sturdy nooks. Slowly.

But these banks are not dry enough, after all, and they betray her. The rock is both sharp and soft at once, cutting into her palm as it crumbles away. In losing both footholds she is suddenly swinging, digging in with the nails of the only hand that still clings to the cliff. Her stomach has already made the fall ahead of her. Her feet will not permit this, however, they have paid too high a price already and will not surrender now. Kicking and scrabbling, they find some kind of grip that gives her a vital pause. A moment, only a moment, but enough time in which to choose a different outcome.

She waits with the slow silence of this second chance and breathes. She can feel the child's heartbeat light and fast against her ribs. She closes her eyes to focus on it. When she opens them a moment later, she notices in quiet amazement that a tiny flower is somehow growing from a cleft in the rock in front of her. Frail, white, fragile, the wishful fruit of some blowing seed that has found a way to flourish where it should not, while all its cousins waste away. Now she knows for sure that they will reach the ground below with safety. She begins to climb again, leaving behind smears of blood from the gash in her palm and giving away one shredded fingernail as a fitting sacrifice.

She needs to jump the last few feet but turns her ankle with it. Hobbling down to the serpent of ice that rests at the bottom of the river bed, she scrapes some of it away to soothe the swelling in her foot, to ease the agony of her torn hands, and to carry some of it onwards in an oiled bladder. But as she shaves away frosted slivers with her flint, leaving drops of her own blood to bloom over the ice, something else appears to be held beneath. She wipes away the scrapings to examine more closely. The backwards spring comes without her choosing as the pain in her ankle is momentarily forgotten. Under the ice she sees a young woman's face. Long frozen but as though still awake, as though still calling out.

She will not look again. She packs tight the ice shavings and limps away.

3

Darius had retrieved the remains. *Darius.* Oh god, she thought, it had to be him, didn't it? But there had been a crucial advantage in this coincidence, a direct line to applying for the project. When he had delivered the bones, personally, triumphantly, to the Institute, they had been polite to each other. The thrill of this discovery had transcended the nonsense for a while. They left the Institute together to drink coffee in one of those characterless clone shops. Awful swill, it made her queasy for little reward, but at least this was easy neutral ground.

Despite the streaks of silver in his goatee and at the temples of his full black hair, Darius looked ridiculously fit for his age. So unfair. While never the archetype of handsome, he'd always been so confident, so controlled in wrapping his mental wrestle-hold over her. When they had been together, Eloise had found herself wondering whether some of his more outrageous opinions about humanity might not, perhaps, be right, before returning to the core of her own, more compassionate philosophy.

Of course he would have aged well, she acknowledged. Darius would bully that bastard *time* into submission.

They talked about the Mount Kenya dig for a while, and all the politics involved, before admitting that they were more to each other than casual colleagues.

'So, are you seeing anyone?'

Was that a hint of hope in his voice? Eloise thought it surely could not be. Darius would never expose a vulnerable flank, and caring about her love life would seem like a weakness to him.

'Why?'

Dammit, she thought. That response should have been much more laid-back, far less defensive.

'Oh, you know, LoLo, I'm only making conversation. Sorry. I'm guessing that means no?'

'Not right now. No.'

(*Oh but I have loved again since you,* she wanted to say. *Loved like never before. Perhaps like never again. Someone you would never have imagined or approved of for me!*)

'Well, you look great. I'm sure it won't be long.'

(*How fucking dare you. Really.*)

'You assume that it's even an issue.'

'We're academics, remember, we assume nothing until investigating. Look, let's start that again.' Darius leaned in, 'You look great, LoLo. I hope you are happy. Truly, I do. And regardless of everything, I know that you are right for this adventure, I would have put every pressure on to make it happen if necessary, no matter what our history.'

'Was pressure needed?'

'No. That's not the point. It seems right, that's all. In every way.'

Eloise relaxed, decided to take off the stab vest. In fact her heart felt surprisingly secure. Darius could still piss her off, oh yes, but it didn't seem to sting so much.

'So how are you? How's… um…'

'Sophie?'

'Yes, sorry.'

This had not been artifice. Eloise had wilfully deleted the woman's name from her memory.

'Not sure. We haven't spoken in months. We split late last year.'

'Oh god. Bloody hell. Sorry?'

'I'm not. Well, of course I am in a way. I hate mess and unpleasantness, as you know. But I don't suppose you're really surprised?'

Darius looked at her, half smiling his familiar cocksure grin, half hiding a new look in his eyes that she did not recognise. Although as ever he appeared more irked than anguished. Inconvenienced. He looked to her now like a small boy who had failed to win at chess and it was the first time he'd seemed anything less than unassailably masculine. He also seemed relieved. Whether that was to be out of the marriage or to have confessed its failure to her, she could not be sure.

'Nothing surprises me anymore, Darius, when it comes to relationships. But I wouldn't wish pain on anyone.'

She meant this, sort of. Eloise was irritated, nevertheless, that Darius could extract so much as pity from her now, whether he was asking for it or not (and she realised that she wanted him to ask her for it.) *He isn't even miserable*, she thought. *He could at least pretend to be miserable.* The divorce from 'that girl' seemed to have dented his pride but not much else. Of course, Eloise had known that it wouldn't last. The man who had told her he would never marry again, who had refused to marry her, had gone off and married that odd, half-cooked (*but breedable?*) creature and had tried to convince himself it was for life. She wanted to say *I told you so* but she would not give him the satisfaction. The schadenfreude was disappointingly dull.

She continued to think carelessly about him (and her) as a creaking Tube carriage rocked its cargo around a tight bend a few minutes before her home stop. The cue to gather up both her belongings and her thoughts. As she emerged from the sickly false light into a bright and lovely evening, the fresh air encouraged more positive deliberations and for the five-minute walk home she concentrated on the real prize of the day. The bones! Female. Partial pelvis, two full femurs, one humerus, half a cracked tibia, a shoulder blade, a semi mandible and an almost perfect upper skull. *Jesus.*

Now, as she approached her front door, she was picturing the scene as her team had laid out each piece like a precious puzzle on the examination table, the stunned, reverential silence as this once-breathing being took fractured form again. Eloise did not want to be depressed, not today. Not with the archaeological find of a lifetime landing in her lap, one that would have sent her beloved father into academic nirvana. How proud, how happy he would have been for her, how intrigued to watch it all unfold. (It also seemed fitting, somehow, that the exchange of a set of skeletal remains represented the high-point of her relationship with Darius.) But when the rush of endorphins subsided, the cobweb of life's ever-present banality caught her out.

As she anticipated the comforts of her light-blessed living room, its Victorian features cherished by a chain of appreciative occupants (her parents included), there it was once more, overpowering everything. The foul stink registered even before she caught sight of it. Recently, appallingly, Newton had become incontinent and had taken to soothing his shame on her priceless Persian rug. She could hardly bear it. In fact she couldn't bear it at all, relented and dissolved under the tears.

Am I the kind of person who would euthanise the afflicted, the needy, when they do not ask for it, ask only to be loved? And who will take care of me, when, if, I ever go the same way?

Despite his delivery (and his personal news) seeing Darius again had not helped. He brought not only the baggage of their own history together but also his connection to her family. The memory of his years as her father's protégé pulled her hopelessly into the past and all its lost promise. With each damp tissue tossed to her ebony coffee table, Eloise could not help but trace a path backwards, to so many memories, names, regrets. To other struggles to meld her life with another's. Or choosing not to try.

Relationship. Her parents had made it seem so deceptively easy. Although quite happy in her own company (and needing too much of it, perhaps), Eloise also enjoyed many treasured friendships. But she understood that her strength was the glue in this network of support, while it had so often been the repellent in her attempts to bond with the male of the species. Apart from one, that is.

The only one she truly regretted losing, however brief and unlikely that interlude had been. The one who had propelled her into the contemporary, to the edge of things, a place both alien and invigorating. One who had been actively drawn to her force of character, even as its application had ripped its way through the possibilities. No. She would not think about that now. Every memory of him, his youthful, loving face, his unrestrained heart, hurt as much as it thrilled. Enough. She would no longer dwell on any of those in her past. Not today. Not now.

She mopped up the last teardrop, erased its trail of endocrine purging (for that was all this was, a much needed chemical rebalancing), threw away the tissues, cleaned up Newton's mess. Eloise knew that she did not have to be alone. It was a conscious choice. One that was necessary for now, or forever if need be. She knew that attraction had never been the problem, many had sensed the passion beneath the presentation.

*

The snow has come again. Not unusual, but this wind. Her lips are burnt, hands raw, fingers deadening. The flakes have become icy thorns that torment her eyes and feel as though they might blind her. She pushes against the softness as it builds around feet she can no longer feel, their worn wrappings sodden and slippery. It is days since they abandoned the depleted valley and now the high, open plain has them at its mercy.

Further. She must go further, make her breath work, keep the stride steady. She knows that if she keeps moving without breaking rhythm it will be easier to keep on moving. She clings to the thought of other long walks in better times. How she would ignore the complaints of her companions on the long trek to the summer camp. No protesting from her as she followed her elder brothers, determined to match their pace and refusing a ride on her father's shoulders. How she longs for those shoulders now.

She slips. Comes down hard on her knees and wrists to protect the baby at her back. It stings, but she worries only that her stumble will awaken the little one – no doubt as hungry now as she is cold, in spite of the fur-lined swaddling of the new papoose. While her daughter feeds faster but less often since their long respite in the valley, her growing weight has begun to wear on her mother so much more.

It's no good, they must stop again, and soon. They must rest before she drops, before her toes are beyond thawing. She needs to nurse while lying on her side so they can each recover, but how, and where? The secretive sun should have been directly overhead by now, but in spite of a world made dirty white, it is dark as the end of day. She pushes on.

Something begins to take shape up ahead, an island of life perhaps, and she moves quickly towards the hope of it. These lonely trees are dead. Once they would have borne berries and nuts, but though barren they are sturdy. The trunks will stand and the branches that she can break with ease have enough sap left in them to bend. She coaxes them into a trellis which she then leans within the lee of the trees, against a pair of close-set spines.

But the task is harder than she hoped and she has never enjoyed such labours, even in less brutal weather. This was always the work of the more willing, the more skilled in such matters. As several of the branches which she'd hoped would be strong enough begin to snap and crack and collapse the trellis, she curses them. Curses her own impatience for not choosing more carefully in the first place. She begins again, until the trellis can withstand its own weight and tension.

Next, she packs some snow over the unrolled hide that she has strapped to the lean-to, its other half hanging loose in front then fixed at the ground with stones. In the morning she will gather up these stones and leave them around the base of one of the trees, as she has done at intervals along the way, whenever finding the right tree. She does this both in thanks and as a signal to any other who might understand and respect the gesture. For many days now she has found no trees sweet or rich enough to tap for their life-giving sap, but even so she honours these elders, these guides.

The task is nearly done. She leaves a small opening uncovered at the top of the shelter, then digs out any snow left within to create a pit for the fire and lays more branches beside it to rest upon. Their dried leaves will offer some comfort. Stripping away a few thin slivers of bark, she adds these to some more of the leaves to act as tinder. The work is slow, her fingers resist her commands, but at last it is complete and she hangs her necklace of shell, feather and ochre at the shelter's entrance in blessing. This will do, so long as the wind lets up, even a little.

Now she pulls from under the front of her deerskin cape the small pouch that hangs around her neck, the charred purse containing a life-giving growth, the powder from a magical fungus that forms on certain trees in the shape of a stag's foot. It takes so long to light but, by the grace of some unknowable spirit, it will hold its smouldering over the course of a day. A spark remains within despite her fears, despite the snow, and it is enough. This secret has kept the many sons and daughters of her tribe alive along so many travels, throughout the turning tides. There is no life without fire. Now under this makeshift shelter, thanks to the spirit of the flame, she can rest a while and revive.

On a good, thin, flat rock she places a few of the dried acorns that have fallen and shrivelled around the trees. She grinds them with a handful of snow then slides the rock beneath the fire stack where the nuts will roast to an edible paste. It occurs to her that sometimes under this kind of tree there grows a flower with a bulb that can be eaten if cooked well enough, and on digging with a stick where some wilted shoots lie she discovers a handful. These flowers will bloom no more, except through the strength they will give her to carry on.

It is a struggle to keep the fire alight, the whip of the wind is everywhere at once and it finds its way under the hide. The smoke refuses to follow a direct path upwards through the opening and she is often forced to breathe it in. The coughing is painful in the deepest part of her lungs, since the first soot that had fallen instead of rain. But at least the stones she has set around the spitting twigs already hold some heat. When they are warm enough, between her efforts to keep the spark alive and to stop the kindling from saturating, she holds the pebbles close to her skin and in her embrace of the infant. Now, at last, she can feed her child at leisure again. How patient the little one has learned to be. Unlike her mother! How fast she has grown over this handful of moons. How well she sleeps now. The hot stones and the suckling of the child bring the kind of comfort she has longed for.

She tries to remember the warmth of another adult body around her, above her, beneath her. The heat of touch and movement. The abandonment to need, the struggle to rise to the sharpest crest of sensation, the desperate dance, like a hand-to-hand duel to arrive at a shocking surrender and a willing kind of death. She cannot bring back that burning. But now, she has something else.

*

Time and space, once the furore had subsided and the circus surrounding the delivery of the bones had left. Alone in the clean room, Eloise observed the evidence. Female X was about five and a half feet, judging from the length of the femur. Tall for her time? *Homo sapiens* rather than any other ancient hominin, as verified by the ventral ridge on the scapula, the triangular diaphysis of the femur, the canine teeth and the shape of the skull.

Precise age undetermined, but a young adult. There was a historical hairline fracture in one femur. Perhaps she limped or perhaps she had overcome it, but there were suggestions of sustained physical activity. Signs of periodic starvation but otherwise she had been in apparently good health. The dorsal pitting of the pelvis showed an indication of possible childbirth. Cause of death unclear – probably exposure.

Isotope analysis to establish diet was due, although waiting on a backlog at the specialist lab, but the radio carbon dating had come back in good time. Between seventy and eighty thousand years, probably closer to the middle of that period (*before or after Toba?*) and possibly during the onset of a minor glaciation event. Middle Palaeolithic. *My god*, thought Eloise, in a habitual resort to 'divine' wonder despite her agnosticism, although today she was immune to its irony.

Perhaps the reference was appropriate after all. The discovery on Mount Kenya had been what many might consider miraculous, this invaluable relic uncovered in the depths of a crevasse at the beginning of a shrinking glacier. An unintended exploration, but the climber had not been badly hurt, even if his adventure holiday had been cut short. Before being hauled out by his team the crampons on his boots had uncovered the corona of an apparently humanoid skull. A few inches to the right or left and the bones might have remained buried for another generation or more. *Good man*, thought Eloise. *Good man*.

And so now it began. Could there be any suitable cells from which to extract a viable amplified sequence? How had these bones survived the cycles of retreat and advance within the ice caps – of periods when there may have been little or no ice at all? Had any mummified soft tissue become separated and ground away at the base of the glacier? Or been slowly scavenged, the other missing bones carried off in the jaws of one or a series of animals? Had she died above or below the crevasse, fallen or been buried there deliberately? So many questions.

The scattered remains were in remarkable condition, albeit scratched, worn and pitted post mortem. Despite the rapid melt at the discovery site the decay seemed minimal.

Eloise took a long look at the skull. The morphology was not quite as she'd expected for the African Rift Valley at that time and, oddly, she felt a recognition scratching around in the recesses of her memory but she couldn't reach it. Then it materialised. Qafzeh! This skull, though smaller, female and from about 10 or 20,000 years later, had arresting similarities to the 90,000-year-old *Homo sapiens* male found in what is now Israel. Her father had kept a replica of the Qafzeh skull in his study, and as a curious young child she had been in that very cave.

Slight brow ridge (though a higher, more vertical forehead than Qafzeh), high cheekbones, distinctive jaw and a defined chin. There were several possibilities for the resemblance. But was it conceivable, could X perhaps share a direct, if ancient, ancestry with those brave pioneers out of Africa who had walked across a briefly flowering Sahara and then crossed a low-level Nile delta into the Sinai about 120,000 years ago? Or perhaps they had waded through the shallow channel across from the Horn around that time and migrated upwards to the Levant – and onwards from there?

Any connection between those older travellers to the Sinai and the much younger remains now in her lab, was a tempting conceit, even if that particular wave of migration appeared unsuccessful in leaving lasting populations, and Female X had been found in east Africa. Nevertheless, Eloise remained tantalised by a notion of her father's, often derided by his contemporaries in archaeology, that the Qafzeh and other early *Homo sapiens* populations who had ventured beyond the African cradle (well before the *direct* ancestors of today's human diaspora) had not completely disappeared but may have left some living signature behind.

These were considerations for another time. There was another more crucial conundrum. Being clearly Anatomically Modern Human, Female X would surely be of the direct lineage of mitochondrial Eve, another hundred thousand years earlier than the Qafzeh people, but was she part of a branch that died out later in a genetic bottleneck, at a time when human numbers had plummeted – or might she have played some part in seeding any of today's populations, African or non-African?

So, who are you, Miss X? And what the hell were you doing way up there on that mountain?

4

The snow has stopped and the wind is weakening. The half-lit horizon offers several choices – from the flat, easy but waterless ground to her east to the suggestion of an old river bed to the west – but it is the hillier terrain ahead that is drawing her. More draining on her dwindling reserves, but with the promise of greater protection and resources if it yields what she hopes it will. She is directly downwind now and catches the pungent hints of life... life that has also enriched the dirt with its death. Better to smell death, than nothing at all?

She is further south than any of her band imagined could be gained with safety but she can see that this territory once offered great bounty. Its uplands must have caught what sunlight had fallen here for much of the day (she tries to remember the warmth of the sun on her face, the richness of the colours it bestowed) but the ravines here would have offered plentiful shade too, when needed. Water would have trickled through in streams, perhaps even dripping from the stonier cliffs, once. Maybe still? This is a chance she must take, although she knows that such opportunity might also mean competition.

She is right to have chosen this way. The loose stones grow into boulders and then into craggy canyon walls and soon open up to pathways between them. There is fresh growth within this sheltering ground and water that runs free of ice. She drinks with joy, the liquid so sweet from its passage through the stone. She senses that other kinds of life may be hiding here but she sees no tracks yet, the snowfall is too fresh. This is a good place to set multiple traps and wait. She takes note of all the best positions for a snare before choosing a winding walkway to explore.

And then she knows that they are not alone.

Her pace quickens with her pulse. Every sense springs to readiness, blade-sharp and alert. Skin prickles over muscles that are tight yet ready for action. She listens beyond the breeze, smells the dusty heartbeat of the earth. This is the feeling of the chase. Except this time, they are the prey.

She has heard it, felt it, knows it is circling them… following.

How big? Too big to fight. Too powerful to outrun. Is there anywhere safe to climb? But then she will have to outwait it and she can't. It is a battle of patience she may not win. She knows she must outsmart it.

*

Impasse. Eloise struggled to hold back her frustration, it was never useful to the method. The teeth had been a dead end, no useable preserved dentine. The skeletal yield was little better, and worse, it seemed the first batch of bone powder had been contaminated beyond the expected presence of microbial DNA.

Despite careful cleaning of the samples with enzymes, tests had revealed the presence of human Y chromosome fragments. As X was undoubtedly female these should not have been there, unless at some stage during the process present-day male DNA had come into contact with the remains.

Eloise could not believe this had happened at her lab, but there was no point in seeking or apportioning blame, these were the risks inherent with handling ancient bones. She did wonder for a chilling moment, however, whether anyone unauthorised could have come into contact with Female X? All staff, from management to services, were fully vetted and trained, access to the clean room was highly restricted, but there was a new senior caretaker being eased in to take over from a retiring predecessor. Could any errors have been made? Could curiosity have got the better of anyone else in the building? No, surely not. Whatever the source of the contamination, the result remained. They would have to start again.

Back at her desk, she logged on and entered her password (a varying recombination of family birthdates with those same four, protean letters: GTCA) and then opened an ominously brief message from Eugene Vanterpool calling her into a meeting. Eloise felt a spasm in her solar plexus. A summons from the Director rarely boded well. The long walk to the west wing of the building did little to help her mood. When she reached the restored oak door of the 'bank vault' (as the Director's office was unlovingly known) it was an inch open. She knocked once and walked in with as much confidence as she could muster.

'Dr Kluft! Thank you for your time. Please, come in, sit down, Eloise. The Java's still hot. A sweet tooth as I recall? How many sugars again?'

'Three. Thank you, Eugene.'

To take up this invitation, Eloise had to move his crocodile attaché case from the armchair he kept for visitors, but struggled to find space for it on his antique desk – despite its imposing dimensions. Eugene may or may not have been aware of this necessity as he turned away from her and towards his fully equipped little galley.

'This is good stuff, you know!' he announced from over his shoulder, 'I brought it back from the islands myself.'

As Eugene busied himself with beverage-making, she realised how much she'd enjoyed the three weeks without scrutiny while her boss had holidayed in his native Caribbean. He appeared well-nourished from it, his white shirt straining slightly at his expensive belt, the salt and pepper in his close-shorn curls a touch more luminous, a glow to his deep-brown skin. Eloise hoped his patience and understanding had been equally recharged.

'How was your trip?' she asked, not really wanting to know.

'Wonderful, wonderful, thank you. The materfamilias is still going strong. Ninety-two, can you believe it? Still chasing the birds from her mango trees. It makes me hopeful for my own hard-earned retirement!'

His familiar baritone had a light and unfamiliar lilt. A little forced perhaps? *Oh dear,* thought Eloise, *if he is this jovial, it must be bad news.*

'So. How are things, Eloise?'

He knows how things are, she thought, she had updated him on their progress (or lack of it) by email only yesterday. She resented having to tell him again. Out loud.

'Well, no change from the last report, but we're still very positive…'

'No, no, with you, my dear, with you. What's happening in your life?' he asked with what appeared to be genuine interest.

Eloise tried very hard not to squirm. Did he really want to know about her personal life, and if so why? Could he be concerned that she was not 100 per cent committed and focused?

'Nothing but this really... Eugene, what's this all about?'

'Well, my dear Dr Kluft. I have just come back from the High Commission. The Kenyans are keen to hear of progress, as you can imagine. They need to know that they have made the right decision for their girl.'

Confusingly to Eloise, Eugene was still smiling.

'And you, of course, assured them that they have?' she asked, smiling too, through the rictus of anxiety.

'Well, of course, of course. I know how much effort you poured into that pitch, Eloise, both on paper and through your various contacts. And we are all in awe of your enthusiasm. Indeed, I didn't mind too much when you went over my head, because, after all, this will be a feather in all of our caps. So long as we can pull it off. However, it seems that we now have another player on the field.'

The knot in her stomach tightened.

'Another player? Who, Germany? Look, I know they would have been the obvious first choice...'

'No, no, my dear. The Americans. A laboratory in the US claims to have developed a new sequencing technique. They are lobbying for a handover...'

No! Eloise wasn't sure whether she had shouted this out loud or not, but Eugene carried on regardless.

'... Furthermore, the Foundation is becoming, well, shall we say, a little concerned. Perhaps if the Americans can push forward faster or can offer more, we may have to hand her over? Though your grant may be portable, Eloise, and we may be able to second you to the project somehow as well? But, yes, there would be a risk to the grant's renewal. I mean, you know very well how our funding has been squeezed, how much competition there is between all of our projects. First, since the financial crisis and now with this EU disaster.'

Fucking bankers. Bloody bumbling politicians and lying bastard, tax-dodging media barons, Eloise cursed silently, thinking briefly yet fondly of the fearless soul who had taught her to profane without remorse (and how, for reasons she was yet to fathom, she had begun to miss him more than ever, even if he might have become that real-life distraction for Eugene to fret about). But this threat to control over her 'baby' was a potential disaster. And she would need that grant renewal, was counting on it if she was going to publish.

If there *was* a hell, Eloise decided, then its depths must be populated by whoever pulled the purse strings against enlightenment. (Even if the same inferno scorched the feet of those forced to make Faustian pacts in order to do the work.) Eloise was tempted to swear again, outwardly, but then managed a more measured voice than she'd anticipated.

'No. No, we cannot give her up lightly, Eugene. We cannot even consider it!'

X belonged to Eloise now and she had grown close, was beginning to *know* her. A rendered 3D print of the skull was in the Netherlands for facial reconstruction, along with scans and measurements of the skeletal remains. Soon, soon, she would meet her quarry face-to-face. Female X was destined to add her own chapter to the unfolding revelation that would change things forever, and Eloise would publish it. She could not risk losing her.

'I will fight it every step of the way, Eugene. And you know how stubborn I can be! Look, if it comes to that we'll raise the money from somewhere else if we have to. We could crowdfund it?'

'Now, now, calm down, Dr Kluft, calm down. I don't want to see this happen any more than you. There have been no decisions as yet, only discussions. I merely thought that you should be, let's say, *aware*. And if the worst comes to the worst, well, I suppose you can go back to your clinical epigenetic work that much sooner. There is, at least, some economic potential in that.'

Eugene was somehow still smiling. Eloise, meanwhile, was arming for a fight.

'Yes, but you know that Female X could potentially inform that project too! Who knows what we might learn... and then share! The Americans will try to take over, try to patent anything they can develop, you know that. We can't give her up, Eugene!'

'Sarah.'

This inexplicable statement from Eugene threw a sudden bafflement into the fray.

'I beg your pardon?' asked Eloise, her eyebrows unsure of whether to rise or furrow.

'Something else you should know,' he said with impossible satisfaction, 'they have decided on a name. Sarah. After Barack Obama's Kenyan grandmother. Catchy, isn't it? And very 'apt' in the light of how much he is missed, don't you agree? A little more media-friendly, too, I imagine.'

Dear god, she thought. Now the bones were part of some political name-checking game, as well as a financial tussle. She had rather liked 'Female X', preferred its wide-open vistas, its lack of imposition or presumption. No matter, she thought. The moniker was a minor issue, she had bigger battles to fight.

The alternative reality of losing the bones, losing the project (and all the fresh inspiration it had brought into an otherwise sterile phase of her life) haunted every step of her walk home, and it had been necessary to power away the cortisol that was coursing through her system rather than suffer the Tube. Finally, somewhere between the pierced, dyed and tattooed throngs of Camden and the gradual gentrification of Kentish Town, Eloise had formed an idea. Darius!

He must surely be on her side, as he had been (somewhat to her surprise) since the first tentative email she'd sent him about the rumoured discovery. Darius could pull some serious strings if he had to, and Eloise had no qualms about calling in every marker that she could.

*

Long before sighting the creature she realises its name, its nature, recognising the rare essence that had entered her soul so many seasons ago, during her first vision quest under the guidance of her grandmother. At the time she had expected (wished for?) a wolf, or an owl, but it was the bear that came to her then... as it comes to her now.

And suddenly, she knows what she must do. She finds a good place, a cleft in the rock face of a small escarpment through a narrow canyon, about three men's height above the ground. No wind. Laying the infant on the ground, exposed, she climbs up and leaves it to cry. The stench of the beast reaches her first, announcing its steady approach. Heavy, hungry.

She waits. Her spear is sharp enough, but is it strong enough for what it must do? Is she? She has placed a few large stones around the bait (oh, please, please, no) in case the weapon and her falling weight cannot finish it, or her aim cannot find that crucial spot between two ribs right next to the spine. But the spear is part of her once more, she guides her intention through to its very tip and feels where it must go. She waits.

5

An interminable delay while negotiations were settled, this unseemly wrangling over the remains. Their transatlantic rivals were offering to build a new museum in Nairobi as her ultimate resting place. Eloise could visualise 'Sarah' (it was growing on her) checking in for her flight. Not fair. Limbo. She had tried to concentrate on other projects (on the gift of some pancreatic cells waiting to have their genetic information extracted and then experimentally corrected, too late unfortunately to save the donor) but she was tethered to this African adventure now and determined to see it through. She found herself present at her desk and yet absent from its demands.

Eloise wanted to hate the poachers, but academic jealousy was never attractive. She might not be justified in resenting their enthusiasm, or their new technology, but certainly she could resent their funding. Where was it coming from? Surely not government, the myopia on both sides of the ocean when it came to investing in science that might enrich the public sector as much as the private was unforgivable to Eloise. Philanthropy was a possible source for the rival backing, and if so this was almost forgivable, even if it had originated in some historically ill-gotten gains. The death-bed bequest of a guilt-ridden dynamite baron perhaps?

Most probably the capital was corporate. Yes, thought Eloise, owning the future by buying up the past and the present. Reprehensible in so many ways, but very smart. The whole morass was exhausting but she needed to stay sharp. Needed to be reminded of the imperative that she resist such professional larceny.

She suited up, went into the clean room and eased open the cabinet containing the bones. Each one was tagged and laid alongside the other, unnaturally, in neat little lines. Her skull in the middle. What kind of a brain had been held within this cradle? What did it contemplate, what were its confusions, its struggles?

'What did *you* have to fight for, my friend,' she asked aloud. 'Did you argue? Did you talk very much at all – and were you listened to?

What did you inherit, what did you change, what did you pass on? And was life really so much simpler for you – or harder than I, for all my contemporary complaints, can ever imagine? Would you care one jot about who gets to keep what's left of you, or what they might discover, or what they might do with that? I wonder whether you would be as pissed off as I am about this undignified tug of war. Or are you furious about being here at all? Do you long for the mountain again, for home… indeed, where or what (or who) was home to you?'

'Sarah. Do you mind the name?'

And how crazy am I to be asking any of this. Is it a fault as a scientist or as a human, or is it a tendency of my particular neurological loading… to want to know the hidden stories, to envision beyond the obvious? But you are so much more than a pile of discarded minerals to me, or some mindless residue for investigation, whatever your name. So much more than a potential profit margin, or a PR windfall, or a tourist attraction. This grail of DNA that we are all chasing once informed a complete human being, a vital and unique individual. And I suspect that you were a battler, my girl, weren't you? Up there, all alone on that mountain. A singular soul, I'm sure of it. I can't help feeling that you deserve whatever destiny you were trying to fulfil, and I for one will be going into battle on your behalf.

Eloise began to close the cabinet drawer, but then stopped. Something didn't look right with the bones. She checked all the tags, then felt a spike of nausea. Two of the smallest fragments were out of order, swapped around. *Oh hell.* A mistake, nothing more, surely? Someone not concentrating. But the kind of mistake that they could not afford. She took a much needed pause for breath and with a gloved hand, moved each bone delicately back into place.

*

The fall is too long. She has mistimed the jump. Misjudged the distance. She will miss the animal's back. It will reach the child before she can recover from whatever damage the hard ground will break upon her body. Worse, the fall will finish her.

No. She must change this. Re-imagine it. She must move the world again until the distance is right. She closes her eyes once more. She has practised this deadly task so many times in the blackness behind her eyes. But there is no time left to perfect it. She must remember the most successful unfolding of this story, and pull it into the light.

Because now, here it comes, in heaving, breathing flesh, no longer imagined.

So much bigger than she had foreseen, rippling with power in every pulse, its hide so thick she wonders how any weapon will pierce it. And yet what it boasts in brute strength it seems to lack in awareness. It treads forward with no sense of what waits for it in absolute stillness, above. Thankfully the child has ceased its whimpering, its cries would only rip at her resolve and shatter her focus. She would struggle to bury her baby's fear beneath her own determination. Yes. She realises it is her daughter now who inspires and directs her courage and she begins to understand from whose destiny she must draw her victory.

Without thought, without doubt, she leaps.

The sound it makes. She has never heard the howl of death this way before, so that it rings within her own bones. Is this death? No, not yet.

The bear still breathes and she must stir herself from the shock of impact and act. She must rise to her knees on its vast, blood-darkened back and force the spear in further. The beast rises too and roars its fury but she holds on hard. She must hold on.

It shakes, it shudders. Its cries are scarlet streams from an agonised mouth, blooding the infant with the mark of her first kill. A kill made in her name, at least. This slaughter must be played out for the child alone and by borrowing from her unblemished spirit, otherwise her mother will have torn away her own totem.

It must be so, or the cavern of darkness that opens up behind her suddenly misted eyes will draw her in completely. Its embrace is too inviting. But while her own passage through this place might be a welcome release, she knows that she cannot go through if the child is to survive. She knows that even if by any unimaginable, unacceptable outcome *this* beloved child does not live that *she* must live to try again. That she *must* withstand that anguish and keep going. Now the mist settles and she can see herself within the cavern, bathed in light, holding out a handful of seeds and then blowing them to the wind.

The vision's meaning becomes clear. She must gather strength from all this scattered future life and bring it back into her own body if she is to complete the kill.

Is it a kill yet? No. Not yet. The animal too has a spirit that will not acquiesce, not without understanding that its sacrifice is essential. Or that its opponent is worthy. She holds on, waving her hips, kicking her legs, using the weight of every life yet to come to ensure that the animal's heart cannot survive, knowing that her own can never be the same. Knowing that what she kills is any hope of loving through the body again. It is the price she must pay for retaining her soul. For saving this child. It is the cost of holding on to a heart that still beats.

6

In the unexpected encounter between a camera case and a shin bone, the shin will come off considerably worse. Eloise had confirmed this fact the sharp-cornered way, and rubbing in the arnica that was a permanent fixture of her handbag was having little effect. Neither had she been able to swear away the pain, having no desire to draw further attention to her stumble.

'Are you alright, Dr Kluft? We'll be shooting your sequence very soon. Thanks so much for your patience. Can I get you a coffee, or a doughnut? Or some water?'

The chirpy young production runner was determined to be useful. Eloise wondered who he was related to, quite sure that nepotism was the way such entry-level breaks into film and TV were attained.

'Yes, yes, I'm fine thanks, no problem. All good.'

The film team documenting 'The Story of Sarah' had commandeered the lab, stopping all useful work, and Eloise felt like a spare part as she waited to be interviewed. She wondered if she should rethink her appearance. *Reading glasses or no?* Some had thought they suited her. One scandalous yet irresistible young lover in particular. ('No, stop, keep 'em on, babe' – he asks as he lifts her on to her kitchen island – 'I like it.') That tiny clutching in her lower abdomen, she smiled with it, tried to hold on to the memory, but then it was gone.

She kept the glasses on, enjoying the new aura of inscrutability those sensations had delivered, and she allowed herself a subtle dusting of make-up, a slash of mascara. No need for strict compliance with the boffin stereotype, after all, a little lip gloss was surely not 'unscientific'?

Eloise had been glad that she'd made the effort when, immediately after, she was introduced to 'The Climber' – the young Australian mountaineer who had found Sarah's skull and who had been invited to the lab today to record his side of the story. Max Michaelson. Eloise had heard his name before, of course, but today she thought it had a suitably heroic ring to it. Indeed, she'd had to resist a sudden urge to throw her arms around him, and not only out of gratitude. Max was strong and mission-fit, of course, but otherwise not quite as she'd imagined him. Arrestingly tall, he was attractive in a rough, surf-dude kind of way with shoulder-length hair that had been sand-blasted into fair, spiral curls but he also had an unexpected authority that was both calming and compelling.

'Hey, Dr Kluft, how ya going?' He shook her hand as if they were about to do business, as if he were bidding for a contract.

'G'day,' she said in return, feeling a complete fool, although he seemed entirely good-natured about her patronising attempt to bond.

'I really don't know how to thank you enough, really,' Eloise continued, trying to salvage something from this first impression, 'I don't think there's ever been a more fortuitous accident, from my perspective anyway.'

'Well, I'd have to agree with you there, Doc! And just as well it was someone with a clue, eh, and not some drongo with an Indiana Jones complex?'

At first the Aussie accent had put her off, reached into the place where she had buried her prejudices and confirmed him as a 'type'. And Max Michaelson was not lacking in bravado, but there was much more to him than this. Eloise knew that he was a fellow of the scientific fraternity but now learned that his specialism was astrophysics at the University of Manchester and that a doctorate was on the way. One of the glamour boys.

Eloise found herself tempted to flirt, to search into eyes that were as blue as her own, and felt that perhaps the Sarah connection between them warranted some exploration, but then she pulled back. Too bloody young. She couldn't go 'there' again, regardless of all the insistent recollections that had been bothering her recently, the rebirth of an ancient longing. Or could she? Should she try to find him again after all this time, the source of all this recurring turbulence? No. Ridiculous. That escapade, as delicious as it was, had ended for all the right reasons. She was fine on her own, she was making the most of her space and freedom, of the ability to focus and to pursue the goals that really mattered. Even if the world beyond tended to regard the deliberately single woman with suspicion, or worse, *sympathy*.

She made a closer examination of Max in order to reinforce her professional equanimity, and yes, there it was, right there on his left hand – a wedding ring. *Good*, she thought. *Good for him.*

Nevertheless, Eloise had sensed some manner of *connection* between them, something that reached beyond this young man's obvious appeal, beyond even their slight degrees of separation in the form of Sarah. And there was more about Max that fascinated her. Despite the aquamarine eyes and the sun-singed curls, Eloise was unclear about his ethnicity. Something about his features suggested a recent ancestry that drew from a gene pool not exclusively Caucasian.

Eloise decided to hover and watch his interview on a monitor. *My god*, she thought, *he's a natural.* The lens was a long-lost lover, found again. He neither stuttered nor stumbled nor blushed, but maintained a beguiling stillness and a vocal flow that made everything he said seem at once very clever *and* readily comprehensible. Not everyone was so charmed. She saw one member of the film crew curl his lip, and a couple of her colleagues appeared most put out by this telegenic intruder. *If the doctorate doesn't work out for him*, she thought, *Max could easily carve out a more financially rewarding career.* He had the scent of stardom about him, for sure.

Max was not the only distraction. Darius was also there, to regale the crowd with his charisma. Eloise had smiled, unable to resist shooting an arched glance in his direction when Max had made the Indiana Jones remark. But otherwise she felt strangely unaffected by his presence, despite the unusual warmth of his greeting to her or the enthusiastic pressure of his kiss to each cheek… and how often she caught him smiling in her direction.

She was deeply grateful to Darius, nonetheless. Not only for urging the documentary crew to her domain so much sooner than planned, after they'd finished filming him at the dig on Mount Kenya, but also for the VIP guest that he had brought with him. The presence of the Kenyan Director of Antiquities was indeed having an effect upon her, raising the stakes to the point of making her a nervous wreck. Eloise knew that she must summon every inherited drop of her mother's legendary charm and channel it into action. But then Darius walked over, almost as if pushed by her parents' invisible hands, to give her shoulder an encouraging squeeze before she was gathered up and ushered into position by the keen young runner.

'OK, Dr Kluft, comfortable?' the director, a wiry, short-haired woman called Marcy asked rhetorically, her time-is-money manner doing little to calm her subject's nerves.

'Yes, thanks,' said Eloise, although she didn't feel comfortable at all. The lighting guy was still fussing around her, waving his hand-held meter in her face to measure its reflectivity.

'OK, so, why don't we start by going through some of the basics: what you're looking for, what you might expect to find, some of the challenges,' instructed Marcy, 'in fact, start right from the beginning, explain what genes actually mean, why the mitochondrial DNA is so important, for the uninitiated. Try to translate for the layman. Don't worry because we can edit down or go over something again in a tighter way if necessary. Just start explaining and we'll go from there.'

Oh hell, thought Eloise. *Please don't let me make a fool of myself.* Then she told herself to get a grip and do whatever it took to keep Sarah with them, keep her connected, let them know what she meant to the team.

Oh, but what do I say, she agonised, *and how many tired old terms should I trot out? Can I bear to say 'building blocks'?*

Eloise heard the director declare that they were rolling – and then remembered nothing of her interview until a few days later, when she was emailed a download link to a rough cut of her section. She didn't know what to do with the uneasy sensation in her stomach as she watched herself, but felt some relief that it was nowhere near as bad as she'd imagined. At least this particular sequence they had edited together didn't linger long over her obvious discomfort, but regularly cut away to a variety of infographics and more general footage.

During a brief, fast-motion clip of cellular division, Eloise heard herself pronounce in commentary (and in a far higher voice than she recognised as her own): 'Our genes, which are found in the nuclei of almost every living cell of our bodies, write the blueprint for our lives in so many indelible ways – and not only in terms of obvious factors such as build, colouring, or abilities etc., but they may also have an effect on our disposition, our vulnerability to certain diseases and many other characteristics that we're still learning about.'

At this point the film switched from microscopic images to a montage of the many peoples of the world, of busy streets, athletes in action, concert pianists.

'Although of course nurture and how our genes interact with our environment – in effect how we 'use' our genetic material – also plays a vital role. Genes are passed down to us in pairs, one half from each parent, and they can be recessive or dominant depending on how each strand of DNA recombines.'

Now they'd spliced in an animated clip of the helix unrolling before switching to an excruciating close-up.

'There are four key amino acids that allow us to read DNA, labelled for short as A, C, G & T. Wait. Stop, no, can I rephrase that, or rather re-arrange it, that combination sounds too much like an aperitif! Come to think of it, I could use one of those right now…'

To her horror they had left in that little gaffe, along with her visible blushes. Eloise made sure to note the time code on the screen in preparation for the email that would beg them to take that out and go straight to the corrected version. The editor might have been amused by her poor attempt at a joke and considered it worth keeping – but, no, no, this was far too embarrassing for broadcast. She hit play again.

'… There are four key chemicals, which are the markers that help us to map out DNA. These are labelled for short as GTCA. Each strand, which is in the form of a double coil, is packaged into chromosomes, of which we each have 23 pairs. The Y chromosome exists only in males and the X chromosome is found in both men and women. But there are two types of DNA: nucleic – and this is where the most variation occurs – and mitochondrial DNA, which is found in the tiny power sources or 'batteries' within our cells. This changes very slowly over the generations and comes to us from the egg, so is inherited only through the maternal line…'

Mercifully, here they had cut away to some magnified film of a fertilised egg dividing and becoming an embryo.

'… It's through this mitochondrial DNA that we can track matrilineal ancestry and which has told us that, theoretically, all humans now alive on earth today are descended from one particular *Homo sapiens* female – a kind of biological Eve, if you like – who lived in Africa nearly 200,000 years ago. Though it's important *not* to think of her as either the sole or the first human female, but rather our *most recent common ancestor*, the one who had a continual line of surviving female descendants.'

After returning to a close-up, but one in which, thankfully, she didn't have the appearance of a cat observing a ghost, they faded to stock footage of a range of indigenous peoples.

'As humans we share about 99.5 per cent of our genetic material in common and we are all so much more closely related than previously appreciated. The apparent racial distinctions that have divided us for so long are no more than minor, mutable adaptations to environment or climate, to diet or exposure to pathogens. Or some tiny percentage of DNA acquired from other ancient hominins outside of Africa, and these are related mostly to hair and eye colour, or to health and resistance, or sun exposure and circadian rhythms. Not so different really to one sister having red hair, burning easily and being a night owl, and another being a brunette who tans better and goes to bed early, or, say, one being a better swimmer and the other good at ballet.

'The rest is cultural, or the result of how race is experienced in a world so sadly inclined to bigotry and 'othering'. The fact is we even share certain universal genes from primordial organisms with every living thing on the planet. In studying Sarah's genetic makeup, once we have unravelled a complete sequence – and we're confident that we'll soon find some cells that have survived the millennia of her icy grave – this could not only tell us about Sarah's branch of pre-historical humanity but also about ourselves today. This is such a significant find because a great swathe of the descendants of mitochondrial Eve, and other pre-historic cousins, died out in a series of natural catastrophes. This reduction may have been caused by changing climate or other environmental and geophysical stresses, but also through competition for resources.'

For this section, Eloise was relieved to be featured only as voiceover above an impressive montage of volcanoes, firestorms, drought, wind-blasted ice sheets. The full apocalyptic playlist.

'We hope to establish whether or not Sarah is, in fact, related to any of our contemporary lineages and how much she might have in common, or otherwise, with people living today. And we may gain crucial insights into certain diseases and into human characteristics and adaptations that are relevant to our current struggles...'

The screen then defaulted to its over-familiarity with a face that, yes, she acknowledged, had needed so much *more* make-up after all – not the false insouciance of less. It seemed the team had been unable to use the longer shots they had filmed of her at first, perhaps because those fidgeting hands they'd mentioned were too much of a distraction. But now Eloise was becoming inured to the magnification of her faults and not flinching so much at the stark reality of her middle-aged self. It seemed that her cursory glances at passing mirrors, especially without her glasses on, had been blessedly deceiving up until now. *Oh well, never mind.* At least the ageing process was also dressing her with a distinguished air, which surely could not hurt in a professional arena where young female scientists were often 'invisible' – even when fully present.

'There's no way of knowing whether Sarah had any surviving offspring or whether she herself is one of our direct ancestors. But the fact that she was found in the African tropical refugia, a safe climatic haven between certain latitudes which was home to several successful *Homo sapiens* groups, makes this is an intriguing possibility. It's feasible that she – or her family group – were a source for our forebears and that the children of Sarah, so to speak, could still be walking among us today...'

They wrapped up her interview with more 'busy streets' footage, followed by an onscreen note explaining that this would fade into the reconstruction of Sarah once it was complete. Eloise clicked stop, closed her laptop and went to find that bottle of Sancerre she'd been saving, which soon proved to have been a good decision.

When she turned on her TV in time for the recapped headlines at the end of the early evening news, she was confronted with the very same footage that she'd previously endured. She caught a moment of a smiling Max before they cut to 'Dr Louise Cruft' (as the caption had renamed her) wondering whether 'The Children of Sarah' might still be walking among us today.

Oh, bloody hell. That first swallow of wine had never been so welcome. No one had warned her they might leak anything to the press so soon. Although she should not have been surprised. When Darius had promised to do all that he could, of course that would mean pulling in his heavyweight PR contacts too. Within a minute of the closing credits her landline had started to ring and her mobile was quivering with incoming alerts.

*

The bear skin is an unbelievable boon. Perhaps the Spirits have come back to her. Yes, there is a cost to this kill, but maybe a gift too? The extra weight is demanding but she is warm for the first time in so many cycles of the blighted sky above. Such a risk, she has barely recovered. Walking is difficult but she can manage. She was clinging tight when the dying beast had fallen and rolled, trapping her leg for a few terrible moments.

She had honoured the animal and given thanks, as she had been taught, yet knew she would always feel the pain of its passing. It had been a relief to confirm it as male. She was grateful no living cubs would suffer from this loss, only those unborn.

The liver and the fat have filled her and the meat will last a few more days before it rots. It is already drawing flies, which she keeps away however she can. Some slivers of flesh have been smoked over the fire, some fat rendered to a thin paste. The best is now packed with snow into the dead bear's stomach and slung across her back, though the aroma will soon be ripe enough to reach the ravenous.

It is a deep shame to her that she must waste so much of this magnificent animal but there is no clan, no gathering to share the blessing and the burden. At least its carcass will serve one final purpose, drawing scavengers towards its decay and away from their onward path.

She had blunted her hand axe in skinning and gutting it. Her hands are raw, but now the hide she has tanned with ochre is wrapped around her feet, her body, her baby. The bear's thigh bone is strapped to her back for a club, its claws are in the hare-fur pouch. One sharp tooth takes pride of place on her amulet. She has been marked by the encounter, both in her body and in her being. She still feels the risk, the bruises, the sprains and the tears (possibly worse within her leg, but she cannot allow that to be. She cannot wait for any fracture to heal.)

Before moving on she has taken some time to tremor, as her people learned to do by watching the animals of the migrating herds recover from a narrow escape. Lying down to roll on the earth she'd let her muscles shake off their fear, so that it would not become buried within and an extra weight to carry. So it could not creep around her bones the way that vines will strangle a tree. Having lain in its blood, having released her duel with the beast back into the ground where it expired, she has set out again, walking as fast as the pain in her leg will allow. She is exhausted, exhilarated. But the course she has chosen is right, she feels it.

The earliest perceptions had come in childhood. Small, quiet knowings. The first full revelation had terrified her. Many times as a girl she had felt the earth shivering and had once heard thunder that might split a skull, but this, these sounds in her head, this sickening roaring and rumbling? A great mountain (many small mountains?), not one she had seen in the real world, not anywhere near, was smoking and shaking and bursting into liquid fire and black sky. Her nostrils flared with acridity. She refused the vision, could not comprehend it, told no one – not even when the changes came, when the skies wept ash and a sharp chill crept into bones and hearts. She did not want to be blamed.

Often since she has wished she'd had the courage to tell them for then they may have trusted, even followed. How could she explain that she knew such a journey was possible? Her grandmother had told her the tales, in sound and sand, of the mothers and fathers many generations before who had left the old lands during the great dry. It was said they had come from even further before then, somewhere long south, in time without memory.

In fading images that tease her deepest dreaming, there is a shoreline. A secret place of lingering life and a sea with drinkable streams that defies its own salt. Once she finds this new coast she understands that she must follow until it turns upwards on itself to the narrowest point, and then she must cross.

7

Sarah was staying. The Americans had agreed to collaborate, but at a cost. Now Eloise had to share her with a stranger: one Dr Kenneth Charles Harmon (an MIT alumnus no less, post-grad Johns Hopkins), or 'KC' for short.

Geek chic, she thought, wasn't that what they called it in the magazines? Those Clark Kent-ish spectacles, the unruly black fringe that he had neither the time nor the forethought to trim before it flopped into his eyes. Cheekbones as sharp as his elegantly forensic mind (Eloise had done her research, read his published papers), a slender build and a disarming, off-centre smile. She was glad that Eugene had arranged the introduction in the cafeteria rather than the airless confines of his office.

'Hey! Dr Kluft! I've heard so much about you! It's a real pleasure.'

What had he heard? From whom?

'You too, Dr Harmon, you too.'

She was pleased with her nonchalance and felt sure it was coming across as unforced, but when she shook his outstretched hand there was a flash of static. *Oh, come on*, she thought. *Seriously?* If Eloise had been so inclined she might have wondered whether the laws of nature were having a laugh at her expense. Both she and her new colleague snatched their hands away with an 'oh!' to shake off the shock, then Eloise gave those mischievous sparks the most innocent of explanations.

'Well, that would be our delightful cafeteria carpet, I expect. Nineties nylon,' Eloise re-assigned the blame, 'a charming leftover which we seem to have kept for nostalgia's sake as much as for lack of budget. But then we are very fond of our relics over here.'

'The air too, maybe,' agreed KC with that dangerous smile. 'It's really dry. And here's me thinking you guys got nothing but rain?'

The ensuing eye contact suggested other factors at play, however. Eloise raised her guard but she was unable to read her newly imposed lab partner well enough to measure his subtler reactions, either to her or to their electrically charged meeting, as polite and professional as he seemed.

After showing him around the building and introducing him to the team, it took a few beers at the nearest post-work pub to properly break the ice. Eloise insisted that her guest sample the flattest, bitterest and most tepid local brew to test his Yankee mettle while she judged every nuance of his gestural language, studied every inflection in his speech. She was beginning to think she could work with him, after all, and was glad of it.

And yet there was *something* that she couldn't quite pin down, an edge that she thought might be there but which he hadn't fully revealed. She saw it in the way he sometimes broke eye contact and looked away to his left. (Perhaps a shyness tic? Or perhaps, she conceded, she was looking for something to dislike, a reason to keep those barriers up?) Maybe Dr Harmon really *was* as nice as he was working hard to appear, and yes, maybe there was some flicker of attraction between them that she would have to manage, but she was wary. What did he *want?* Had he been instructed with any deeper brief by his pharmaceutical backers? Was she being paranoid? Probably, but not without cause.

There had been plenty of friendly male colleagues before, happy enough to work with her, happy enough to take any credit they could. Willing to acknowledge her abilities but equally willing to explain what she ought to know / do / understand. Always wanting to take the emotion out of the workplace – and, no doubt, out of any sex that she might have offered up too. She never had. Hopefully, would never be tempted to.

Eloise decided to concentrate on what the Doctors Kluft and Harmon might have in common professionally (and philosophically). Which turned out to be plentiful, especially when it came to their passion for the work. Reassuringly, KC appeared to be more enlightened than many in terms of gender issues, whether or not this would turn out to be the proverbial sheepskin disguise. Eloise had no desire to dwell on politics but it was a difficult beast to ignore and they soon found a way to commiserate about their countries' mutual tragedies with bouts of rhetorical one-upmanship.

'Well, look at it this way,' KC offered, hoping against hope, 'maybe sometimes a wound has to be purged of all its pus before it can begin to heal?'

'Or maybe we have to go through the Black Death to eventually reach the Enlightenment?' Eloise had returned, using the heft of European history to win that round.

As the alcohol went to work, they shifted from the depressing to the inspiring and spent the rest of the evening exploring themes from chaos and convergence to the possibility of a predictive pattern, and from the mathematics of morphogenesis to the seductive notion of a unifying scheme. New-found compatriots in the unbounded country of the mind, they indulged a shared infatuation for the magnificence of the genetic chronicle, from Precambrian bacteria through exponential speciation and on to *Homo sapiens sapiens*, emerging Venus-like from the tree of life. Eloise felt, at last, a stirring from her lengthy hibernation.

So she relented on the trial-by-ale and switched to a classy single malt as a conciliatory nightcap, its rich flavour spoiled only by a late supper of dry roasted peanuts and salt and vinegar crisps. As each decided to head home Eloise cast aside restraint and followed a sudden urge to set up a re-match. While she was relieved they seemed to be on the same page in so many ways, she needed to investigate the sharper corners to KC that she suspected – and in more relaxed situations than the workplace. She needed to know whether she could trust him.

'But you do appreciate now, don't you, Dr Harmon, the critical difference between a crisp and a proper bloody chip?' asked Eloise, 'because this will be vital to our working relationship.'

KC looked at her with amusement.

'Well, I think I do now, yeah. Thank you. But I've obviously got so much more to learn.'

She was struggling to get into her denim jacket before KC reached out to help her.

'Yes. Quite. Oh, oh… thank you. Yes. The sleeve. Always does that for some reason, so annoying! OK, so, successful beer initiation notwithstanding, I feel it necessary to continue your induction into

London life. Allow me to organise further culinary forays into our national dishes of, say, a kebab or a curry sometime. And absolutely, Dr Harmon, with the aforementioned authentic chip experience thrown in.'

'Sounds good, Eloise. I look forward to that. But only if you start calling me KC.'

'You might have to give me some time on that,' she said, as she shook his hand again to say goodbye, half expecting, half hoping for a replay of the static but the stained floorboards and soggy air of the saloon bar would not oblige.

Eloise strolled home that evening in a more buoyant mood, even when drenched by an unexpected shower (and without berating herself for the lack of an umbrella).

*

How long, how far? She knows the exhaustion of hunger all too well, but this latest fatigue, this slow draining of her soul, feels deadlier than any she has fought before. She is alone and yet not. Sometimes she wishes that she was, after all, and then feels sick for having given shape to such terrible thoughts. She knows it is only for the child now that she stays alive. She understands for the first time, if only for a fleeting moment, the old stories of terrible days when mothers had been forced to inflict a horrific kind of mercy on the most vulnerable, if only to save and feed those young more able to fend for themselves, more likely to make it.

But this is not something she can allow herself to contemplate. Not after the heart-ripping sacrifice of the bear, her spirit animal. Too much has been taken from her now. And there are no others to save. Perhaps anywhere? No life more liveable, not even her own without the child. There is no reason to go on except for this little one, however much it puts her mother at risk. However heavy the child has become, however irritable when the milk is too stubborn, or the body that offers it too drained to keep trying. But this unspeakable feeling, this unbearable resentment remains. Her burden is a boulder strapped to her back.

She stops to rest for a while under the cover of some thorny scrub. Pulls up some of its deepest roots to chew on. She knows this plant.

There will be scant nourishment here, but enough that she may find the strength to get up again. Over the cycle of the last moon, they have suffered less snow across the vast, open plains, but she wonders whether it was a mistake to leave their last place of respite? The hot spring was but a few days walk behind them. Perhaps they should have stayed there, made a home there, even if nothing but green slime could thrive in its odorous waters? This cruellest of havens had been discovered by pursuing a hint of steam on the cool morning air, towards the dull creep of daybreak.

She had been sure those faint wisps were not smoke and she had been right. The spring itself may have been undrinkable but its rising steam cooled upon the rocky walls around it, enough to drip slowly into a gourd that was fed by a series of reeds. She had been tempted to stay, though she knew that she could not. Bathing in the warm waters was a comfort she might have succumbed to forever. Or, until starvation released them both into the final sleep.

The heavy heat had brought dreams, memories. Once she had felt the warmth of her mother near and then remembered with a remorseless ache that she was gone. Was anyone left? How she wishes for her mother now, with all of her laughing, scolding flock of friends. She wishes every one of those women back to her now.

She saw herself weaving nets and baskets with them to gather the succulent life from the shallows, remembered that soft, sweet, salty taste – the energising freshness of her favourite food. She saw how her mother deftly inserted the sharpened stick into exactly the right spot to tease open a reluctant shell, recalled the reeking mounds of shells that marked the best places to find this tender flesh. Those vital lessons in how to tell when they were ready, when they were in season, when they were good. She remembered how her grandmother would force feed some poor soul the burnt wood from the base of the fire, if he had been unfortunate or foolish enough to swallow one that was bad.

In the rising mists, she had remembered her father teaching her to make her first bow. The feel of its tension. Being allowed to follow the hunt away from the rock pools and into the deep forest. Running under the broad lacing of leaves that spoke to each other through the breeze, watching the shapes of light fight with the shadows on the dark, rich earth.

She had fallen behind as the group chased a trail, but she was not afraid to be alone. She had climbed one of the trees and waited. Her father had been angry when he'd found her again – but not once he saw what she had caught. Watching, hiding, hearing, holding her aim. Asking permission from the mother of life to take this life. A small hog, yes, but big enough to feed them all. They had celebrated her that night and the boys had been resentful. After that, they'd tried to trip her, keep her behind, hide her arrows. But she soon learned how to wrestle back what was hers, how to use another's weight or weakness against him. Then as she grew to womanhood she found subtler forms of revenge and a new, enticing, dangerous power. But she never missed another hunt.

Now, the dry earth seems to drag at her feet where once it had spurred her forward. Now, she feels nothing of her ability to play or choose. At least the cold here seems to be shrinking, but they are off track again after the diversion of the hot spring and need to alter course to reach the envisioned shoreline that, even now, even in such emptiness she trusts they will find. To move away from that heat had taken so much out of her, but with every measure of will that she can summon she walks onwards into the west, towards the unseen setting of the ever-shrouded sun.

*

Soon the new lab partners were spending most coffee and lunch breaks together. Eloise nursed her resistance to saying 'KC' out loud, the unsuitability of the soubriquet for one who seemed so much on her wavelength continued to jar (as did the prospect of too great a familiarity) and she often defaulted to 'Dr Harmon'. KC insisted, however, and at last she relented. The turning point was when he asked her, 'So, which version? The Ryan brothers or The Damned?'

That he knew (or had researched?) her song intrigued her and she'd replied, 'Well, for my parents the original, of course. But for me? Oh god, The Damned. Dave Vanian giving it all that, in sexy vampire mode. How could any teenage creature of the night resist?' KC seemed surprised by this more personal and revealing response, and perhaps a little too encouraged. He smiled, inclined towards her and asked her more about her musical tastes. But this resulted in only a greater and more dangerous sense of compatibility for Eloise, rather than reinforcing her detachment.

More often their conversations were of an academic nature. Occasionally, Eloise tried to play devil's advocate, if only for the sake of it. She didn't want to agree with every word the man said like some doe-eyed fangirl, in awe of the MIT / Johns Hopkins axis of his qualifications, and she needed to keep setting a few hurdles between them. But KC had so much to share and he shared it willingly. Back home he had been working on targeted vaccine delivery and DNA replacement using viruses that had been stripped of their power but which nevertheless could stimulate the right immune response, or deliver the right new information to a sufferer's cells.

His team had also begun exploring the creation of synthetic virus-like mechanisms – very exciting, very controversial work, but with so much potential for realising the evanescent dream of pharmaco-genetics. They shared an 'almost too good to be true' sense of thrill about another new procedure that exploited sequences of palindromic code that had formerly been considered 'junk' within the genome. This promising advance used the simpler RNA molecules as guides and enzymatic clippers to target defective DNA in both strands of the helix, snip it out and even replace it. The potential for addressing inherited disease or frailty, or even the genetic damage inflicted by adverse environment or life events, was staggering.

But it was the new method for the work on Sarah's cells that was the primary game-changer for Eloise. Its application of high-throughput sequencing technology in combination with a genome analyser and a machine-learning algorithm had put their work firmly back on course, and it was gathering pace. As KC had boasted, 'this thing can sequence the heck out of anything.' So far they had managed to capture only fragments and were having ongoing and infuriating problems with contamination, but they were getting close. Very close. Both to the clues that would unlock the enigma of Sarah, and to each other.

KC was married, of course, but Eloise had expected as much, at their age it was almost a given. He didn't wear a ring (hygiene protocols, perhaps) but smiling out from his phone (left on the table one lunchtime) there she was. The well-fed Midwestern wife with a helmet hairdo and a brace of orthodontically-corrected kids. Eloise had held back from asking KC any direct questions about his marital status, felt it might suggest an interest that she would not admit to, even if she felt sure it was there. She was relieved by the knowledge of his family, however. It cleared the path to a purely professional relationship.

When he came back to their table with two plates of shepherd's pie (another essential step in her programme of his cultural assimilation) she reinforced her resolve by asking him about his children. She listened attentively, made appropriate noises of approval over the pictures he then swiped through, duly congratulated him on the soccer prowess of his daughter, offered sympathy for the bullying experienced by his son. Were they becoming friends?

To resist such uncertain traction she refrained from asking him about his wife, but KC chose to tell her anyway. Apparently 'Gretchen' had been his college sweetheart, a humanities student and the first among his fellow freshmen (outside of the bio-chem club) to give him the time of day. *Probably the first freshman with a cleavage to take notice of him at all*, thought Eloise, rather unkindly. Despite the mercurial and unspecific current between them, she recognised that KC's type was an acquired taste and he could hardly have been considered a stud, especially in his teenage years.

Then, during their next caffeine-powered conversation (in which he'd told her about his environmental activism as a student and there had seemed nothing more romantic than standing in front of a bulldozer to protect an ancient forest, and its reserves of genetic information) KC confessed that he felt no other woman 'got him' in the way that Eloise did. That no other was such a kindred spirit.

She wasn't sure whether to be flattered, sympathetic, or suspicious.

Perhaps recognising the hazards ahead and reflexing to defuse them (or worried that this was a move too far, too soon?) KC added with a stutter, 'I mean, you know, it's like I've found my long-lost British sister, or something.'

She was irritated. Was he playing with her? What had she done to deserve that? Was this part of some manoeuvre, some conjuring trick to make her feel more secure? And what the hell did he talk about in all those private conference calls back to the States? She decided to ask him. Then wished she hadn't.

'OK. So, the contamination issues are becoming a serious concern,' he admitted, 'and they want to move the whole project back to the US. But they want to invite you over too, and they're happy to organise a visa. And, hey, I'm sure your secondment deal and per diem would be *very* generous.'

Eloise had never been in a fist-fight, but she imagined this was how it felt to be sucker-punched. She realised immediately that she could not show it, that she could not overplay her hand. She had to get in to see Eugene first, to email Darius – before letting KC know that this was never going to happen. On US soil they'd be subject to US biotech laws and US patents. The human past that Sarah embodied could be horse-traded like market 'futures'.

'Oh, wow, really?' she said. 'Wow…'

Then Eloise was tripped up for a second time, as KC declared, 'Yeah, but I said no. I really think she should stay here. She's your baby. And we are right on the cusp, it would be crazy to break the momentum. Unless of course you like the idea of a few months stateside?'

'Well, who knows… I mean, maybe. It's an idea. Why don't we think about it? Let me talk to Eugene,' she replied, preparing to call his bluff. Or at least buy some time.

Eloise forced herself to set aside all the teasing static between them once again. She spent a few fevered days securing assurances from everyone with influence, persuading Eugene to get CCTV fitted both inside and outside the clean room to catch any breaches in security, but she had no idea whether or not she could trust KC. On any level. She kept finding excuses to take more lunch breaks alone and off-site. She tried to concentrate on the work, keen to learn what she could from him but cautious to protect what she should.

*

There is nothing to burn. Not even a dry bush. Stupidly, in her exhaustion she has failed to gather or carry any new wood or kindling. Such a fool! She shouts her fury at herself to the darkening night. The child at her chest wakes and cries, whether from shock or fear or cold she cannot tell, but such suffering is her fault alone and she is unworthy of this living gift, for all its torturous wailing. This unforgiving blessing of motherhood. She does what she can to comfort and quieten her again and the child responds. By some miracle, her milk still comes and she welcomes it, no matter what it may steal from her own body.

The bear skin will offer some warmth, some protection, yes, but even this cannot shield against a rising northerly wind. There is not as much as a tall rock here to break its heartless blowing. She must keep moving to keep them both warm. This in itself is a risk, making them vulnerable to whatever living things here are graced with the secrets of the night. Anything that belongs to a pack, anything big enough, fast enough, sharp enough, quiet enough. Anything with poison in its teeth or in its tail. Any creature guided by the same spirits that are laughing at her now, mocking her pride for imagining that she could kill her totem and not be punished. She is so tired. But if she stops to sleep they will die. She must find the energy to march until dawn.

At least the wind has thinned the dust clouds a little and she can make out a few familiar stars. She must follow them or she will turn herself around and lose the ground that they have gained.

Fool. Fool!

8

'Eloise, you got a minute?'

'Yes, sure.' She smiled brightly at KC, not sure at all what to expect.

'In private?'

'Oh, OK. Where?'

'Sun's out… How about a bench in the courtyard? I'll meet you there with a couple of lattes?'

Eloise loved the cloistered courtyard, its time-textured stone, its mottled sunlight and criss-cross of shrubbery, its 'in memoriam' benches to academics gone before, but until KC turned up bearing caffeine it had taken on the oppressive aura of a dentist's waiting room. *What the hell is this all about?*

He sat next to her. Close, but not uncomfortably so.

'Hey, so I know you've been worried about it but I wanted you to know that I've persuaded my guys to drop the move stateside. Makes no sense right now – and the new security should keep the bean-counters off our backs for a while,' KC revealed, without breaking eye-contact before she did.

OK, thought Eloise, *great, but what backroom deals have been done?*

'OK, great!' she said with as much confidence as she could muster. 'Yes, it would be too much of an upheaval, really, wouldn't it? But thanks for letting me know. I do appreciate it. And the latte.'

'You're welcome, Eloise. But that's not all. I just got a seriously tempting offer to speak at a conference up in… Leicester? Did I pronounce that right? OK, good! And I really want you to come too. I want to shift the focus of the talk to archaic DNA. Keep that spotlight shining on Sarah.'

Eloise was flattered, excited. Confused, concerned. The more she talked in public about Sarah the more she stayed connected with the project, but this also would mean a night away in some melancholy hotel. With KC. She wasn't sure that she should go but her lab partner was persuasive, said that his 'money men' were fully behind the idea. The funding gods must be appeased, after all.

So she went – and the inevitable moment arrived.

A moment after an enjoyable day, after a dinner of further discoveries as to their mutual tastes and influences, heroes and passions. After too many drinks. In the corridor – as they said goodnight.

KC leaned in, his height matching hers so the move required no clumsiness. He pecked her on the cheek a little too firmly and held her wrist a little too long. As she began to turn away he switched to kiss the other cheek and their mouths brushed, ever so lightly. Eloise nearly responded. So nearly. But *godammit*, she thought (as the image of his full-cheeked, wide-smiling wife loomed large), how could she betray every principle for this – whatever it may turn out to be?

As KC apologised, saying, 'Oops, sorry… never sure with Europeans, how many times, which side and all.' She smiled and turned away, fumbling for her keycard. Naturally, the lock would not go green when she swiped it and then swiped it again. She flushed. KC reached in and took the keycard from her and she let him hold her hand for a moment as he did so. With the first swipe, for him, the light switched to green. Even so, Eloise had heeded the warning of all those preceding red dots.

In an absurd falsetto, she tried to appear unruffled.

'Thank you, KC. Good night! Sleep well,' she said, and slipped inside her room.

'Good night, Eloise,' he agreed.

But then he waited, swaying slightly, eyelids heavy, until her door was fully closed.

The infant, her weapons, her tools, any surplus food that might last long enough to carry with them, it's all too much now. There is no part of her body unburdened. And now she has learned the hard way that they must always carry a little firewood and some extra kindling in case the fungus has lost its smoulder, and her scooped-out circle of flint will have to go to work. They have seen too many days of empty ground.

At least the terrifying night-walk had brought food instead of death, at least the only life they had met was a surprised groundhog that she could take with ease. Even better, by following the stars they had come to a place where a family of trees had once flourished. Now their blanched and broken branches reproach the sky as it waits for the coming dawn, but there is wood enough here. Dead as it is, it burns well and she can sleep at last, once the flames are raging.

She wakes again with hope, but knowing that she has a serious task ahead. The load she bears has become too much for the simple slings across her chest and back, for the small pouches around her waist, too much for her arms and shoulders and hands. She needs to make a basket. The kind she can strap to her back, the kind the women of home would carry when walking between camps, or when harvesting from the trees.

There was a place, in the autumn, a place her grandmother knew where the cane was plentiful. Strong and supple. The old woman had made certain of it: tended the sodden ground, taken out the smaller, weaker plants, cut away any rival growth and burned the roots back into the soil when the reeds were cut away during the dry season. Many had not understood what her grandmother did every year, or why, and some had laughed at her efforts, but the women who weaved understood.

How she wished now that she had heeded them. Stayed longer while they selected and cut, then wet and worked the cane, not grown bored and restless and run off to follow her brothers in more exciting pursuits. For she has struggled to find a faded sapling here with the right softness in its roots or any tree with twigs that bend instead of snap, or to know which type of stripped-away bark might work instead. She has tried and failed, again and again. She has strained to remember any pattern of weaving that held itself and did not unravel. Fought to control fingers that sting from slices and splinters, that ache from such delicate yet futile work. She has failed to hold back her cursing, despite how her anger disturbs the little one.

At last, after a precarious branch-snapping climb up one of the taller trees, she has found some kind of parasitic vine that has outlived its withered host and perhaps not long since given up the last of its leaves. She strips away the supple ropes and sets to work again. After several attempts she has wrought something that she hopes will work and she

lines her new basket with the bear skin. It is ugly and she imagines it
will fall apart quite soon. It sits crookedly on her back and cuts into
shoulders that she must now wrap with a thicker layer of hide, but she
has done it. Made something new. Made something necessary.

The little one, now able to sit without assistance and lift herself
up to grip the rim of the basket, is thrilled with this new thing. She
tries to copy her mother as she packs it with useful things, picking up
handfuls of the pebbles all around her and putting them inside. She
cries when her mother casts out this excess weight, then giggles as
she picks them up and puts each one back again into the basket. Her
mother cannot help but laugh a little too.

*

Facing another night alone in a wretched hotel room, Eloise was torn,
remorseful, tempted. This was not some crazy and uncontrollable
desire, even if she'd done little to discourage KC's wine-fuelled
flirtation over dinner. And yet she felt a touch regretful for not taking
the bait. More, she was resentful of her own self-righteousness (and
not for the first time in her life). Or was this nothing more than
cowardice?

After she'd closed the door on KC she'd hesitated, held the handle
for a moment, begun to open it again, so nearly walking out into
the over-lit corridor to knock at his room, before finally releasing
the handle and leaning back hard against the inside of her bedroom
door. She had sacrificed so much in the service of *doing the right
thing*... How could she do the wrong thing now? How could she
render worthless all those other decisions to let something go, to
deny herself? For what might well be a dire disappointment and an
excruciating morning after. Or the ruthless self-ablation of realising
that she'd fallen for the long game. Or deadliest of all (and, she
suspected, the most likely outcome) a devastating entanglement.

She poured a nightcap from the minibar knowing she would suffer
for it in the morning, but unsure whether the extra alcohol was
intended for the courage to give in or the courage to resist. One sip,
one thought about KC's family and she knew that she would not open
the door again that night. While she had no offspring of her own,
Eloise could not bear the thought of children in any kind of anguish,

and certainly did not want to be the cause of it. Various rounds of volunteering with the Samaritans had taught her not only how to listen but also about how much emotional damage can be inflicted in youth and the insidious havoc it might wreak over a lifetime.

Eloise had debated nature over nurture, endlessly. She understood how much in terms of physiology was dictated by those tiny spirals. The true markers of anything resembling 'destiny'. And yet, not intractably deterministic, not hopelessly enslaving. Lifestyle choices, or trauma, or the right therapy could re-write the agenda and flick so many of the switches on or off, altering the behaviour of a gene without altering its code. Could acquired damage (biological or emotional) soon be corrected? Would the inherited indicators of future pain finally be overcome? Yes, she wholeheartedly believed so, the mind-blowing possibilities were already unfolding before them. As far as disease and disability were concerned this was her passion, her mission. But what about the genetic effects on behaviour or character?

Her best friend, Anna (another who had fallen foul of the mating lottery), had adopted from Asia after long, expensive and dispiriting failures of IVF, and Eloise was a conscientious if secular godmother to the child. She often wondered why there were so many reproductive cul-de-sacs in her own pioneering but sacrificial generation. They had shattered ceilings for sure but not without splitting heads and splintering hearts. May-Lynn, Anna's feisty little daughter, had settled well and clung to her new life with insatiable curiosity and affection – but Eloise had made it a long-term if discreet project to watch and see how the girl 'within' emerged and how she responded to, or was affected by, her transposed world 'without'.

She might have made a good mother herself, Eloise felt that now. It had taken an ailing and incontinent pet to teach her, if slowly and painfully, how much practical patience and forgiveness she had to offer. Admittedly she may not have been a laugh a minute, and yes, she would have been a dedicated (though gentle) disciplinarian, but she hoped that she would have been wise and warm.

No. No regrets, no room for that. Eloise knew that she'd done the best she could based on who she was, and what she'd known, and the cards she'd had to play at any time. When she got together with the few friends with children that still made time for her, yes, she might feel sharp pangs over a giggle or a cuddle but also absolute relief in being able to walk away from tears or a tantrum. They all seemed so exhausted. Not to mention obsessed. Although, considering the labour overload on the modern woman combined with the media's manipulative hysteria and a mystical cult of motherhood online, this was hardly a surprise.

She could not remember her own sensible and studious mother, a renowned anthropologist and photographer, ever fussing or fretting so. Even as adventurous and accident-prone as her young daughter had been.

In her more sanctimonious moments, Eloise was tempted to think that her childlessness was a kind of social and ecological sacrifice, considering the twin bogeymen of exponential overpopulation and mismanaged resources.

Oh bugger it, she thought. She was tired of turning it over and over, tired of worrying for herself and the world. She wished she could live instead like some impulsive hedonist, without a care, without a shred of guilt or remorse. She finished the miniature vodka, decided against another and contemplated the attractions of her vacant hotel bed.

They failed to convince. Eloise recognised that she was too much in her head, as usual, and there would be no sleep for a while. The only answer was to get back into her body, to move about, to change the record. Yes, that was it. Records! The fail-safe cure. If she'd been at home she would have made a cup of chamomile tea and put on some music. Here, the only option that would not disturb her fellow guests (particularly KC next door) was her museum-piece Sony Walkman, packed on a whim when she'd suspected the hotel's televisual offering would be of little comfort, if comfort were required. Eloise loved that the old device was still (just about) working after all these years. Still cradling that cherished compilation of Northern Soul, a love token from the only college boyfriend to have earned the gift of her heart.

Eloise pressed down the play button with a satisfying click and felt her body begin to move. Soon she had pushed the pointless hotel chairs out of her way and was twirling around a strip of cheap carpet as if she were 19 again, up at some riotous weekender in Wigan. There was insufficient space to break out all of her moves but it didn't matter, she was working up a sweat and writhing away the frustration. As 'Tainted Love' segued into 'Needle in a Haystack' her mood had shifted and that painful old needle was no longer sticking on its favourite emotional scratch.

Ah hell, she conceded, parenthood had never really been on the agenda, even if she had found, in time, an engineered cure for her own inherited Damoclean sword. That damnable Kluft curse that lay coiled within her cells. (Or if any one of her relationships had worked out.) Ultimately, she was and always had been a free spirit. Maybe not so spirited anymore but still free. The horizons of opportunity may have hazed over with time but she still had the freedom of choice, and the sanctuary of solitude whenever she chose it.

And yet… perhaps when it was all a little too late, Eloise had begun to feel that she might make a good life partner now, after all – albeit any partnership faring better if part-time and non-cohabiting. She had no illusions. No expectations beyond kindness. She did not need anyone to complete or appreciate or flatter her. No need for social status or financial support. She was certainly much less intense about affairs of the heart (or body) than she had been in her youth. Crucially, she no longer needed to be *right*, nor did she have any strict criteria for what would be right in a partner. She was diligent these days about avoiding all the 'shoulds' or 'should haves' (for herself or anyone else). Learning to spurn the bitter seductions of blame.

But what about jealousy? To her great surprise, Eloise realised that she was no longer quite so concerned about the sacred cow of fidelity. Encounters like the one she had just resisted could happen so easily – and were not always beyond forgiveness. In a momentary lapse of control she could have been in a different hotel room right now. The loyalty that really counted meant someone being there for you when you needed them most.

And she understood all too well that passion ebbed and flowed through a relationship. Although a sound deposit of erotic chemistry in the bank should be a given, something sweet and satiating to draw upon whenever need or opportunity presented itself. Good Lord, she asked herself, otherwise what would be the point? For as self-sufficient as she was, she missed a physical relationship. She found herself in middle age no less – perhaps more – in tune with her own sensuality than in her youth.

For now, however, she would keep on dancing and forget about everything else. Forget KC. There were other, better routes to happiness. It was all about choice. This oh-so-tempting transgression in the guilt-free 'Vegas' of a forgettable hotel, however flattering, however natural, however easy – she could not, would not do.

9

Her scanning of the wide skyline stops at the white bedrock. This is what she has been hoping for. Where there is the soft white stone there is a good chance of finding flint, as essential to her as any other resource.

Yes, there, in a line below the layer of white, there it is, loose and easy to gather. She doesn't even need to hack it out. She picks a few choice pieces and examines them for faults, for fitness. One tiny shard is almost perfect as it is, fitting neatly between thumb and forefinger, its edges will soon be sharp enough to straighten and refine the shaft of an arrow. Another will make a good bone scraper.

She readies a hammerstone to refine the blades but then is drawn to look closer at the small piece that she is about to work, for she has never seen anything like this. There is something curling and complete within the rock.

Surely it cannot be alive and yet it looks like something once living, perhaps crawling in a tidal pool, but now forever entombed. She strokes the smooth surface as if somehow her touch might coax a reaction. It is enchanting. How did this thing so like a sea creature come to be so far inland? They are still many days from the coast, she senses it, but cannot smell it yet. There is no answer to this puzzle, but its mystery makes it even more special. She will keep this prize deep within her pouch and not risk it on any task. Though, if she must, she would consider using it in trade. If she gets the chance, if she meets either the opportunity or the need.

Will there ever again be such times of coming together? Families meeting, friends finding each other, old enemies or rivals in love watching each other at a distance. Learning who has been born, who is no longer alive, who is now throwing the furthest spear. Excitement and squabbles over the swapping of skins, ochre, amber, and so many jostling to choose one of her father's bows. Sometimes, they had joined for the honouring of a lost but much loved elder. Many had heard the horn and the howling and had come for her grandmother. She who had eased others through their passage to the end of life, who had been carried for days as she faded, who had been mourned for many more.

The wise one. The one who could smell trouble on the wind, see the wasting sickness before it took hold. Humble, quiet, kind. Never insisting, never diminishing the pride of the long beards or mocking the antics of the strutting stags, but these same men would do little of importance without consulting her. When would be the best time to leave one camp, one valley, one shore for another? When would the rain come, the herds return, the heat abate? Would this one live, could that one be trusted? How should a quarrel be solved between siblings, how to ease the pain of toothache, failure, loss? This remarkable old woman also had knowledge of how to set a bone, if there had been a clean enough break. This was among the greatest miracles yet seen and a method she had discovered only through the will to try. A skill that had saved many from certain death.

Her grandmother had not always had the answers but somehow a touch from her, a smile, a nod of reassurance, a pat or a stroke of forgiveness, a smudge of burnt herb or taste of bitter leaf was enough to move a matter forward to its rightful, natural conclusion.

One such gathering had been tense with the taste of bloodlust, the itch of revenge. The more skilled that some became at killing, or in the making of tools that could more quickly kill, the more dangerous the dispute. A great beast had been brought down with two spears, one belonging to a man who had taken something from the thrower of the other. It was claimed he had taken the other's daughter, without the consent of either. But that daughter could neither confirm nor deny this claim for she was now dead, having bled too much during childbirth – a birth she was at least a year or so too young to have risked. One man insisted that all had been willing, but the other could not be persuaded, or placated for his loss. And now they both claimed the kill.

The men at the gathering took too easily to one side or the other. The heat of the fire that had been readied to roast the beast was at risk of spreading and so it had fallen to her grandmother to settle the score. She had examined the carcass, the position and the depth of each spear, one to each lung.

She concluded both blows to be equal but decided that the one who had lost his daughter should have the animal's hide, a dowry of great value and a thing of comfort. He who had lost his mate (whether she had been willing or unwilling) should take the horns, one for himself, one for the orphaned child that had survived his mother's demise. One horn should be carved with the mark of the child's father, one with that of his grandfather and both should be blown when the latter ended his life's walk and then be cast into the fire that would mark his end. That night, the old woman had declared, the entire gathering would feast on the meat, but the heart of the beast would burn in tribute to all those children who had died before their fathers, and to all those children who lived without a mother.

Now her granddaughter ached for such times again and all that they meant. She wished for the many, she wished for even one other. For at those gatherings (perhaps, she realises now, the real reason for this coming together) there had been the young men – and their needs. Present in the air, the smell of effort, the quest to find one who was willing, ready, one who might also want what he wanted.

At the last meeting that she could remember, before the great death, she had been of age but had seen no one who might give her what she needed, what she deserved. No soul who looked like the one in her visions. None like the one that she had met much later, along this broken, lonely path.

Now she understands that there is no longer any place for pride. No chance for choice. There is no longer any sense of rightful, natural conclusion. And she may have to exchange whatever she must for whatever she can. If she ever finds any other left alive.

*

Eloise was still not sleeping. Back home after a long and sometimes awkward (though more often stimulating) drive with KC, her top-of-the-range bed was suddenly too soft to resist her restlessness. Insomnia was a nemesis that she had vanquished with various strategies over the years but guilt and confusion always outflanked her.

Am I falling in love with this man? Or rather, she asked (hoping it was so), *is this nothing more than a troublesome series of synaptic sparks? Does love live only in the frontal lobe, where it can be so easily excised by injury?*

(Or influenced by hormones.) Is it merely an adaptation, a mechanism of attachment, a learned behaviour that ups the ante for mating and survival? Why, then, why, does it so often lead to self-destruction? Or the ultimate in self-sacrifice? Could 'love' be an emergent property, somehow greater than the sum of its parts?

Eloise struggled to stop her thought train from grinding steel-on-steel, but it would not slow down, it merely sparked and took another track. She began to re-live various conversations with Darius, those repetitive arguments about the biological imperative to polygamy, their angry words to each other returning in audio fragments and merging into a single recollection from a miserable holiday at Yellowstone. It had been their last together and almost as explosive as the massive thermal cauldron that was bubbling beneath them.

As she sank into the quicksand of her memory-foam mattress, she could hear the proud, booming bass notes of his voice but she couldn't visualise him clearly. Somehow her midnight memory had sucked the steam from the geysers all around them into the cramped Winnebago in which they had cruised the big sky highways. (And in which, in every way, she had miscarried her last hopes for happiness with him.)

'Eloise, you are dreaming!' Darius was shouting at her now. 'Monogamy is not natural! The nuclear family was a necessary restriction of the age of agriculture but it's a social construct, nothing more. Look at the promiscuity of your beloved bonobo apes, for *fuck's* sake!'

Darius liked to swear only when he thought it was witty to do so.

'Oh, bollocks, Darius,' she had replied, 'that's so boring. This helpless compulsion to spread a dynastic legacy – it's nothing more than a convenient excuse for masculine self-indulgence. And if anything, agriculture was the worst thing ever to happen to sexual and social equality! It may well have been the worst thing to happen to our ecology at all!'

'Now come on, LoLo,' he'd countered with his most dismissive tone, 'at best monogamy is a quasi-religious imposition to control the spread of disease and keep people in line, keep them parenting. But 'free love' is genetic, my darling, it's nature's best weapon for multiplication.'

'There's no bloody proof yet that promiscuity is either genetic or inevitable, Darius, or even beneficial except perhaps in highly reduced populations! It's a specious argument... and you know it is, because if that were the case, everyone would be shagging anything they can get their hands on!'

'They are!'

Eloise remembered looking away from Darius in disgust, making a mental note to add some new behavioural comparisons to the twins study that was due to start right after Yellowstone.

'Look, my love,' Darius continued, 'I know you'd prefer to think that humanity has always yearned towards a lifetime of singular love...'

Yes, she knew that was true. Like the wolf, like the swan. Like her parents.

'... but that's because you're a well-brought-up and well-meaning woman...'

Patronising git. How had he always managed to turn a strength into a weakness?

'... and it was the female of the species that learned to demand commitment to enhance the survival of their offspring. Hah! Even though a good half of you girls would happily source these from a healthy bloody prick 'n mix – or, at the very least, the most impressive presenting candidate! And as for the male of the species, we are more than happy to oblige. Hell, we'll kill each other to oblige! You know very well your own mother observed such violent reproductive competition among the supposedly blissful natives of the Amazon – and what an anthropological wrecking ball that was! We came out of the trees that way, my love, and we may have tried to smother it in a self-hating Victorian veneer, but we will always be driven to both violence and sexual variety.'

At the time she had been too exhausted about everything, about the whole played-out drama of 'Darius & Eloise' to fight back with any gusto.

'But that doesn't have to be the case, Darius. There really is such a thing as self-control. And anyway, humans have far less sexual dimorphism between the genders than in truly polygamous species.

And once we invented weapons that equalised male-on-male combat, making it much more dangerous, the harem was out and pair bonding crept in. You know very well that humans have nothing like the canine teeth you see in any species dominated by the alpha male – or even the matriarchal society of the bonobos. And despite the huge variations in culture around the world, we have observed in several ancient hunter–gatherer tribes today – those with relative equality among the sexes that is – that monogamy is the norm and polygamy is a rare exception. An urge to promiscuity simply isn't a compulsion for everyone, Darius, and not everyone who seeks the constancy of monogamy is weak. On the contrary, it takes some serious strength!'

'My point precisely! If it's such a struggle, how can it be natural?'

His questioning smile had made her feel quite sick at the time and she had visualised him as some kind of movie-screen silverback, roaring and beating his chest. But now she saw that this comparison was unfair to the beauty of that beast. The cult of misogyny did nothing but warp true masculinity. Those sad and angry men, so very afraid that if they were not more powerful than a woman then they were not much of anything, had greatly misunderstood the dynamic. The role of the alpha male in the higher primates was not to bully, oppress, or abuse – it was to protect, encourage and support. Unless directly threatened, unless in a situation of real and present danger, one rarely saw anything but gentleness from the most successful of silverbacks.

'You're missing my point,' she had tried to explain to Darius that night, 'humanity has probably been inclined to mate for life for many millennia and there are very tenable theories that the Old Stone Age was a time of egalitarianism for both gender and social groups.'

Yes, a peaceful era of plenty. This had always made sense to Eloise. After all, how could endemically selfish societies cohere and thrive for so long? Even if it was, as some argued, a selfishness that was directed towards the survival of familial DNA at all costs. Or with the understanding that human violence was often born out of some misplaced sense of morality or justice. But Darius had always accused her of sentimentality, never failed to seek the Achilles heel or undermine her sense of objectivity.

'Fantasy, LoLo!' he had pronounced victoriously. 'Life has always been the "perpetual struggle", not some elevated utopia of Quaker brethren. The vulnerability of pregnancy and the dependency of nursing young has always required the protection of the most vigorous mate available, who meanwhile would be looking elsewhere for comfort while one consort was otherwise engaged. No, I'm sorry, but we are all hard-wired to put our own needs, our own DNA first. And mankind is the most ruthlessly efficient machine this planet has ever produced.'

Yes, she'd thought, and no better representative than the man in front of me right now. But she had known better than to say so.

'Well, actually,' she had replied instead, 'I would argue that we have some serious competition in that department from the virus. But, come on, Darius, "survival of the fittest" doesn't necessarily mean the most aggressive – it means the best adapted, maybe even the most intelligent, or the most capable of living in balanced harmony within its system. And it certainly isn't an expedient excuse for "slaughter of the feeblest" or "reproduction of the most rampant"!'

'Careful, Eloise, my darling, you are starting to sound like some airy-fairy hippy.'

At that point she had sighed and made a strategic retreat, if not quite giving up the battle or her opinions. Now, however, as she juggled her feelings about KC and pondered their attraction – and the recent temptation so nearly taken – Eloise was less sure. Perhaps Darius was right, after all? Perhaps we are all programmed for ego-centricity, for instant gratification at minimum effort. To seek power. To take whatever we want, whatever we need, whatever the cost. Perhaps patriarchy, oppression and war have always run amok and always reared their brutal, grinning heads. Especially if, or when, Darius's type had ever been dominant. And how that monstrous tribe was rising again now.

Did Darius deserve such comparisons? No, she conceded. Her ex may be *challenging* – a complex blend of the liberal and the conservative – but he was hardly on a par with the populist exploiters, or about to jack-boot up to join the resurgent right. His opinions could be harsh and uncompromising and he might lack empathy from time to time, but it was too easy to demonise the man she had once loved, once admired, and this did nothing to heal the damage wrought by the misplaced expectations of her youthful passion for him.

At last, Eloise let the mists of Yellowstone reclaim Darius and draw him back into her distant past. She tried to forgive him (once again). She tried to forgive herself. And then, with greater success, she tried to forgive the stubbornness of sleep.

10

The small mounds ahead seem unnatural to these surroundings, to this flat, featureless land. As she comes closer invisible fingers rake the back of her neck and she hesitates to approach, but there is no living movement and she is compelled to explore.

The first curled cadaver, by now almost fully drawn back to the earth, stops her still. This one died how... of hurt or hunger? There is another nearby, face down, reaching out, as though collapsed in crawling. She sees no more corpses, only this handful of mounds, decorated with pebbles, horns, twists of twig and what once had been some kind of plant.

Further investigation finds tracks leading from this place. Walking (not running) two-footed. A pair of men (not so much bigger than her). Survivors of this group? Or the ones who had given out the dying? Then she sees that they had been dragging something. Something small and struggling, but also two-legged. Her heart sounds an angry alarm and her eyes graze the horizon all around.

When she is sure they are not still near she looks again at those left above the ground. One, and perhaps his mate? And now she understands that these were not her own kind. These were the Others. Different. So strong, and yet, as weak as any in these times. They hunted well, by crowding, thrusting and stabbing but they threw no spears, nor slingshots. They had no bows (although she had heard of no others outside of her own tribe that did) but they were powerful and never to be underestimated. She had never seen the Others before, only heard tales of them, but now there is a mysterious bond that she is unable to rip away.

It is a waste of energy that she should not spend, even though she has fed well from a lucky find along the way (a tough old long-horned goat, gored in a fight, ready and willing to give up his struggle to more merciful means than a long, slow bleed would grant) but she sets about finishing the work of the burial. The pair left above ground had somehow lived through – or come back to find – whatever had happened here, lasting long enough to honour those who had fallen.

She covers their remains, if only shallowly, shares some of the death-gifts from the other mounds, if only a scattering. But these fellows, too, deserve to follow their kin.

As she works she hears her grandmother's voice. The chants that the old woman would offer for one lost. There were certain sounds for those who died of sickness and other more powerful and deeper laments for those taken suddenly or too young. More for those who died in the hunt, or who had been taken by the anger of men. She cannot know what sounds these souls may have made to each other, or for each other. But she thinks her grandmother would not scold her for lending them one of her own people's songs. There is no other to hear it. Only the small and crawling creatures of the sand.

And as she sings and works, she understands, suddenly. The distance between all that exists is nothing. The tiny grains of dust that claim us all had birthed us all. In each that lives and loves there is the same and everything is better for it. And in this she finds a quiet yet immeasurable peace. Now she understands the look in her grandmother's eyes as she was dying.

She finishes her work, but then awakes from the sacred and is aware once more of momentary fears. Striding on into the cover of the coming night, she knows that she must change direction, yet again – and walk far away from those terrifying footprints.

*

Back in the lab, Eloise had to work alongside KC and act as if the hotel moment had never happened. If anything, she thought that he must also be relieved. It was as though something lurking in the shadows had stepped briefly into the light, and having been recognised and avoided, was now fading into soft focus. She felt sure she had made the right decision.

KC acknowledged both the awkwardness and the greater intimacy between them with a gesture that pointed, she hoped, towards a potentially rewarding if sensibly chaste companionship. Eloise returned from lunch one day to find that he'd left a book on her desk, not inscribed within but rather with a post-it note on top, something that would appear casual to the impartial observer, transparent, out in the open. But Eloise could tell that KC had thought carefully about what he had scribbled. It was a kind of code – hidden in plain sight.

The book was an early edition of Jonas Salk's *Survival of the Wisest* (he had clearly gone out of his way to source it) and the inscription referred to a conversation they'd had over dinner in the hotel, on that so-nearly night, about this heroic virologist and 'bio-philosopher' (and also about some of the troubling errors that had been made along the challenging road towards immunity). It had been another of those clear yet confusing moments in which they'd found themselves in complete harmony.

The note was addressed to 'Dear Dr Kluft' – simply calling her that was a nod and a wink to their own private joke, as he was the one who insisted on less formality – and it read: 'As we discussed, cometh the hour, cometh the (wo)man. Much of value and relevance here, if not everything we might have hoped for? Enjoy!'

The gift had both warmth and meaning. Was this the turning point in their relationship and could she now let go of all her misgivings about her colleague? Eloise unpeeled the yellow post-it note from the cover and was about to crumple it, but then paused for a moment and placed it inside the back page of the book. She smiled inwardly and looked forward to thanking KC in person.

Nevertheless, she considered it wise to maintain a safe distance. The libidinous aspect of the ego did not take well to rejection and this, after all, had been the ultimate reality of their evening together at the conference, however subtle his approach, however discreet her refusal. She remained perplexed by their relationship. While there was a real and compelling physical lure between them, that much was now undeniable, Eloise knew it was one that she could and should resist. What she wasn't clear about was KC's take on it and she felt unable to confront that directly.

Was he as convinced as she or might he yield to the undertow of a disastrous affair, given any further opportunity or in any moment of mutual weakness? Was he happy to remain at a healthy arm's length, as nothing more than amicable colleagues, or was he interested in forging a true friendship (an appealing outcome to Eloise, if possible). How safe would that path be? Could they turn this affinity into a fruitful working relationship that extended far beyond the Sarah project, or did there remain some hidden agenda with KC, personal or otherwise?

Eloise knew that the boundaries now in place were indispensable and yet she was always in some way aroused in KC's company, whether intellectually or physically. Might this come to taint any occupational partnership in the end? Indeed, how would a growing closeness between them be perceived by workmates, or management, or reflect on a reputation that she had fought so hard to establish? Eloise wondered whether anyone else had sensed this electromagnetic pull between them, more powerful than gravity, threatening to sweep her right out of her professional sangfroid.

As she leafed through KC's gift, a calendar notification popped up on her phone asking her not to forget her godfather's birthday, but more effectively reminding her that this circular rumination was a waste of time and headspace. Eloise returned to her research, excusing herself, nevertheless. As natural as workplace attractions seemed to be *(didn't a significant percentage of couples meet this way, weren't they often the most successful?)*, Eloise had never experienced anything of this nature before.

KC waved from across the lab as he made his excuses to leave for the day and she waved back in casual acknowledgement, as she would to any other of the team, feeling rude for not having thanked him for the book straight away. She sent a brief but sincere text and received a thumbs up in return.

Not long after this, Rory, her lab assistant, ambled past her desk to check whether she wanted anything from the vending machine, but Eloise soon realised that his slower-than-ever gait indicated that he had something to say. She declined the offer of a chocolate fix but smiled at him in encouragement even so.

'No thanks, Rory, sugar quota already maxed out for the day. Nice win for the Magpies last night though, bet you were happy?'

'Aye, ecstatic, aye.'

He stood there, smiling, but not moving.

'Was there something else, Rory?'

'OK, so, I saw that book that Dr Harmon left you. Yeah, nice. Great book.'

'Oh, you've read it?'

'No, but um, I'd like to when you've finished it?'

'OK. Sure.'

'Great. Thanks.'

He smoothed back his lank pony tail. Smiled again.

'Was there anything else?'

'OK. So, I really need to say this. Otherwise I might regret it. But please be careful, Dr Kluft.'

Eloise knew that her cheeks had flushed but hoped he hadn't noticed. She cleared her throat, feigned bewilderment.

'About what?'

Rory pulled up a stool from the workbench opposite.

'You know, I'm really not sure about that guy,' he said, indicating the book still on her desk, but Eloise knew that he meant KC, not Jonas Salk. (If Rory was an anti-vaxer then he was working in the wrong place.)

'Oh. Why?'

Despite the involuntary swallowing, Eloise felt sure this came out calmly enough.

'So, the other week, the day when you came in late, you took your cat to the vet, I think?'

'Yes, that's right.'

'So, I saw Dr Harmon coming out of Eugene's office. I didn't hear what they were saying but they looked way too friendly and 'agreeable' if you know what I mean.'

'OK. But why wouldn't they be?'

'No, no, it was more than that... I don't know. They shook hands like they were in a club of some kind, you know?'

Eloise had always liked the hot cocoa of Rory's Geordie accent, its 'what's the hurry, man?' pace, but now she wanted him to pour out his point.

'No, I don't.'

'Well, OK, so that meeting might have been nothing more than a bit of diplomacy, but... ah wey, I know I shouldna been listening, but

I overheard him Skyping his bosses, or whatever they are over there, and I only caught the end of it but he was saying something like he was 'working on it' and that he knew it was a problem but he had a few ideas for sorting it. Or something like that. That's all really, but… you know, I just thought you should know.'

'OK. Thanks. I think? I'm sure it's nothing, Rory, but yes, don't worry. I'll get to the bottom of it. And really, please don't worry about me, my eyes are wide open.'

'Right then. That's good then.'

Right then. Eloise knew that any of Rory's tale could have meant anything at all. Or nothing. Those overheard conversations would have been before the CCTV went in, before KC had admitted to her what was being discussed, so this was nothing new. But Rory had picked up on *something*. At least he hadn't sympathetically warned her not to 'get too close' – at least this seemed nothing more than a hangover of suspicion from when the whole team was aware that the project was at risk to a rival US bid.

But shortly after, Eloise was forced to wonder whether her work really *was* being impaired by the 'KC factor'. Was all this crackling interference now creating other problems? Of course, she knew it could not be so, but something very strange was happening to her terminal. She'd opened an email, supposedly from the lab that had worked on the carbon dating of Sarah, with a link that she was pithily encouraged to click. When, without thinking she did so, it took her not to where she'd expected but to a bizarre page of biblical quotes, in a font that bellowed of both righteousness and entrenched tradition. Eloise thought it had to be some kind of joke when she began to read:

Proverbs 19:23 – The fear of the LORD [tendeth] to life: and [he that hath it] shall abide satisfied; he shall not be visited with evil.

A vague tingling at the back of her neck told her something wasn't right before she realised that this was no prank. She closed the link straight away, but now various programmes and files were opening and closing of their own accord. Oh fuck. *Fuck, fuck, fuck. Have I been hacked?*

Eloise unplugged her terminal before it could infect the server (she hoped) but felt stupid for not having been more careful, for having been so preoccupied. Here, surely, was the most punishing answer to all those mind-wasting questions about KC. She summoned the IT department and hung back helplessly while they went to work, knowing there was nothing more she could do, but feeling that she ought to stand penitent at the site of her transgression.

'Who did the email come from?' the not-long-out-of-puberty expert asked her. 'It was probably a spoofed address, but it would be useful to have it.'

'Oh damn, I couldn't tell you the exact address off the top of my head, but wait a minute, I threw out an old email from them only this morning. It should be in my recycling bin... oh, no wait, that's weird, my bin's been emptied? That doesn't usually happen until the end of the day. Oh dear, no, I'm so sorry.'

'No worries, we can find out with a phone call. We should let them know anyway.'

'OK. Yes. Here, I have their number on speed dial...'

As the wall clock flashed red past eighteen hundred, Eloise was drenched in another wave of guilt. This would make her late for the Samaritans. She hated letting down her shift-mates, or worse, any caller in dire need of their now divided time, but realised she would have to consider a break from volunteering for a while. She could not commit while the project possessed her and, in truth, she was struggling to cope with the interruptions to her delicate sleep patterns that came with the night shifts. After tonight she would request a sabbatical.

There was a tug of regret, however, that went beyond abandoning the needs of callers. Eloise realised how much she would miss her weekly contact with John. An unlikely friendship, but one that had so enriched her life. She was determined to join her shift at some point this evening, as soon as IT gave her dispensation. With everything that was going on, she needed to see John.

The Reverend John Evesham had been a Samaritan volunteer for over two decades. He ministered at a well-attended progressive church, as well as prisons, police cells, hospitals and psychiatric facilities, but was trusted to reserve his spiritual guidance for his willing flock rather than inflict it on callers to the helpline. He was part of something called the 'Integral Christianity Movement'. While Eloise was not sure quite what that meant (or that she wanted to know) she had found his equanimity and unswerving compassion more appealing than several in the scientific fellowship.

John's gentle mentoring had endeared him to her, as to all who worked with him. In a series of difficult calls in her early days Eloise had been tempted to get angry with the aggressive, indignant with the hoaxers, contemptuous of the heavy breathers and impatient with those tragic regulars who seemed unwilling or unable to jump out of their vicious circles. John had offered a very clear observation on their purpose.

'Eloise,' he had consoled, 'I know it can be upsetting, especially when you worry that perhaps more genuine or critical cases might not be getting through, but we can never guess at their intentions, or motivations. They *all* need some empathy, some human contact. Someone who will not judge or betray or dictate to them. Someone who is there to listen, simply because they want to be.'

There were other misgivings about her suitability for the role that Eloise had not shared with John. Sometimes, in flickers of shifting static, she was not completely convinced that suicide was *always* something to be saved from. Knowing that depression was usually treatable and not the immutable state that those despairing in the middle of an episode often believed it to be, Eloise felt that if she could help even one soul to see past the darkness, it would be worth the attempt. But what of the terminally suffering, or those whose quality of life was as hopelessly dire as their ability to rationally choose was clear? And what would she do if the course of her own life ever brought her face-to-face with that reality? The horror of her mother's last weeks had never fully left her.

Eloise was clear, however, that it was not their role as Samaritans to forcibly dissuade, but rather to offer a guide towards any chink of light. If someone had picked up the phone, it indicated that at least some illumination might be creeping under the door. And far better to help them well before, while suicide was only a sly, unwanted thought. To let them say the unsayable.

Eloise did not know how she would cope with the ultimate 'failure' if she ever experienced it. John had recounted a couple of heart-wrenching occasions during which he'd had to accept his part was simply to stay with the terrible reality and bear witness. For those who were determined to do so, not to have to leave the world alone.

Eloise had often pondered the paradox. Despite the mystery of mass strandings, no other healthy animal actively suicides. They cannot contemplate it, driven only to live, reproduce or die trying. Was this the curse of consciousness, she wondered, of that chemical crucible for all our outward *and* inward looking intelligence? That together with the ability to seek ourselves, know ourselves – even to laugh at ourselves – comes the cost of realisations that we cannot bear? As a species, humanity was blessed with a vitalising richness of emotions and yet, insanely, these were sometimes so dense and dark that we were unable to support their weight.

Sometimes, Eloise found it hard to prevent those reflections from seeping inside. One caller had asked of her in agony, 'How do you stop wanting the things that you know you will never have?'

Even if it had been ethical to impose an opinion, Eloise could not have. She had no answer to that question.

She also had no answers that were of any further use to IT and so, remorsefully, she slipped away.

*

She watches her sleeping, the tender breath coming slow and easy. Eyelashes fluttering in gentle dreaming. Watching. This is her task alone now.

When the men of her kind became fathers they received their markings in a ceremony that women were not permitted to witness, but she had seen it once, well-hidden and quiet. A very fine, sharp arrowhead was warmed in the fire. Deep sounds rose and fell in humming. Hands were held behind the back, but no force was used or needed. This was for pride. This made a man. Three quick cuts, like fingers, on each side of the upper chest, then widened and sealed with a stick, ember red from the pit of the fire.

She is both mother and father now. She is a whole tribe.

She makes a decision. Prepares the fire, blesses and heats the tools, comes to stillness and looks long and deep into the flames. Elusive yet alive with ways and wisdom beyond understanding, the voices of the ancestors could be heard within its silences. But this treacherous attraction has also left its mark upon her. She knows both the beauty and the fury of fire all too well, the skin of her forearm tells the pitiful tale from a careless moment of play. Pain she will never forget.

Her flint is not fine or sharp enough (is it hot enough?) but she does not care, she needs to feel. Something. To know that she is not made of stone and dust. She closes her eyes and begins to deepen her breath, turns back into the sacred place until all has slowed to nothing.

Then she drops the stones she has been beating, but keeps the humming buried low within her gut. Now. She winces as she draws the first cut, but makes no cry, the child still sleeps. The cut is jagged, the blood flows too fast but she stops it with the smouldering. The smell. She had forgotten the smell, different somehow when it is your own flesh. The next cut is better, faster, cleaner. She gets the angle right, keeps all the cuts high and close. It is done.

In the morning the child notices, reaches out to touch but she pushes her hand firmly away. She avoids her questioning gaze, draws deeply on this new authority and they move on. Her father, her brothers are with her now once more and at her shoulders again.

But what of the child's father? Where is he now? For all her determination to forget, she sees him each time she looks into her daughter's eyes. What more might they have exchanged, what more might she have learned from him? How might he have found and fed the softness in her, now all but gone.

She recalls how her mother and father had been with each other, their looks, their quarrels soon forgiven, their care for each other. Not all pairings were so blessed, she understood this, she had seen some couplings come and go, had seen the bruises of the battles to mate in other members of her clan. She had witnessed the fear of those left alone, whether by death or choice or theft. And then there were those other times, during the gatherings, those forgiven nights of the year under certain moons when pairs might be permitted to separate and find another for only a few hours, if all were willing, if all agreed. Not every pair took this path, but for some it was a way to feed a threatening hunger, or to welcome fresh seed into a bond that had been unable to bring new life to birth.

But she had always believed it would be her destiny to have what her parents had enjoyed, she had been determined to settle for nothing less, to resist any attempt at a trade between tribes, unless it suited her. She knew her gifts were valued above many things, and she knew she might bring good to her band if she agreed to an advantageous match with a long beard, or his son, or with a water talker or a herd runner. But she had known also that she would never be forced. She knew that she channelled a different kind of force that must be free to flow, could not be coerced.

Perhaps she had taken advantage of that, perhaps her brothers (those whose company she has pined for since) were right to resent her pride. And would this pride have tainted her own attempts at partnership? Would she have tired of the one with the sunburnt hair, would he have tired of her? Could he have looked away from her faults and she from his? But these things are beyond answer now and pointless to ponder. She knows that she must find and sharpen the flint within her own blood once more. No more dreams of softness.

11

Eloise finished her last call at the Samaritans for the foreseeable future and joined the others in the Phoenix. This gathering was a necessary ritual to rinse away the sorrow that lingered long after the phones were put down, and many a thirsty pint after an evening shift had led to easy, good-natured debate, in particular with John. Tonight turned out to be no exception. Eloise was unclear how she and John had formed their tight huddle of theological ping pong (despite his strictly 'civilian' identity when on Samaritan duty) but she always enjoyed a one-to-one with the only man of god she knew personally, no matter the topic.

'Look, John, I fully recognise that people can benefit from the practices of stillness and the soothing brain waves these can induce, or from a comforting sense of communion with others, or a sense of connection to something greater. We are a kind of hive mind after all. And yes, OK, the core of most faiths does contain some sensible guidance for happy or healthy co-existence. But I'm sorry, John, far too much horror, exploitation and madness has been done in 'His' name. I mean, come on, the arrogance, the intolerance...'

John countered with typically fur-lined incision.

'Indeed, Eloise, indeed. Though I am not sure that religion has the monopoly on arrogance or intolerance?'

'Of course, yes,' she conceded. 'Politics, tribalism, the market economy, even some factions of academia can all be guilty of hard-line dogma. But that doesn't mean we should remain enslaved to the violent and dysfunctional history of some displaced desert tribe! Or of any historical people who were seeking to make sense of their troubles and establish a moral superiority over their oppressors.'

'But there's so much more to the Bible than that, Eloise. Parts of it are sublimely beautiful, an exquisite love song to the divine with so much deep wisdom. And in the New Testament, the teachings of Christ are all about moving on, about peace and forgiveness,' insisted John.

'Hm...' Eloise was undecided about the Jesus story. Was it merely a useful amalgamation of ancient religious myths or figureheads? Campfire folktales adapted to make 'the one god' more loving and forgiving than had been his habit... perhaps so his luckless followers could feel more valued or more hopeful, or be kept more docile and compliant. Or *was* it rooted in a real history, in the pacifist mission of a more enlightened teacher and healer of the time? Either way, she did not deny the nuggets of beauty, wisdom and compassion she found at the heart of his attributed preachings.

'OK,' she replied, as kindly as she could, 'maybe some of those fusty old fairy tales have worked well enough, for want of anything better, as instructive allegory if you will – or as psychological archetypes to guide the human journey, but do we really need them anymore, and in that form?'

'Maybe they contain more than rules and regulations, Eloise, maybe there are hidden codes and answers in the sacred texts – of many religions – that we don't yet fully recognise?'

'Oh, come on, John,' Eloise was incredulous, a little disappointed that he had taken this turn. 'That sounds like fantasy to me, or the red herrings of conspiracy theories. Elaborate stories to frighten children. Entertaining perhaps, but they distract and seduce. I'd say some are even dangerous in the way that they dehumanise their supposed enemies. But what's worse, they throw us off course from immediate solutions to immediate problems. I mean, seriously, how could any intelligent being dispute the scientific facts that are so clearly laid out before us? It's a collective delusion. No, I'm sorry, your God holds us back now, John. All these insane crusades or jihads... all the disgusting political manipulation.'

'Eloise, I completely agree that faith has too often been exploited in the name of unspeakable horror... or simply to turn a fast buck. And there is no greater sin or blasphemy than to commit murder in the name of God. I mean, if you want to kill, at least have the honesty to acknowledge its source in the base human urge for violence, whether that's driven by rage, revenge, avarice, or even in defence. But don't try to sanctify it with excuses.'

'Hear, hear!' Eloise dropped another shred on to the pile of torn-up beer mats in front of her. There had been times when she'd almost wished she was a smoker, or a 'vaper' as they had now become, such a useful diversion for the hands that had been ruler-rapped at school for doodling in the margins. She was vexed, but not at John. Not at the soft grey eyes that were the same shade as his steely quiff. Had he been a rock'n'roll fan in his youth, she wondered, perhaps in his days as a Cambridge undergrad? Eloise had often found solace in those eyes, as they smiled behind crinkly creases and saw deeper inside another person than most, eyes that took the time to look.

As a couple of their party decided to call it a night, John stood up to offer his trademark two-handed shake. Eloise swallowed the last mouthful of her now warm and flattening lager and looked back at John.

'One more for the road?' she asked.

'Oh, go on. Just a half though, thanks.'

At the delightful old wood-panelled bar, and in the reflections of its etched mirror behind, Eloise surveyed the easy warmth all around her. There were times when she hated people, concurred with Sartre on the nature of hell, and times such as this when she felt bonded, forgiving, hopeful. Until, with a jolt, she remembered the violation of being hacked a few hours earlier at the lab. Who were they? And what had those cunning, track-covering bastards been after? *Why had they gone after her?*

Now, as she replayed that unpleasant threat (or invitation) from Proverbs to 'Fear the Lord' she recognised what had stimulated her irritation with such zealotry, but also realised she should moderate her tone for such a likeable moderate as John. Their bond, their mutual support mattered more than dogma or dialectics. On the way back to their booth Eloise spilled some of the overfilled glasses, splashing the sticky froth on to her trainers, but neither this habitual clumsiness nor thoughts of the hacking attempt (which fortunately seemed to have reached no further than her own terminal) could change her mood. John stood up for a moment to relieve her of his drink.

'Lovely, cheers.'

Each took a contemplative sip before returning to the theme.

'You know, Eloise, Jesus was no fan of religious hypocrisy,' John continued, keen to get to the heart of his point, 'I feel he was trying to guide us to a more personal relationship with God and to the wisdom within, to the "Christ Consciousness" rather than the self-interested control of any hierarchy. Despite everything that may have been edited out or tacked on around it, his greatest message was only to Love. To treat others as you would be treated. And the day that we all wake up and realise that the "promised land" is not some arid hunk of real estate but rather a state of being, well, that will truly be the definition of rapture.'

'I admire your optimism,' Eloise offered with little conviction, but she was happy for him to carry on. The sound of his voice was soft, sweet and lyrical. She wondered briefly whether he sang and what glorious heights he might attain in chant or in choral harmony. No wonder he made such a 'good' Samaritan, she thought, that voice was a soothing balm. An anchor to salvation.

'And I'm a great admirer of your calling, Eloise. For me, the enquiring mind embodies the gift of intelligence, the desire to understand and to make life better. I'd even admit to some admiration for the courage of the atheist. It's a brave, if potentially desolate journey to live unguided by a greater power and rely entirely on your own resources. To recognise no reward for your actions beyond their own merit...'

He stopped to clear his throat and sip his cider, but Eloise knew he had more to offer and did not jump in.

'... but the fact is, Eloise, this connection, this yearning for reunion with creation, it's something that you *feel*, that you experience. And once you do there's no turning back. Once you begin to access that bliss, that oneness, everything unfolds from there. Good behaviour comes naturally and the promise of heaven or the threat of hell becomes unnecessary as, in effect, you want to do nothing other than act from that place of compassion and understanding. And even along the rocky path towards all of this, you can't deny people what they hold in their hearts, Eloise, what relieves them from isolation and separation. You can't deny them hope.'

'Perhaps not, but many of those same pilgrims would in turn deny humanity its freedom, its choices, its progress.'

'Yes, but only those who are afraid. Fear is the most dangerous and destructive thing on this blessed earth, and *my* God is not one who demands fear, only love. And respect. Oh, and a little humility doesn't hurt. The only true voice of God for me is the one which asks you not only to love, because that's easy – but to love *all* of life – and such a love asks that you do no harm.'

'First, do no harm. Well, yes, I can certainly relate to that!'

'Ha, of course, yes, the Hippocratic oath! But even when so many of us do stumble, Eloise, even when we cannot help but cause some harm, there's always a way back. For me, God is no more the kind of parent who would eternally punish his children than any one of us would. He, she, it, us… whatever form or non-form this force takes, asks only that we try to know and to feel it. And in seeking it come to better know and love ourselves, and everything within and around us.'

'Which would be all very well, John, if every believer was like you. But these states of bliss and ecstasy you mention can be replicated in the laboratory – or even at the beginning of an epileptic fit! They're neurological conditions, not divine. And this 'force' you mention, there's never been any proof or measurable evidence that such an intelligence exists.'

'Or that it doesn't? What do they say? "Absence of evidence is not evidence of absence"?'

'Yes, but it's unlikely there'll ever be any convincing evidence, either way.'

John sighed, leaned back against the scuffed leatherette.

'But does there need to be, Eloise? We each will be faced with our own "confirmation bias" in any of our experiences, will we not? And science cannot yet answer all our questions. Indeed, it usually raises as many as it solves. And it can be equally culpable of leading to terrible deeds. From the machinations of the big pharmaceutical companies to the arms race… or pollution, or eugenics… you name it.'

'Oh, come on, John! Genius can't be blamed for its discoveries, nor how they are used!'

'And you can't blame most well-meaning believers for the actions of a few fanatics. Or the greedy, or the angry or the power hungry. Take out the noisy fundamentalist cults, take out those only paying lip service and most people who go to church, or mosque, or synagogue, or temple, live in the simple hope that they and their families will be healthy and happy. They just want to try to lead good and meaningful lives.'

'Yes, but so many belief systems or apparently "spiritual" experiences are too easily twisted to fuel those fundamentalist fires, John. They set up such corruptible frameworks for all of the bullshit.'

'And we should also remember the role that peer pressure plays in any belief system, spiritual or cultural. Behaviour can spread rather like a disease. And some people hold on to their ignorance, because, after all, it's all they have. The relief of certainty. The ease of slotting into their tribe, and letting go of all responsibility. Because this "living to your full potential" thing doesn't feel available to many. And even if they felt they could reach for it, it's too hard. Too lonely. There's little worse to most humans than loneliness. And then, we should also consider how something as banal as the ego plays its part?'

Eloise looked down at her mini-mountain of shredded cardboard beer mats and re-arranged it.

'Hm, you have a point. Yes, perhaps it's less the sheep we should be angry with and more the self-interested shepherds. But believe me, John, I'm all too familiar with the evils of the ego.'

'And you should give yourself a break, Eloise. Have as much compassion for yourself as you have for others. Forgiving oneself is as crucial as forgiving the "trespassers against us". And it's not as hard as it may seem at first, you know, intention is a very powerful and transformative thing. As is prayer.'

'Well, actually, John, I do accept that paying attention to a problem, or applying some good will, or even the simple human touch can be intriguingly healing, but isn't that just the positivity effect at work, the conscious or unconscious stimulation of beneficial biology? Of feeling cared for?'

In between sips, Eloise had inhaled a little froth and had to excuse herself for coughing before continuing, though she was both keen and apprehensive to do so. '... OK, so maybe... maybe, I will consider that something goes deeper. I could be academically lynched for indulging the kind of "spiritual" appropriation of theory that infuriates most scientists but then there's still so much "weirdness" in what we see. I mean, all the mind-bending discoveries of sub-atomic physics, the changing behaviour of particles depending on the attention paid to them. Wave function that collapses on observation and particles that are entangled, or can be in two or more places at once...'

Eloise took a breath, nodded her willingness to negotiate.

'So, yes, I suppose there might be some as yet not understood effect of intention or concentration. But if that's the case, then that's what we should be harnessing, without chaining it to stagnant religions. Or leaving it to modern day witch doctors to enrich themselves by packaging it up for sale! And crucially, any form of prayer or remote "therapy" if you like, should be applied only alongside all the other safe and proven medical tools at our disposal, it shouldn't replace them. I see what you're saying, John, but for me, the notion of traditional prayer is too bound up with closed mythologies. Too open to exploitation.'

'Well. I'll tell you what. You work in your way, Eloise, and I'll work in mine.'

At which point the bell rang for last orders. John began to tell another anecdote to support his point of view and Eloise engaged with it, although she was also ready to draw the evening to a close, so gradually the conversation came to a natural end. But as she gathered her belongings John offered a postscript that stayed with her for some time afterwards, something that hung about her thoughts like an echo, if only because she understood its truth as keenly as the struggle to action it.

'You know, Eloise, perhaps the best that any of us can do is to learn to live thankfully in the moment and love whatever is available to us.'

*

As her footsteps trace the skeleton of a dry riverbed, she sees the shapes of the rivulets where water had once found the easiest routes, how it had split and splintered the ground, over and over, finding and forming new pathways. Like the branches and twigs on a tree that have been stripped by winter. Like the veins in her arms, like those on a leaf, or the lungs of an animal. She has recognised this same pattern in so many things and understands that this is how the living earth moves and flows.

She recalls how as a child she would examine a feather or a flower and notice that its form would repeat itself, many times over, small and large. Now she realises that this is how one thing is passed to another. As the many mothers before have passed their memories to her, and perhaps to others like her. If there are any others left in the world like her?

Once she had been pleased to feel special but now it is a weight she would happily share. All this knowledge is hers alone to bear and yet sometime, somehow, it must be shared again, as the river springs back to life under the rain, forming its countless streams to return to the land and finally the sea. She must hold the wisdom, she must carry it forward.

Was this why her back-bent grandmother had protected her and rushed to form the circle around her that first terrifying time she had witnessed the damage that men can do? She will never forget the heart-piercing scream that alerted her band to the coming danger. The clan had found that woman later, the one who had cried out while gathering sticks, before her throat had been emptied. She had struggled and bitten and sacrificed herself to free her tongue and warn them all.

Without words they all had reacted to that scream and had done what they had known they must, remembering how to survive such brutal, sudden blood-letting, even though it had been a generation since such evils had come. They had learned, and they had remembered.

The attack was brought by a strange and distant tribe of people, unknown and unknowable. Of shared bloodlines perhaps, but not the same way of being. It had been a dry summer. They must have been desperate, hungry, angry… but without the wisdom, without the sense to trade or to talk or to ask for help. When they had come upon her kin with violence instead, the group had not scattered under the ambush but had formed circles within circles while keeping to the highest ground, quickly gathering up sticks and clubs and stones, arrows and spears and nets.

A ring of the oldest men at the outside had met the initial wave of attack. They had struck out and then let the others strike, allowing themselves to receive those first furious blows. Then from behind this line the strongest of the young men had surged, surprising those now drawing breath once more, their arms still raised in anger, their trunks exposed. And, from behind this ring, those women who were strong enough but beyond childbearing picked off any who had pushed through or finished off those who might be wounded but still dangerous. Meanwhile their men regrouped.

The youngest and the very oldest of the women guarded the children, while letting out a shrill chorus of cries and sounding the horn that one clever soul had found the sense to carry with her. This inner circle had huddled together and called for the other clans. Called out angrily on the air for this violence to be turned back against their tormentors. Until, finally, it was over.

Their losses had been hard to bear, horrific for the youngest to witness, but they were not too heavy to survive. The invaders were all but finished off. Those who had realised the fight was lost and were strong enough to run had been intercepted by others coming to aid her clan. Two young women, wise enough to submit, lying on the ground as if still in the womb, were left behind, and with them a young boy.

They had brought some trouble these three, never truly healing from their misfortune or from the foolish mistakes of their fathers. Although her grandmother had tried to help, with smoke and chants, with patience and good will. But in time, this burden had been shared out among the other clans and two of the strangers had become of use, found the way to be. The other's fate was never spoken of. Unlike the story of their own famous victory, a tale that was told over and over again.

This same tactic had almost worked for her family one other time (the last time) after the dread, the dark, the dying, but they had been too few, too weak, too frightened. She had wanted to fight with them, but the circle had held long enough to hide her for one last time. Their only salvation had been that equal numbers of their aggressors had fallen, giving them time to flee, while carrying with them the

greatest wound of all. The knowledge that this latest horror had come
from within their own kin. She had never imagined that one of their
own could turn on them in desperation, join with strangers that he
believed to be stronger, and die at her feet for his mistake. The world
had darkened in too many ways.

12

Eloise slept well after her evening with John but woke early with fragments of the conversation becoming confused, like a poorly edited replay of something half-heard and hardly remembered. She let it drift away, there were notes about the challenges of the Sarah project to write up and so despite the temptations of a Saturday lie-in, she heaved herself out of bed to make coffee. She knew that writing was going to be a struggle, but also felt these preliminary thoughts might form the basis of any future book, a way to share all that they were learning, all that she hoped they would learn still, and she needed to set them down.

First, coffee. What was needed most was inspiration but for now a strong dose of caffeine would do. And music. Eloise shuffled through her new smartphone until she found the duet from Lakmé that never failed her. She was forced to admit that this play-listing capacity alone was worth the gadget's price tag and wondered why she'd held out for so long against such technological delights. Eloise recognised that her natural thriftiness, together with an ingrained resistance to any change of routine, had often denied her a little harmless indulgence.

She hit play and let the music build towards its crescendo. As she stared out of the kitchen window, waiting for a potent enough brew to percolate, her gaze settled in soft focus on a tiny finch that was fluffing up his feathers in her bird bath. Instinctively, she looked more closely at its beak (seed or nectar feeder?) but the connection with her hero, and an idea for starting her book that this contemplation had hatched only came together once she sat at her desk and her attention wandered to the small plastic bust of Darwin that Rory had given her one birthday, a souvenir from the Natural History Museum.

She looked away again in case she was discouraged from switching on her laptop at all. Whereas some writers might torture themselves by setting up the Bard as an impassive observer, Eloise had her own idol to live up to – even if this benchmark often caused her to refuse the first hurdle. Oh, but how she wished she could talk to her hero.

She had so many questions to ask him. To *talk*. To exchange ideas. Such a singular human blessing.

This notion of conversation reminded her of the work of a colleague, who in researching a cure for an inherited muscular wasting disease, had made a genetic discovery that set alight new theories about the origins of human speech. Eloise found herself looking long and hard at that little statuette again, and then embraced a long-denied temptation. She clicked open a fresh white page full of digital possibility and began to compose the letter that she had always wanted to write.

My Dear Mr Darwin,

Oh, how you would have loved all this, living today. How it would have lifted your heart to know not only that speciation by natural selection (along with other mechanisms that we are exploring) is correct, but also how it works! (Even if it doesn't quite take the linear, hierarchical structure that you imagined. Perhaps more of a crooked bush than a neat and tidy tree.) But how you would have enjoyed your introduction to the wonder that is DNA! To understand precisely how all those tiny little messengers in living cells inform and instruct all the variation. And, my goodness, everything that we've discovered since! For example, that within the human genome what at first looks like an aberration or an omission of letters that could cause a terrible muscular handicap may be partly responsible for our speech... and thus perhaps for the flowering of our intelligence. Indeed, for *your* beacon of brilliance and all that your ideas have given us.

They ridiculed you for tracing our roots to a common ancestor with the apes, drew your benign head upon a monkey's shoulders. Little did they know that all their slack-jawed chattering was a clue to the truths that would one day reinstate your dignity.

For my dear, dear Mr Darwin, there are so few genetic differences between us and our closest primate relatives (the

Human Accelerated Region notwithstanding), but it seems that one key distinction between your magnificent head and that of the chimpanzee may result from a mutation that makes our bite so much weaker than theirs. Because of this missing code in the MYH16 gene, our jaw muscles now have but a fraction of the power of our cousins – and it's possible that this 'accident' allowed us to vocalise so much more fluently.

So did the weakening and loosening of those muscles then create the extra space for our skulls (and therefore our brains) to outgrow the chimp's, blooming gradually into the rippling cortex that enables not only complex language, but music, art, imagination, advanced mathematics? The idea makes me want to break into the museum at night like a ninja vandal and chisel a wry smile across the sombre expression of your statue. Oh yes, you would be smiling now, Charles (may I call you that?), I am quite sure of it.

So, are we really what evolution intended? (If you will forgive the figure of speech, Charles, because of course there's no evidence for *intention* at all.) But are we its pinnacle, its optimal outcome, so far and in the here and now? How might it have happened on earth in a different form, or has it, is it happening somewhere else?

We know that convergent evolution comes up with common solutions across radically dissimilar species that are separated by millions of years of divergence. Bilateral symmetry (in almost every complex life form), the camera eye (the clever octopus sees very much as we do), the wing (insect, bat and bird have all learned how to fly), a problem-solving mind with the ability to deceive (humans and crows). But what has accelerated the process so dramatically in us? Why and how in our short time on the planet have we evolved so much faster and apparently more intelligently than, say, the dinosaurs?

Our mammalian progenitors survived the Permian

extinction not only by being small but by being *adaptable*, from food source to habitat to temperature. A quality that, much later, along with an inclination to co-operate with other bands of *sapien* brothers, would serve us very well (and which may well have been the decider in the ultimate competition with those unlucky, isolated Neanderthals).

Although, of course, we now know that we had, in fact, some low-level interbreeding with these and other archaic hominins before they completely disappeared. For as one wave of anatomically modern humans spread out from Africa and encountered new pathogens, so we needed to acquire some fresh immunity from the 'locals' who had arrived from that same continent millennia earlier, in order to create the enormous differentiation of leukocyte antigens that we see in non-African populations today.

The dinosaurs had millions upon millions of years and yet still couldn't come up with opposable thumbs, significantly larger brains, complex language (a reasonable supposition), tools or technology. Of course the apex predators among them may have been very canny indeed, but surely they had none of the abilities we see in the higher mammals (or even cephalopods). Perhaps they had no need, no spur, especially during a more settled environmental period. So how have we managed in only a couple of million (if taken from a more ape-like than truly human start) to get anatomically to where we are now? To shed our fur and then replace it when necessary with another's, or with the warmth of fire, so that we could sweat away our body heat to walk and run and hunt – through burning day and frozen night – right across the globe? And then in another few hundred thousand years to begin the process of civilisation, and in only ten thousand to go from farming into space?

Were the reptilian kings no more than a long, slow dead end that was never going to get much better? (Until of course their smaller cousins evolved into birds, whose attached parenting encouraged considerable intelligence, held back only by a lack of fingers that were sacrificed for wings.) But were those big lizards merely a dead-end branch of cold-blooded, thumb-free losers? Or will their angry ghosts have the last laugh if, for all our arrogant smarts, we can't make it past the next generation? Burn brightly, burn out quickly. (And perhaps, as some say, humanity has been nature's greatest mistake.) But what else, apart from birds, might the dinosaur family have become given a little more time and a few more molecular accidents, or essential adaptations? Or, dare I say it, *interference?*

Please excuse this mad, momentary speculation, my dear Mr Darwin. I blame it on my companion of last night, he wrapped me up in the sense of *something* greater, something other, and he can be most persuasive when in the full warmth of his passion. (Although I think he is someone that you might have liked too. At the very least you would have been polite. And equally kind I'm quite sure of it, even if you lost your own faith in increments.) But didn't even Francis Crick – unraveller of the helix, Nobel Laureate and establishment darling – develop a version of the Panspermia theory in which all life was originally seeded from one molybdenum-rich place in the universe, and then was spread outward? And who was it that likened the odds of the higher life forms emerging into such complexity over such a short evolutionary timescale to a tornado sweeping through a junk-yard and assembling a Boeing 747? Ah, yes (excuse me, but I have just googled it, Charles, another of the wonders of our times) it was Sir Fred Hoyle, noted English astronomer and the provider of many such a pithy observation.

So, did we all begin in something resembling your notion of a 'warm pond' – or maybe in some dry, thermal, boron-laden, RNA-friendly wasteland? Was it the effect of cosmic rays on the essential elements for organic matter that eventually brought the DNA molecule to life? Do those odd recurring numerical patterns, symmetries and sequences inside the code actually mean anything or are they nothing more than a mathematically improbable display of chance?

The questions are endless. And yet, everything (or *almost* everything) it seems can be explained with the new understanding that you set in motion, Charles. An understanding that has itself evolved by taking into account all the environmental stimuli of our volatile home planet – whether that be the movement of our tectonic plates (so deadly and yet so life-giving) or the wobbles of our axis and the magnetic flipping of our poles.

How I wish I could ask you what you think of it all now, Charles. To invite you, together with Sarah and a few other VIPs to my ultimate dinner party and thrash it all out over some fine food and wine (or for Sarah's sake perhaps an al fresco hog roast?). There are so many questions, still so many questions…

Eloise stopped typing and stemmed the stream of consciousness for the time being. She recognised it as an exercise in vanity, a rather embarrassing unburdening of her soul to someone she considered to be the greatest Englishman (a handful of other luminaries notwithstanding) but she decided to take some distance from it before judging it too harshly. She printed it out, put it aside and went into the kitchen to make more coffee.

Halfway through the process she regretted that decision. Yes, she had needed a change of cognitive direction but now she was dismayed to find herself thinking about the state of her kitchen and how badly it needed refurbishment. Eloise comforted herself with the notion that if she waited long enough this hand-painted Shaker look that her mother had so loved would surely come back around again. (Hopefully with the 'distressed' version of the aesthetic being particularly in vogue.)

As the brew deepened to the precise bite of bitterness she preferred, Eloise temporarily discarded dreams of a sleek, minimalist, high-gloss scheme with all mod cons (and maybe one of those fancy new percolating machines). She poured herself a fresh cup, breathed in the Pavlovian effects of its aroma and went back to her desk to pick up the printed missive to her hero. As she read it back she knew that it was silly, just silly. Certainly not the way to start her book about Sarah. She crumpled it up and binned it. (Even if she saved the digital file in her personal folder, perhaps as one might treat an unwise outpouring to a long lost lover. The writing of it had been catharsis enough. No need to stamp and post it. No need to click send.)

Nevertheless, Eloise was not entirely ready to abandon her whimsy. She rummaged in her desk drawer for a marker pen, lifted up that little bust of Darwin and drew upon it a slightly smug, subtle smile.

*

Perhaps it is better. This being alone. Perhaps it is right to start everything, all of life, all over again? Or maybe it is wiser to let everything come to an end. Here, now, on her knees, watching her blood mingle with the dirt. Mourning the waste of both warmth and moisture, as the tears tumble from her cheeks. Maybe the carnage she has seen before setting out on this quest is natural to her kind, and will always be the way it goes when death stalks the living as patiently as the spider. When it knows that all it must do is wait and watch and savour the foul struggle within its web. Hunger is the cruellest hunter. At least the sharp-toothed beasts kill quickly.

But why has the spider left her until last? Is it a special kind of triumph to savour the death throes of the strongest? And will her child, perhaps the very last child, taste sweetest of all? Pride again. She is neither the strongest nor the best. Perhaps she is the weakest and the worst and her punishment is to be left behind to witness all of this withering loss.

She sucks in a few shallow gasps of air and then purges them, too quickly. What use such thoughts? She still draws breath. If she can choose to get up again, she knows that she can still walk, despite the pain, and that she will still walk. She knows that she will stand and strain against the web with her final shout of fury. Yes, she will shout and scream and cry and rage and make herself too sour, too bitter to the taste. The spider will surely spit her out again.

Whether she is good or bad, whether she is worth the sacrifice of the others or not, she can still move, she can still fight, and that is enough. Even for those unseen watchers, those cold-hearted web-weavers. Even though the moments of her life seem to stretch and contract in turns and the earth now takes so much more from her than it gives. The Mother who no longer cherishes or supports her, but gashes her knees as she stumbles exhausted into her jagged embrace.

Yes, she still breathes, however sharp and gasping as it leaks away her strength. However heavy the growing infant lashed to her aching back. The child that cries now too, taking her moods from the heart she is wrapped so close to. No. She must stop this foolishness. She must inhale until her lungs are tight, hold it there and then give it back slowly, slowly, slowly.

There is a ritual that her people practise to prepare for the hunt. Right before first light those who wear the skins and claws and teeth of famous kills, those with the taste for what must be done, gather to welcome in the rays of the sun and encourage their warmth with the sound of their breathing. Slowly at first. Long cycles of fresh morning air. They light no fires, seek no other comfort but the closeness of their skin to the cold, damp soil, drawing the heat they need instead from deep within the belly.

Gradually, the cycles grow shorter and stronger, breath squeezed in at the throat, making a hiss as it emerges. Rising, turn by turn, into a growl that forms from the root where birth begins, calling for new life to replace what they will take. In and out, through nostrils now drawn up into a snarl. Preparing to put aside pity. Praying that they are worthy enough to play the part of the beast. Knowing that they must.

The heat builds and the breath creates new sight. The path is envisioned, success is foreseen, gifts are requested, gratitude given. When the cycle recedes to a natural end, he or she who has seen most clearly the animal they must pursue leads the way. The others trust, because no matter how mistily, they have shared the same dream.

Yes, she will breathe this agony away. Then she will stand up again and walk. She will rise up and roar like the bear and keep on walking until she falls out of life itself.

13

Hampstead Heath could save your life, thought Eloise, and not only on a day as glorious as this. If you came up here in the autumn rain with some rope and a black mood, this hallowed ground would not permit such desecration. Before you could find the hidden spot or tie the noose, a dog might bark and shake its coat of mud and smile at you. And even if that were not enough to make you think again, surely the branch would break and a sodden carpet of soil and leaves would cushion your fall?

If there was anything in her life akin to regular church attendance, for Eloise it was her Sunday morning run to the Gospel Oak entrance of the heath and then a sprint up Parliament Hill. This initial exertion was followed by a more leisurely power walk in a wide loop around the ponds, before a gentle jog back home. Of all the city's green spaces, the heath was special to Eloise. A fertile oasis offering both expansive views of the metropolis, and along its more secluded trails, a means to leave London behind altogether. To forget its proximity.

Before winding through the woods, Eloise stopped for her customary tribute to the panorama from the top of the hill. It was a clear day and reaching up above the leafier neighbourhoods the urban skyline drew a jagged sketch of cohabitation and commerce, hope and hubris. A flock of metal cranes bowed their heads and prayed quietly towards St Paul's, taking their Sabbath rest from the city's state of constant construction.

The heath had always welcomed a diversity of visitors, but today a curious gathering caught Eloise's eye, if only because a few of their number seemed to be looking pointedly back at her. She could not imagine why. They stood without speaking, in a ring, holding hands. Not the usual preparations for a picnic. Eloise puffed hard and bent forward, hands to her upper thighs, but she kept a discreet sideways watch, intrigued. It was no surprise to see group activity up here; revelry, nature-worship, self-improvement rituals, discreet assignations, memorials, sponsored walks, the latest fads in keeping fit. It all happened on Hampstead Heath.

However, this crowd did not have the aura of neo-hippies or keen adventurers into self-discovery. Indeed there was something distinctly conservative and sober about them. Praying for a lost friend who had loved this place, perhaps? But the gathering came across as neither celebratory nor inclined to heartfelt mourning and its participants appeared untroubled by any readable emotion. Almost robotic.

It was for this reason that they looked out of place, Eloise realised. They had chosen to gather here in this haven of nature, preserved by and for the city dweller, and yet they felt wholly unnatural to it. Despite the reverent poses they were oblivious to their surroundings, neither noticing, nor honouring, nor enjoying them. As if they were here by necessity, out of duty perhaps, or on some deadly serious mission. Each wore a variation on the theme of beige, but several had a subtle detail of red or maroon, in the form of a pocket handkerchief, a ribbon, a headscarf, or a belt. Then Eloise noticed that one among their rank, a long strip of a fellow she could see only from the back, was wearing a roll of thick brown packing tape looped around that same red belt. Odd, she thought. *But hey, each to their own.*

When more of the group turned their heads from the circle to stare at her she felt an unpleasant twist in her diaphragm, still pumping from the run up to the summit. Normally from here Eloise would switch into a fast walking pace to better take in every seasonal detail but instead she coughed, turned away and decided to pick up her pace again, at least until her path diverted out of view.

A few minutes on and she felt comfortable enough to ease out of her jog and let her heart rate settle, to let her senses relax into a softer awareness of everything around her. To allow the sun to seep through her skin and into her bones. She had forgotten the gang on the hill, more or less, but their peculiar congregation had revived an old meditation on the rituals of community, of hope, grief and loss.

The many ways in which humanity coped with suffering and how that pain might be reduced or eliminated were familiar reflections for Eloise, but lately she'd found herself wondering whether suffering was somehow a fundamental force of the life experience, a spur to the forming of bonds, to compassion and ultimately to growth. Should all suffering (and the forging of character from the effort to overcome it) always be eliminated? How different a person might her father have been, for example, without the burdens that he had to bear?

Eloise wanted to explore this theme further but felt it could be a difficult conversation to have with her colleagues. Especially those working on cures for childhood illnesses, or pain management. For who would not move heaven and earth so that a blind child might see, or a paraplegic could walk again? But since forming the outline of her book about Sarah, she had discovered a new kind of discourse, an alternative means to contemplating the difficult questions. As she selected a favourite pathway, one she knew so well it required no conscious navigation, she began making mental notes for another of her private 'love letters' to Darwin.

Before she could form any coherent arguments on her theme, Eloise was distracted by a last waltz of white butterflies making the most of the late summer sun and beckoning her from the paved track towards an overgrown trail. As she weaved further into the woodland, the heath began to work on her in its own particular way. The peaty tang of the soil, the ripening perfume of the ferns. Soon she abandoned the contrivance of her secret correspondence and released her thoughts to find their own emerging twists and turns. She embraced a different kind of dialogue, engaging now with the vitality of her surroundings rather than with one long dead.

How much longer would those butterflies live, she wondered? Their primary cause to fly must have been fulfilled through mating by now. Yes, there was still some nectar, a last round of pollination for some species, but otherwise did they dance today purely out of joy? Their genome remained the same whether in caterpillar, chrysalis or butterfly form, so did they remember anything of their former lives? Could they recall the struggle to change?

Eloise understood that metamorphosis was less about how something looked and more about how it lived – perhaps to feed in a different way, absolutely to seek others of its kind, to reproduce and carry on this remarkable code. It was not merely shape that shifted, but behaviour. It was a response to a new set of needs and the process of transforming into something capable of meeting those. In that sense, a poetic soul might consider this as much a metaphysical phenomenon as a biological one.

Finally she came upon her 'fairy glen', a hollow of ancient trees that leaned towards each other in slow conversation, like misplaced characters from Tolkien, or refugees from the felling of a primeval forest. As she touched their time-wrought gnarls and knots and stood under a halo of vibrant green, Eloise felt something stir within and it was easy to see how nature, fantasy and imagination had become so intertwined in the human psyche, especially for the more innocent of minds. To understand how shamanic tradition had emerged from an instinct to worship and to wonder, and a desire to enter more deeply into that wonder. (From there so easily to shift to fear and superstition, and on to organising, monetising and controlling all that unruly 'magic'.)

On the other hand, she could understand why some felt something was lost when everything was seen purely from a reductive and mechanistic point of view, even if for her this essential process had brought only a deeper appreciation. But, she wondered, could there ever be a new synthesis, some kind of rapprochement or a 'third way' for those who felt left behind? Perhaps not to be found in the wilder fringes of pseudoscience and its proliferation of cults (some no better, if not worse, than the major religions to Eloise) but maybe a more measured yet fulfilling embrace of the bigger picture, and the health and happiness of whatever ingredients made up the human soul? For what was magic or miracle after all but something with the ability to alter the state of something else, be that a flame, a catalyst or an enzyme? The negative ions in fresh air, a beautiful view, the care and company of friends, a sense of value and purpose.

'Oh... hello.'

'Hello. Gorgeous day!'

Her reverie was disturbed by a young couple who had also chosen to go off-path and wend their way towards a more secluded spot. They seemed surprised to find her there but smiled even so. Eloise moved on through the woodland, and thought for a moment that they might have been following behind her, perhaps trusting her knowledge of the glades more than their own (to her bemusement she was so often stopped and asked for directions, wherever she was in the world) but it wasn't them. It wasn't anybody, although she was sure she'd heard the twig-snap and leaf-rustle of a meaningful footfall. A dog no doubt, pursuing a scent too far, worrying its owner to distraction. But nobody called out or summoned their wayward pet to heel. The sounds had been too weighty for a squirrel hopping around in a tangled bank or a crow dancing in the undergrowth. Perhaps a badger, though unlikely. A fox then, surely? The scavenging urban variety had lost not only its fear (and health) but its nocturnal restrictions too.

She stopped as if to examine some wildflowers but used the moment to glance behind her and around her. It was silly of course, but Eloise wondered whether one or two of that strange, silent gathering from the top of the hill had somehow caught up with her, were shadowing her. No. Of course not. Why would they? No. She would not allow any paranoia to pollute her affection for this place. Although her new vigilance had reignited a recent yet persistent desire to bring a companion up here sometime, to share all of this with someone else who might appreciate the potency of 'Dr Heath'.

And now another of her captive memories had slipped its bonds. She recalled how delighted she'd been to discover a young Londoner as enamoured as she with this urban illusion of wilderness, even if his affection had been shaped by a history of forbidden teenage bacchanalia more than bucolic appreciation. One night they had consummated their mutual passion – for each other and for the heath – in a secret spot he knew about. A place she felt unable to revisit these days, either out of embarrassment or the denial of how much she missed him. She was not sure which sentiment was worse.

Oh, stop it, Eloise. She would no longer indulge such useless nostalgia. Maybe it really was time for that dog. (Ah, but then he had been a dog lover too, once suggesting that they rescue a few together, desperately imagining a future that they both knew she could not offer him.) Where was all this longing coming from, for the fictional salvation of that discarded love, that missed opportunity? It was hardly helpful and she didn't need any of it. While Eloise didn't get to see her closest network as often as any of her friends might like, as busy and spread out as they all now were, she kept in touch via digital means and these deep connections were sufficient. More than that, the 'self' was sufficient. And the work she was doing was everything.

And yet. Eloise was aware of her tendency to seclude herself beyond what was healthy. So maybe she should consider inviting KC to join her up here one day? Their current condition of 'compatible colleagues' owed much to continued assurances – from both KC and Eugene – that Sarah was going nowhere, and also to Eloise putting aside the notion that KC was under orders to do *anything* to relocate the bones. She had confronted him about his supposed secret meetings with Eugene, about his clandestine negotiations with his backers.

'OK,' he had said, reacting more calmly than she'd anticipated, 'I can understand how the way our collaboration came about and some of the stuff that happened early on might have spooked you all. But please trust me, all I want now, all *we* want now is to make some real progress here and to share everything that we find. It might not mean a hell of a lot right now, but with my hand on my heart I can promise you that much. And you know what, Eloise, good for Rory for watching your back and all... but you do realise the guy has a thing for you?'

'Oh, don't be silly, of course he hasn't.' (But she knew of course that he had, harmless as it was.)

'But, hey, who can blame him?' KC had added, with his sideways smile.

So, no. Maybe she shouldn't invite KC up here after all. Maybe that would be tempting fate too far? The heath had a way of bringing out the romantic in her, which could be risky to her relationship with him in more ways than the carnal. Indeed, KC had already called her out on her inclination for the fanciful.

A solar flare having enhanced the borealis to a spectacular degree, the pair had flicked through a social media slide show from around the various northern latitudes over a shared coffee break. Eloise had mused aloud about what Sarah might have made of it and how, for all their understanding of the earth's protective magnetic shield, this extraordinary light show of charged particles had an eeriness about it that 'touched the human spirit', stimulating an innate desire to praise the wonders of such a finely tuned universe. She had gone so far as to ask whether such phenomena might manifest, in part, in order to inspire the observer.

'What?' KC had replied, in an incredulous tone that took a sharp departure from his customary diplomacy. 'You mean that cold, mechanical set of physical laws that would crush your supposed "observer" to dust outside of the fragile system that allows it to live? Or the nuclear explosions that enable complex planetary life to occur but which would fry or let freeze that same life the minute it stepped out of the Goldilocks zone? Come on, Eloise. Be careful of falling for the woo woo. Magical thinking isn't gonna get us very far in this field. And better make sure that your "baloney detection kit" is in good order there, Dr Kluft, 'cos I reckon you get too easily drawn into the wilder theories sometimes.'

To quote Carl Sagan against her was cruel and this had stung. Not only because she now felt diminished in KC's estimation but because she'd endured enough of being dismissed in this way, in both her work and her love life. That this poetic aspect of her personality, this tendency to be open to potential without *believing* in anything until persuaded by empirical proof, must always make her somehow 'less' when she felt it might be the door to 'more'.

She had responded. 'But there has to be a balance, KC? There's a fine line between what many reject as magical thinking and the openness that we need. Without which so many of our great steps forward could not have happened at all, or were far too delayed... The freedom of the imagination, KC! Of simply asking the question "what if?" I'm sorry, but I'm with Einstein when it comes to valuing the imagination. What was it he said? That "imagination is more important than knowledge"... yes, that's right, something about it embracing the world, stimulating progress, even evolution? No, sorry, but I won't apologise for a mind that's open to *potential*, KC, or for projecting that same sense of wonder on to Sarah. Because if we're going to get the public interested in this and behind this kind of work, then it needs to be relatable?'

An entente cordiale had soon resettled but the exchange had ramped up her wariness of him again, hardened her suspicions that they might not be such 'kindred spirits' after all. (Not enough for an alliance of the heart, anyway.) Indeed, Eloise had been tempted to wonder whether KC might be capable of turning any perceived 'weakness' against her if their working partnership ever had cause to be prised apart.

No, better not KC then. Her chosen companion for hiking the heath should be someone close, yes, but not in danger of coming *too close*. Or adversarial, if push came to shove.

Anna? She lived near enough. But as much as she loved her old medical school compatriot, their conversations about what each was discovering and what each was duelling with, Eloise knew that Anna's now toddling baby would only slow them down, or the pushchair limit them to the path more travelled.

What about John, then? *(And there it is again, that bloody rustling.)*

As Eloise pressed on more purposefully away from those unseen noises, she contemplated her relationship with her fellow Samaritan. He was so often an unlikely source of inspiration, the grit that forms the pearl. She recalled something John had shared the other night about a supposedly 'scientific' experiment conducted 'in some teaching hospital or other' to investigate the efficacy of prayer.

The very idea of it had seemed oxymoronic to Eloise, but he had assured her both of the study's credentials and of some provocative results. Apparently, the observations suggested that beneficial intentions from a group of volunteers (whether religiously inspired or not) had produced quicker and more effective wound healing in another group of volunteers (unknowing recipients of the 'prayers') compared to a control group (who had not been prayed for at all). She had questioned the criteria, argued that people healed at different rates for a variety of reasons, but John insisted that all this had been accounted for. Eloise resolved to do some digging, doubtful of the conclusions or that such results could be reliably repeated, but nonetheless intrigued.

Oh, for fuck's sake, what IS that?

Her heart was tripping spikily now, instead of the satisfying rhythms of a well-paced walk. The unsteadiness in her knees made them feel more degraded than ever. No! This was ridiculous. She would not become frightened of this place, she could not permit it.

She looked around again, this time more directly, searching the gaps between the trees and the undergrowth. There was nobody there. Perhaps that was the problem? Her precious *imagination* was filling in the blanks. Oh, the irony, she was forced to admit. So, should she go back to the concrete path, out in the open? No, goddammit, much better to push past this silliness, to employ a distraction technique.

Yes, keep thinking, Eloise, keep thinking. That's always your shield. (Anything but admit to your vulnerability.) Look for hard evidence, not for those creepy occultists from the hill. Listen for realistic clues and natural movements, not for the wandering phantoms of every regretted decision. Make a positive plan.

Eloise resolved to look into some local self-defence classes. And to bring her phone with her next time, along with its ill-fitting earphones, much as she resented how modern life had conjoined humanity to this devilish device. Music might have helped her right now. Or not? Would getting lost in melody only expose her to whatever (harmless thing) was making those noises? She wished for a Bluetooth speaker instead, the kind she loathed having to listen to anywhere public, but especially anywhere that ought to be peaceful. She fantasised for a moment about a blast of wailing guitar and some thrumming bass... a Celtic war cry, a rebel yell.

The thought amused her, sanding the splintered corners from her fears. It also reminded her about a set of exotic experiments conducted by a physicist in Japan who had played either uplifting or angry music to snow crystals as they formed in the lab. The flakes that were treated to the arias made more beautiful, intricate symmetries, while the metalheads became all deformed and chaotic. She wondered if perhaps the fellow had been trying to prove a point to his teenage children, but it was an interesting exercise and one whose observations came as little surprise to Eloise.

She'd once had a flatmate so fond of playing AC/DC at absurd decibels, despite her pleas, that she'd briefly but alarmingly contemplated a violent resolution (a brutal bout of PMS not helping the matter). Now she understood the false courage it had afforded him and was inclined to be more sympathetic.

Music. Such a fascinating field for investigation, with all its mischievous and measurable effects upon the human brain. Eloise eagerly consumed anything published on the subject. If it hadn't been genetics, it would have been neuroscience. She was fascinated particularly by those tiny cerebral clusters responsible for states of ecstasy and excitement, for good or bad.

It seemed ungrateful to question their purpose but they had been the source of so much human happiness and also of so much madness, so much danger. Perhaps that same arrangement of neurons that brought her to tears during the duet from *The Tales of Hoffmann* also made men kill each other for the love of a woman, or persuaded religious and nationalist cults to go to war? Of course she knew that the primary function of such excitement would be to stimulate reproduction, but even so, did such altered states also make life worth living, or create experiences that were worth dying for?

Eloise preferred those studies that suggested the human brain was wired more for kindness than for killing (admittedly less so when the override switch of starvation came into play). Yes, it was a remorseless kind of resilience and adaptability that had enabled the species to survive – and a simple need for movement that had spurred the earliest of neural systems – but it was sociability, surely, that had encouraged the hominin brain to keep growing. The forming and maintaining of relationships. And the bigger and more complex that set of relationships, the more *Homo sapiens* intelligence evolved to keep up.

We came together to make love, to make music, to make exchanges through trade. To create common cultures and beliefs, even before the age of agriculture. It seemed to Eloise that such acts of *communion* must be in our best interests, in every way.

She believed that it was only after the emergence of land ownership and hierarchy that the joy of ceremony was tamed and turned into organised religion, *ruining everything*. But this deep need in humans for connection and redemption, the need to help, to give thanks and to supplicate remained a powerful instinct. Eloise acknowledged that she was more often drawn to those such as John, those who had chosen a life of service to all of this over more traditional advancement, ambitions or desires.

As she emerged on to a wide-open and sunlit pathway (with some relief, though proud that she'd maintained both her wilder route and her willpower) Eloise pondered a familiar personal paradox. If someone had asked her whether she would rather be stuck in a lift with, say, the Dalai Lama, or with one or two of the more famously aggressive atheists in her community she couldn't help thinking that she would choose the former, if only for the kindness of that smile, the lightness of that giggle and the calm quietude of all that 'mindfulness'. But would she, could she, ever admit that out loud and among colleagues?

*

She has walked through many days that seem to her as though they must be the same day, but she knows they cannot be. She looks for any change to mark and to remember, the shape of something, the feel of something else. Along the way, in the repetition of steps, she has come into a walking trance and imagines that her own thoughts weave together with the thoughts of everything that lives, perhaps with everything that exists. She becomes, for a moment, an empty vessel, a hollow bone.

She remembers now the quiet talk among the few within her grandmother's trust, of times such as these, journeys such as these in other days long dead. She realises that all of this has happened in its own way many times before. That the earth would shrug and change its face, and all that was to be done was to live as long as the living would allow and to keep moving, keep changing with it.

At least it has been easier going across this flat expanse of former grassland. Are they nearing the coast at last? Then she trips on something and the surprise shakes her out of her timeless thinking. The loose stones now under her feet signify the trials she will soon face. The earth has risen. Should she scramble up over the steep hills ahead or try to find a way around? No, she senses that this way will lead eventually to a shoreline. It will be tiring and perhaps even dangerous if black ice sticks to the smoother surfaces but she also knows that this kind of cracked and curling high ground can hold hidden treasures. Better to find food and firewood, however, before attempting it.

She sees no clues of any meal that will be easy. No larger prey left here. Surely something lives in the warmth and damp underground? This is ideal earth for burrowers. Yes, there, the tell-tale sign of droppings. Only a few small pellets, but fresh. Is there time enough to find the opening of the warren, to set a snare and wait? But she is not alone in her plan to raid the shelter of those that dart and dive, fast and agile, those too small for spear or arrow. They have other enemies. Sly, cold and slithering. Less worthy of the feed than her. She knows that this is an unworthy thought but the times have led to it. There. There! The ripples of its limbless sliding are drawn into the loose top sand.

She follows the sweeping lines, they are new. And now she sees a little sand-rat, mouth full of young grabbed up by their hairless scruffs, running, finding its mark, disappearing below. The snake has seen it too, tasted it upon its tongue, and it follows. This one will not distinguish between young and old. It can fit through their tunnels, corner them. It will stay as long as it can be filled. Leaving nothing, no hope of another cycle of living.

Its prowess is worshipped by some, but not by her kind. There is fear, for sure, but there is also respect. This is an ancient thing, a thing that can dream a path through adversity and survive in strange, sleepy ways that others cannot. A thing that can shed its own skin when it no longer serves and when it is time to grow again. The slider will surely not taste as nice as the little runner but, this way, both she and the burrowing sand-rat can win.

*

On coming home from the heath, a workout that had been as invigorating mentally as energetically, Eloise went directly to her desk to type up the letter to Darwin she'd begun to compose on her enforced jog down the hill, away from the cold stares of that circle. (Were they still up there on the hill or had they spread out? She had twitched at the suggestion of any beige-clad human she had spotted on the way home, accessorised in red or otherwise.) Enough of that and back to work. She wanted to capture her thoughts from the heath in a more concrete form, before the cognitive re-set of a hot shower and an icy rinse. Eloise was feeling both inspired and unsettled. So many things were playing on her mind.

Dear Charles...

(She felt familiar enough now to abandon formality, especially with no living readership to rebuke her.)

... I wonder whether you would worry as much as I about where we are headed, about the risks, about the ethical quagmire? As in your day, there are many who feel deeply threatened by our work and by what it might mean. The dangers could loom from many directions.

My good friend John (I have mentioned him before) raised these anxieties for me again in our last conversation, along with the spectre of eugenics. Of course, I utterly reject every horror committed in the name of genetic purity and foolish notions of superiority, from the concentration camps to those enforced sterilisations of the 'feeble-minded' in the US last century. And if I'm honest, I'm apprehensive about how some of the work I'm doing now might be used in the future, the idea of engineered enhancements or misuse for personal or national gain (as challenging as commercialised or weaponised design may actually turn out to be).

But surely we must push forward in the quest to understand and to improve quality of life, to apply our own kind of compassionate selection by choosing to edit out the damage in every affected cell before it can cause devastation? I wonder how your own intimacy with the torment of ill-health (and the worst kind of grief, the agony of a child lost) would affect your view on our present dilemmas. Perhaps it is our role to interfere, Charles, even our duty now that we have 'evolved' enough to do so? (Some argue that our own evolution has already been redirected by civilisation, by our self-domestication as such.)

Or should we let go, trust nature and allow her to take her long, painfully slow course, with all that cruel, 'dispensable' damage along the way? For as much as it can be risky, the free rein of reproduction has been the most valuable stimulus to growth, up until now. Indeed, it's the very mutability in the risks of replication that has resulted in some of the greatest evolutionary leaps – and yes, these reproductive errors can be disastrous, but they can also be magnificent!

For example, what if we experienced another spontaneous 'accident' such as the complete duplication of the SRGAP2 gene? It's believed that when this happened in some distant common ancestor it effectively doubled our brain power. How wondrous might that be? (Or how horrific, if manipulated for only the privileged few?) So, should we wait and see what evolution has in store, or should we now take up the reins and attempt to further steer the process along... and can we be trusted to get it right any more than the trial and error of nature? So much is happening so quickly, Charles.

Some international laboratories – and even a few renegade 'Biohackers' experimenting on themselves – are moving forward at breakneck speed with CRISPR gene-editing, despite the possible hazards and lack of agreed regulation. But how can we not explore the full potential of these new frontiers... especially when it allows us, for example, to replace the shredding skin of a suffering child?

Improving health, immunity, longevity, limiting needless suffering and premature loss of life (freeing myself and others from the shadow of what they fear to pass on), this has always been my ambition, Charles. But is there a price that must be paid either way, an equilibrium that must be maintained? Are some evolutionary sacrifices necessary, after all?

She finds that snake meat is surprisingly good. At first she had attempted only the tiniest morsel and then waited for most of the night, despite the pangs of complaint from an impatient belly. Anything with scales was always a risk, not only in the catching of it but in the safe digesting of it. Often colouring or patterning is sufficient warning, but sometimes, when the need is greater than the fear, the only solution is to try.

She decided that she would not take a chance on drying or smoking any of the flesh, but instead charred it all to a crisp and consumed it in one sitting. The best place to store this meal is within. She is uncomfortably full now, and so sleepy, but pleased with her own resourcefulness, with her willingness to overcome her misgivings. Now that her resistance has been mastered, now that she knows how to anticipate the creature's rapid movement, she has found a new source of food. And while the bigger animals remain so depressingly few, the slithering and the scuttling ones are in no short supply.

14

It was not unusual for the detritus of various misplaced marketing campaigns to collect on her doormat, walked over rather than worth the effort of a creaking deep knee-bend, but something on quality lavender paper stood out from the various fast-food leaflets as Eloise arrived home. A handwritten note.

In careful, elegant script, its graphology spoke of another era of patient consideration. It was from Mrs Templeton, in the house on the corner, asking her to come and see her as soon as she could. Intrigued, Eloise walked right over but then hesitated at the door, unsure whether the old brass bell had worked or not as she'd heard no sound on pressing it.

After an impatient pause she chose the lion-headed knocker instead, which gave up a more purposeful and satisfying noise to announce her presence. Eventually, the door eased open and Eloise adjusted her gaze downward to meet the bespectacled eyes of her neighbour, who seemed so much older and shorter than she remembered.

'Mrs Templeton, it's Eloise Kluft, you left a note, are you alright?'

'Yes, dear, I'm fine. I'm so sorry. It's about the cat.'

Oh god, thought Eloise, her heart plummeting several storeys at once, although the clear, calm and remarkably youthful voice that delivered this anxiety gave little away.

'Newton? Oh, oh, right… what's the matter?'

'Well, dear, when I came into my kitchen, there he was. Not a surprise to see him, he visits me often, but I knew something was wrong. He was simply lying there on my floor. He was breathing, but there was a little blood, you know, from the nether regions. I'm sorry, I don't have your work or mobile number, so I asked Mr Singh next door to take us both to the nearest vet. I didn't know which one you used, dear, but he's at the Middleton. They are expecting you.'

Eloise had never liked that practice, felt they overcharged to cover the cost of too fancy premises. She had sought some treatment for Newton elsewhere when his continence issues began, and that vet's reassurances plus a change in diet seemed to have helped, at least temporarily. He had even lost a little weight, which at the time had seemed like a good thing.

The comforts of denial, she thought now, feeling horribly guilty. Perhaps she should have spent more money on him, done more, but she had so wanted to believe that he would be fine. He was getting old, that was all. Despite her contrition (which Eloise felt must be as obvious as a hair shirt showing beneath her silk slip), the nurse at the Middleton was kind enough when she walked in, seemed to know immediately why she was there and took her in to see Newton. He was on a drip, eyes half-open, they flickered when she stroked him. Then the vet came in and all Eloise could think was that he bore an uncanny resemblance to her old maths teacher. She did not know why she found that comforting, she had never been particularly good at maths and that struggle had very nearly cost her a place at medical school.

'Well, I'm sorry to say,' the vet began, confirming her worst fears, 'he's not a well animal. Not at all.'

Eloise took in very little of what he said next, re-entering this new and unwelcome reality only with the heavy portent of his final question.

'So. What would you like us to do, Dr Kluft? We can run some more tests, maybe try some treatments but at his age he's not likely to recover, I'm sorry to say. Indeed, any intervention may only stress him further, drag things out, if you know what I mean. Lovely old fellow, mind you. Well. We'll give you a few moments, shall we?'

By the time Eloise pulled back into her street an hour later there were no parking spaces. Of course. Arsenal were playing at home. Damn, she thought, as she made a mental note to compose yet another angry letter to the council, insisting they extend the match day parking controls to these streets too. She was weary, tired of everything, all the stupid little stresses that wore away at her resilience, gnawed at her soul. She kept the engine running in the middle of the street, did not know what to do. Newton was wrapped up on the passenger seat, she had opted to bury him herself in the garden they both loved. She had splashed out on a small fox-proof coffin but had hidden that away for now, out of sight, in the boot.

After a moment there was a knock on the passenger side and she jumped. It was Mrs Templeton. Eloise leaned over and unwound the window, manual and stiff, on her beloved old Golf.

'Pull into my drive, dear, please. Right there, behind mine, I won't be going anywhere tonight. And then come in, dear, don't go home quite yet. Come and have a cup of tea.'

Tea. *Yes*, thought Eloise, *the British answer to any crisis.* Tea sounded good.

She had never been inside the old corner house before, only spoken briefly at the door about this or that. It was the only detached property on their street of Victorian terraces and the only one with its own parking. They were all envious of that drive, such a valuable commodity in London.

The interior was exactly as she might have expected. Cosy but classy. Tidy, but not intimidating. Rather like Mrs Templeton. How long had she been a widow? Eloise had no idea. She recalled hearing that she was a retired teacher and several generations in the street seemed to know her very well. Her mother had known her, but she'd barely registered on the scale of awareness for Eloise. Although she'd suspected that the old lady might be one of those in the neighbourhood who fed Newton and kept him so fat and happy, she'd had no proof until now.

Eloise was guided to sit down and she gave herself up to an unfamiliar armchair as if she had been seeking its particular form of solace all her life. Mrs Templeton (Iris? Was it Iris? She didn't have the energy to ask) came back with the tea. Not in chintzy china cups, as Eloise had expected, not even in a teapot, but in tall, elegant white mugs.

'I'm so sorry, dear. Really, I am. He was such a delightful old thing. I shall miss him. Eleven o'clock sharp every day, in he came for his saucer of milk. I know I shouldn't have but it was only a drop and always semi-skimmed. I knew he wasn't well but I could only hope.'

Eloise could not be angry with her, even though this unhealthy treat would hardly have helped his digestive problems. Unlike his namesake, Newton liked company.

'I know. Don't worry,' Eloise absolved her neighbour, 'I'll miss him too.'

Mrs Templeton put down her tea, weaved her gnarled yet beautifully manicured hands together and inclined her neatly coiffed head.

'Of course you will, my dear. Of course. You must allow yourself to grieve, you know, you really must. You must find ways to face the pain. Without falling down the rabbit hole, of course. It really doesn't do to dwell. It will always be with you, yes, but even though each loss changes us a little, we can learn to carry them. But we must never bury them, my dear, or deny them. You have to keep busy, you see. That's the key. You have to stay open to life, to joy, no matter how much death has taken from you. My mother always used to say that "industry is the best cure for melancholy" and she was right, you know. I have learned that only too well. I have lost so many people.'

Eloise had nothing to offer in return for this information. So she simply nodded and sipped her tea. She nestled into the winged-back velvet of the armchair and looked around. Framed photographs everywhere, faces old and young, many in uniform. Colour, black-and-white and sepia.

Mrs Templeton noticed this silent study of her life.

'Yes, dear, there on the table beside you, those are my men. My grandfather, killed at the Somme. I never knew him, though I think we would have got along famously. They all said that I took after him. My elder brother, lost in a Lancaster over Libya. Only twenty-one. My father, next to him, he died in a POW camp in Malaya courtesy of the Japanese. My mother and I got out of Singapore just in time, but he stayed on. "Duty", don't you know. He starved to death. Or maybe it was malaria.'

Eloise felt the loss of all those precious men, each the bearer of an important nose and a defined brow. The same features that this lovely old lady wore with pride, despite the loosening effects of a long and full life.

'I'm sorry,' said Eloise, 'So many terrible things were done in those wars. In all wars.'

'Yes, but life goes on, eh? We might forgive, we might trade with our former enemies, but we don't forget. You know, my daughter adores it, but I have never been able to contemplate eating sushi.'

Eloise couldn't help herself, she laughed. Had to spit back some of her tea.

'Yes, dear. That's right. Life is a marvellously mad comedy, after all.'

Mrs Templeton had the kind of smile that surely would have fascinated the suitors of her day. Eloise indulged a vision of a happy young woman, floating in taffeta about some gilded ballroom, laughing and flirting – but never cruelly, never simply for the sake of it. Such a young woman would have been tempted by many but would have chosen wisely.

'And this one?' Eloise reached over and picked up a slender frame with the image of a youth in a bright-red uniform, a bearskin swamping his handsome head. Coldstream or Grenadiers? She knew little of regimental distinctions but understood that this uniform carried prestige.

'My grandson. George. He's in Afghanistan, or Iraq perhaps. Some such place. Not sure. Not sure it's official at all, actually. He's a crack shot apparently. One of the best.'

'Oh god.'

'Yes. One worries, can't help it. Especially with our family history. Still, he signed up, a career soldier. In the blood, I suspect. Do you suppose that luck can be inherited, dear, passed down?'

Eloise was halted by the question, a random conjunction of the esoteric with her own field of expertise. She paused, wondering how best to answer without giving offence.

'Oh... Well, no. I don't think so. Certainly not in any sense that I can comment on. Actually, I'm not sure I believe in luck at all, as such. My father had the odd pertinent saying too, you know. He used to say that "luck is just opportunity meeting preparedness". But I suppose that applies only to the good variety. Bad luck? I don't know... a series of chance circumstances colliding with unsuspecting choices, probably? Maybe there's some element of the subconscious involved in getting us into certain situations. Was his father in the forces? I mean, were there any strong influences encouraging him to join up?'

'Good Lord, no,' Mrs Templeton insisted. 'It came completely out of the blue. It was the last thing we wanted. My daughter is a bit of a leftie, you see, and she married another teacher, so, no, he was hardly encouraged.'

'I see.' Eloise searched for the most comforting, least patronising response, but then wondered whether Mrs T (yes she decided, that was what she would call her from now on) was aware of her medical specialism. Why would she be? Nonetheless, she decided to make an offering of her professional opinion.

'Well, it might be that his inclination for things military could be somehow inherited, there's still so much we don't know about how certain genes, or their chemical "epigenetic" tags may affect behaviour or tendencies – or react to them. It has been seen, though, that certain epigenetic changes related to responses to trauma, for example, can be passed down and can affect the next generation. But perhaps your grandson's choice was more about a desire to be of service in some way? I mean, that does seem to be a part of his background. Perhaps that was a subtle influence? Anyway, it's an interesting idea. I might have to look into it more, one day.'

Eloise felt no urge to leave so she settled back and sipped some more of her tea. It was good, remarkably so. She thought she might have to consider the occasional switch from coffee.

'I remember your father, you know,' offered Mrs T, in return. 'Very well. A fine man. Fine family. It's no surprise that you are such a success, dear.'

'Am I?'

'Oh goodness, yes, dear, don't you think so? All of our achievements must be appreciated. But we can't have everything. Perfection is a pipe dream and expectations are born to be confounded. That's what they all seem to have forgotten these days.'

'Yes. Quite.' Eloise was thankful for this small serving of colloquial wisdom, or for its intentions, at least. 'You know, I'm sure he'll be alright... your George.'

'Oh yes, I think so too. Praying like mad, of course, storming heaven with all my might. And I know that he has enough old warhorses watching out for him up there.'

Perhaps he has, thought Eloise, in a moment of wishful submission. She almost wanted to believe that it was so.

'Yes. Well, thank you so much, Mrs T. For everything. But I think I'd better get home now.'

*

She is unsure of what to do with the snakeskin. There is no tradition for its use amongst her people. She has let it dry in the sun and now holds it to the light to examine it closely, the tiny flakes that lay over one another, its curious give and stretch. There is a beauty to its patterns, for sure, but she feels unable to measure its worth. She strokes it, but it is cool to the touch and not comforting like fur.

There is little enough that is comforting now. Other than her caresses with the child, the soft strokes of a love whose worth too cannot be counted, but for different and better reasons. She recalls the touch of her grandmother, the steady circular passes of those leathery old hands around her back. Her mother's touch was softer, lighter, more playful. She had seemed, in many ways, a child at heart herself. Those lovely long fingers that would rake and comb through her hair. She recalled her father's firm pressure on her shoulders when she had learned something well or his tight grip around her waist as he lifted her to the sky in celebration. The pats and head tousles from the others in the clan. The pinches and prods from her brothers, the linked arms and the held hands of her childhood companions.

Companions. Sometimes she had resented them, walked away alone to keep her own company, the noises of her kind too much sometimes, too crowding. But she had always been glad to return. What sort of woman might her own child become without such connections, without other voices, without the touch of others? She is growing fast, reaching out to grab and pull and stroke and shake. Rolling and crawling now when her mother feels it may be safe. Trying so enchantingly to mimic her mother's words of love. But her mother's love is all this little one has. For how long will they be alone, for how long will her daughter be alone, if the girl lives long and strong enough to see her mother die?

This snake too had been alone. Had it ever loved – could it love?

Was it this lack that made the creature so cold to the touch, so hated, so feared? So free.

Before beginning the climb into the rocky high ground, and now revived on its roasted flesh, she wraps and tucks its skin tightly around her wrist. She will keep it a while longer and try to understand the source of its strength.

15

Eloise carried in the little shroud and placed it near the back door. She would bury Newton in the morning. She had spoken to Anna while at the vet's, waiting, hoping for the right decision to come. But now she wanted to call someone else. She tried another old friend before remembering that she was off traveling with Médecins Sans Frontières, as her voicemail confirmed. Who else might be available?

KC? No. They were getting along well enough and their working styles had a pleasing balance and compatibility, she thought they might be forming that friendship after all – but calling him now would be too weird, too needy. Besides, he hadn't known Newton, it could mean little to him. She thought for a moment about KC, his family. (Did they have pets?) This didn't help.

Then she tried to focus on the work and thought of Sarah, hoping it would distract her, trying to picture her. How would she have coped with grief? Death would have been so commonplace, so visible, so unremarkable, a daily occurrence of one form or another. She would have had the closeness of her tribe and all their traditions to mollify against loss. If they had allowed themselves to feel much of that at all? Surely Sarah would have felt no sentimentality over the death of an animal?

But this detour was only sharpening her sense of separation and could do little to pin back her pain. Eloise needed to call on her own tribe now, her own traditions. She thought of John. What was his number? No, he had too many other people to care for. Besides, there was a good chance he was on one of his regular visits to Pentonville prison tonight.

She rummaged around in the storehouse of her consolations, looking for an alternative, for something or someone who could lessen her pain, or at least appreciate and commiserate with it. Who else had known or loved Newton? And who had Newton loved in return?

Oh no, she thought, *here we go.* She had resisted the rush of remembering *him*, the young lover she had once been so passionate about, but she was too raw, too enfeebled to keep fighting it. As she lost all resolve, he swam upwards from his padlocked chamber to surface into her consciousness and she acknowledged that he was the only living person that she wanted now, the only one who might offer the comfort that she needed. But as quickly and as willingly as he might have come (in person and not mere memory) even after all these years, she had put him beyond her own reach. Where he must stay. It was for the best, yes, she still believed that to be so. He, like John, had others to care for now. At least she hoped that was the case, otherwise what would all that wrenching apart have been worth?

What else could she do? If she opened a bottle now she would finish it too thirstily. Then she would sleep, yes, but badly. And she knew enough about hangovers to know that one the next morning would only exacerbate her mood. When ambling through the middle ground of life Eloise was more than comfortable with her own company, even craving it, whether in a relationship or not. It was only at the extremes of good or bad that it became difficult to be alone. Eloise had never felt the house so empty.

She wondered how Mrs T coped with her own solitude, surrounded by her family photographs, her reminders of those lost. They seemed to give her succour. Eloise could not remember where all the old Kluft family albums were kept, perhaps in the camphorwood chest up in the attic along with the Thai silk and the Indian cashmere? She decided to go and search for them, at last finding them in a cobwebbed and battered metallic trunk, the kind the family had once used for long sea voyages. This one was still wearing its scratched and fading stickers announcing a series of exotic destinations.

The covers of some of the albums were torn, the satin or leather binding beginning to wither, the paper card yellowed, the glue that had once bound each photographic print to the page no longer sufficient to the task. But here, held within, was her history. She flicked through them, not ready to linger yet, wanting only to skim the surface of her childhood and to feel its unspecific warmth. *Oh, look, yes*, there they are at Borobudur in Java – a monkey on her skinny shoulders and a gap between her teeth. Now they are leaning on the rails of a P&O liner as it cruises through the Suez Canal, next she is hand-feeding a llama in the Peruvian Andes, and here they are standing beneath the golden dome of the mosque on Temple Mount.

Then an image that still shocks her, still floods her with the abrupt confusion of her first encounter with injustice, her first confrontation with the brutalising power of poverty. It is Bombay (as it was then known) sometime in the 70s, and behind the cosy huddle of the Kluft family looms large the decorative façade of the Taj Mahal hotel (and what horrors that grand old institution has suffered since, Eloise regretted to think). They had been strolling along the high-smelling waterfront, having recently arrived in India. Eloise remembered the odd sensation of jet-lag, as if her head was in a balloon, as she had attempted to describe it to her mother.

To the left of them in the photograph there is a beggar and he holds something aloft, balancing it precariously in the palm of his hand. It is a long bamboo pole and something sits above it. Oh god, yes, of course… Eloise remembered less the sight of the tiny toddler strapped into a chair atop this pole and more the sound of her cries. That child did not want to be there. That child was not enjoying the experience. Young Eloise had not understood how the girl's father – how any father – could do such a thing.

It took some considerable explaining by her mother to help her see that this man had little choice. That this action was his misguided way, perhaps, of loving the child and it was so that he might feed her. The fact that a father might not be able to feed his child other than by frightening and endangering her was something quite beyond Eloise's six-year-old comprehension. She had come to understand the ever-present reality of deprivation all too well since then, but wondered now whether she had become too used to it, too inured to its harsh truth. Eloise worried again whether she did enough, or gave enough. Perhaps she should sponsor another child?

She chose to park all the unpleasantness of the outside world for the moment and continued to flick through the precious legacy she had uncovered in that old metal trunk. Digging further, she found some of her parents' own family albums, generations both English and Norwegian, captive in black and white, solemn and unsmiling as they sat through the laborious photographic process – until the happy advent of Instamatic, Kodacolor and a developer on every high street. Eventually Eloise came upon an album that she'd thought was long gone, donated to the Royal Anthropological Institute along with the rest of her mother's academic photography.

Within its first page was carefully preserved an old cover of National Geographic, a photographic study of the Padaung, those colourful women of the hill tribes of Burma with their ringed and elongated necks. She looked at the date on the magazine – that particular expedition had come well before she was born, before her parents had married, at a time when the young Frances Fletcher would have been freer to travel, to risk and to commit to the work.

As she turned the pages, Eloise came upon the Pueblos of New Mexico. A series of polaroid snapshots seemed to focus more on art, jewellery and pottery than on faces, though there were some scenes of the Buffalo dancers, and a few bashful smiles. *Oh, yes,* Eloise remembered now, that exquisite turquoise and silver inlaid neckpiece that had been gifted to her mother in acknowledgment of her sympathetic treatment of the camera-shy Kewa culture. They'd had a story that needed telling, but they had not wished to trade their souls for it.

Then Eloise came across a series of pictures from Papua New Guinea. *Of course,* she thought, the de rigueur re-assessment (for any anthropologist of her mother's era trying to make their mark) of Margaret Mead's work on gender and culture. She remembered now how her mother liked to 'quote' her heroine, offering Mead's apocryphal encouragement to her daughter whenever she felt dispirited by human frailty to 'never doubt that a small group of thoughtful citizens can change this world. It is the only thing that ever has.'

The pictures in this collection were both candid and insightful. Her mother had loathed any kind of cultural exploitation, her mission had always been one of understanding and then sharing that knowledge, but she had rarely been sentimental. Nevertheless, in all these images there was a certain intimacy, a relationship between the subject and the woman behind the lens. These seemed to be more photographs of friends than dispassionate observations. Perhaps this was why her father had held back this particular album?

Towards the latter pages Eloise came across a series of images that she'd always thought she must have dreamt but now she retrieved a memory that, apparently, was quite real. A very young Eloise (four? five?) sits astride a shaggy-maned pony, held securely in its ornate saddle by the strength and the smile of a Mongolian horseman. This must have been either before or after a dig in the Gobi Desert? Her father is not in any of these shots, so perhaps her mother had left him to his fossils and brought her young child to the steppes to experience some life.

At once Eloise was bathed in a stream of reminiscences, of wide skies and biting cold, of warm yurts and rancid milk, of tame eagles flapping their vast wings and of red flags flying above the dust from pounding hooves. The thrill was more vital than anything in recent memory and she relished until it began to slip away, but she knew that she would return to this treasure chest again, and soon. Tomorrow perhaps, after she buried Newton... and thus the joy subsided and Eloise shuddered at the thought of this unwanted obligation.

Feeling the need to hold on to a touch of their comfort, she tucked a couple of albums under one arm to take downstairs. As she navigated the retractable ladder down from the loft, a single photograph came loose and floated to the floor. Even before she could pick it up for closer examination, Eloise recognised the virile posturing of the tanned young man in the picture standing proudly in front of the Buddhas of Bamiyan. It was Darius.

Her father must have taken the picture. How he would have wept at the senseless destruction of those treasures since, she could hear him in tones half-despairing, half-raging as he mourned for art beyond value that belonged not to those warped and angry vandals, not even to all Afghans, but to all humanity. It would be as monstrous to him as the Spanish conquistadors burning Mayan libraries in the name of the church, or all the other inestimable losses at the hands of various cultural 'cleanses'. Eloise was mystified, however, as to why this particular photograph had been included in their family albums.

This was taken long before she and Darius had become 'an item'. How odd, she thought.

Darius. Now there was someone who had known Newton well enough. Though he'd had no special fondness for cats, a friend of his had been moving abroad and after an excess of farewell drinks, he had returned home one night to present her with Newton. This was about six months before he'd left her. But she couldn't hate the pretty cast-off tabby for that. Especially when he turned out to be far better company than her ex. Eloise continued downstairs to the kitchen, placed the albums on the table and made some herbal tea. She left the photographs where they were for now and went into the living room to surrender to the generosity of her red velvet sofa (so painfully lacking the presence of that sweet little soul curled up at the other end of it, likely only to have stretched and yawned and changed his position in lazy acknowledgement of her arrival).

She half considered the diversion of a recorded documentary, but knew it would not satisfy. For the first time in a life full of so many hopes and joys and yet so many losses, Eloise felt an overwhelming sense of abandonment. The ache of isolation cast her back once more to the one she had tried so hard to forget, believing the brevity of that experience could override its intensity. Believing that Newton (or she) might be capable of loving anyone else as much. Before she could think better of it she had picked up the house phone. *What was his number?* But no, she had banished it from both phone and personal memory some time ago, to guard against temptation. It was pointless. Even if she could drag it out from the depths of her mental archives, would he still have the same number?

No. It was as well she could not remember. It was *she* that had given him up (against both their wishes) and she could expect nothing from him now.

Her mind was drawn back now to that fallen photograph from Bamiyan. To the man so tightly woven into her history there was little wiggle room for wilful amnesia. Yes, there was another number that she *could* remember with no trouble at all, etched in deep from the days before stored electronic memory. Darius had been one of the first to acquire a mobile phone with international capability (how proud he had been of that). He may not have bothered much with the cat that he had given her as a consolation prize but he deserved to be bothered by her bereavement now. She picked up her landline and pressed in the digits, not caring what it might cost him or what hour it was, wherever in the world he may be.

'Darius.'

'LoLo? What is it? Are you alright?'

'Darius, it's Newton.'

She could say no more. But no more needed to be said, Darius, it seemed, had understood.

'Oh. Oh LoLo, I'm sorry. Really. I'm so sorry.'

He knew her well enough, the tremors in her tone when she was trying to be strong. He knew she was in pain, yes, but this time apparently he cared. She could sense the sincerity in his pauses, in a voice less icily hardened, less convinced of invulnerability, a voice becoming thawed by the friction of life.

*

The climb had been the right decision, despite its difficulty. From here she can make out a coastline, at last... yes, she is sure that is what she sees disappearing into the distant yellow mists. Too far for them to reach quickly, close enough to allow for a lasting rest. And there is sustenance here, she has discovered a flock of fat and slow ground-nesting birds. She has taken what she can of them, and from them, without taking more than their numbers or their spirits could recover from. Those already without mates, those with more than one egg.

And in the heart of this high ground she has found a good cave, rare and precious, no one's territory now but hers. She has burnt the rotting carcass of the strange animal that had come here to die, though what it once had been, she could not tell. Other than the rancid aroma that will pass in time, this is the perfect place to stop for a while. In its cool silence (so warm when the fire was new) she has allowed herself to let go of her aches, her fears, her doubts and to retrieve a long-forgotten chant for the child. The smile, the gaze it brings lurches deep into something she did not know was possible.

In this stillness she has also felt safe to trance. Powerful, but mystifying, it is nothing she can cling to or recognise. Strange but revealing in ways she may never understand. Are these spirits or people? So, so many people. Creatures hard, sharp and angular like rocks carved by some giant elder, and they moved so fast. A colourless human, perhaps, or a ghost, is looking at her. It keeps looking back at her.

She let it be. Let it settle somewhere where one day she might be able to recall and read the signs. Not now.

Now she examines her necklace, those pretty shells that had required such skill, patience and precision to work without cracking. But these are not the kind of treasure that she needs in this moment. She breaks a piece of carved ochre from the centrepiece of the necklace, crushes it and mixes it with melt water. She rubs it into the parts of the bear hide that have begun to waste.

This is important work. She was taught well by her mother how to treat any hide before letting it near a living body. How to avoid and to carefully check herself and others for those nasty crawling pests that would sink their tiny teeth into your flesh, hang on and steal your blood before you noticed them. Or worse, before they gave you the red fever and the agonising aches. She finishes with the hide and resolves to check again her own body, between her toes, her hair, and that of the child. Although they have made no close contact with any other warm, living thing for so long, it is unlikely that they have been travelling all this way alone.

But before touching the child again, she wipes the paste on to the rock and the trail of her fingers remains. There will be no rain within these rocky walls to wash the lines away. How long will this sign of her presence stay?

An old temptation returns. Will she try something she has often imagined but was never brave enough to attempt, as she could not know whether it might please or offend? There are no others now to ask. It is only for her to make the choice and so she begins. She prepares more paste. The figures flow from her fingers with instinctive grace. Along the smoothest striation of the wall, they soak in and start to mark out the episodes of her odyssey.

16

Her eyes were tired and still red and swollen, despite the misdirection of some extra make-up. Rory had noticed her unhappiness and asked if she was OK but Eloise declined to talk about it, afraid the tears were too imminent. She had never been good at sharing her own sadness, however instinctively she gave encouragement to others. There was too much to do, but once KC had left for his regular conference call with his colleagues across the water, Eloise sent Rory home too.

There was little of significance for KC to report. The head of Sarah's femur, which they'd counted on as their next best source for harvesting the right cells with the least risk of damage, had turned into another dead end. But there was a glimmer of progress. To everyone's relief, there'd been no further contamination issues since the new security measures had gone into place (and no successful email breaches since the new firewall parameters) and this was good news indeed, barring the disturbing inference that *someone* in the building was not to be trusted. The next step would be to compare every staff member's DNA against the source, but that would steal time and resources they could not spare.

Eloise caught herself wondering (in spite of how well they seemed to be getting along, both personally and professionally) whether there was the remotest possibility that KC himself had been sabotaging their work, setting up cause for a full handover to the US? Surely not? He was certainly under pressure from those responsible for the 'bottom line' but this would be Machiavellian beyond all reason. There was no clear cause anymore for that level of mistrust.

Eloise put all such outlandish notions of dark plotting aside, laid all concerns about Sarah to rest for a while and reassigned herself for the evening to monitoring the progress of the corrected cells in the pancreatic study. A simple, suspicion-free project running parallel with Sarah that had a good chance of yielding applicable results. It seemed that no distraction today would be successful, however, and her thoughts kept looping back to the morning's sorry task. To the shovel that she had forgotten to return to Mr Singh, to the sealed grey box underground that was denying, against the all-rightful demands of nature, an easy meal to her neighbourhood foxes.

No. She needed to let thoughts of death subside with all the other heaviness and worry of her world right now, wanted to think about something vital, something energising. She needed to lose herself in the vigour of another.

So, in the lull of her working limbo (and the failure of Mrs T's 'cure' of industry) Eloise closed her eyes to remember. The shock of it still stirred her, seven years on. The pictures, the sensations emerging so clearly into the present. She is having sex in a dark stairwell. Wild sex with a thrilling but entirely unsuitable new partner. Not 'making love' as she had done with Darius, those complex chess moves on Egyptian cotton sheets or that half-hearted submission to enervated duty, but she is greedily shagging with complete abandon, and it is bliss.

Afterwards she had felt a little nauseous with the shame, but the addiction had begun. She had known her eager new admirer for only a few days and he was so much younger. So absurdly delicious. She had tried to dismiss it. *No. No, no,* she had reproached herself at the time, *this is impossible, this cannot be.* But she lacked the belief to resist it.

Eloise had met Tom when she was thirty-seven. Two dry years after Darius. She'd been running on the track in the park, in the days when she still trained religiously. The whack of filthy leather had come from nowhere, booted with venom (at Tom, not her). She recalled the jolt of the blow and the acknowledgement that, yes, a football in the back at speed is rather painful. Winded, she'd dropped to all fours. When able to feel anything again, Eloise had felt a hand gripping her bare shoulder.

Yes, yes, she thought, as she let herself remember it all, as real as it had ever been, entering the moment as if it were happening right here, right now…

'Fuck, Shit, are you alright? Fuck, I'm so sorry, are you alright, darlin'?'

Her breath came back slowly.

'Yes, I'm fine. It's nothing. It's OK, just the shock.'

She was not a wimp, not frail. She was strong, she would not make a fuss. She looked up at him – and then had to look away again to avoid a wave of unexpected desire. She wasn't ready to move yet but he helped her up and she surrendered to it, let him hold her.

He is so young, she thought, *how old can he be? Twenty? No more than twenty-five.*

Her calculation was interrupted by cat calls from his friends.

'Oi! Come on, you wanker, she's alright!'

Eloise ignored the sequence of obscene gestures and recommendations that followed.

'Fuck off, you cunts! Oh, sorry, darlin' – 'scuse my language,' he both cursed and apologised, as he kicked the ball back towards his cohorts.

It was a weekday afternoon, during some welcome 'get-things-done-at-home' leave for Eloise. None of the players wore a team strip of any description and they were an odd number for any-a-side but they seemed harmless enough, despite the vulgarity. Eloise did not share the snobbery of many of her social strata, those who might make educated excuses for their disdain. ('Barely bipedal,' she imagined Darius deriding, as he condemned such lads to their fates, 'the natural world would have selected them for extinction by now if we weren't keeping them on benefits.')

But this young man was still there beside her, still touching her shoulder, still smiling at her rather than returning to his 'losing' team.

'I'm sorry,' he offered, with playful sincerity and a half-bow.

'Oh, don't worry, it's not your fault, it was an accident.'

'Yeah, I know, it wasn't me – but it was meant for me. If I hadn't been watching you.'

Eloise looked down at the ground, afraid he would notice the dilation in her pupils. Was he feeling what she was feeling? His bold touch on her shoulder told her so.

'I've seen you here before, you know. Running.'

She felt a little hunted, but was surprised by how much she was enjoying his shameless flirtation.

'I owe you an ice cream, or something,' he offered with persistent charm.

'No, no you don't, it's fine really.'

And yet Eloise had found herself eating an ice cream with this boy after he had abandoned his game and his friends, sitting at a weathered picnic table across from a face she could not figure out. It was alluring in parts but there was something elusive that would not crystallise. A proud nose. (Good.) His lips were lush and full and might not look amiss on a Hollywood starlet, and under his arched eyebrows his eyes were a little too narrow, a little too close together and an indistinguishable colour... but when they looked at her she was intoxicated.

The human eye. Such a magnificent accomplishment of adaptation, she thought, as she remembered that feeling of *connection* with her new companion. Its very complexity had become the battle cry for the deniers of evolution, despite computer modelling that revealed how its progression from simple light sensor to a full optical lens was both possible and natural. To Eloise, the eyes were a window not so much to the soul but to the countless generational changes that enhanced awareness of prey or hazard. (Or perhaps, she admitted, from a more whimsical perspective, a richer appreciation of the wonders of this world.) As far as she was aware, the human eye remained superior to any computer algorithm when it came to recognising certain patterns. How much more might it evolve, she wondered. How much more, in time, would we be able to see? *Or do we see only what we need to see in order to negotiate this limited consensus of physical reality?*

She had unlocked herself from his gaze to more coolly assess her audacious suitor. Tom, as he had introduced himself with a zealous handshake, kept his hazelnut hair tribally short and was pasty in the poorly nourished way of young men who eschew healthy eating in favour of beer and cigarettes, but he was hard, defined and kick-about athletic. The Celtic spiral tattoo that curved around his triceps (a perfectly formed triangle that presented itself for her admiration each time he twisted his Cornetto) was badly executed, but the pattern was entrancing as it flexed. The most curious thing, the feature that had reeled her in beyond return, was an identical scar to her own right under the chin. Eloise did not subscribe to divination and yet this shared marking had seemed somehow... prophetic.

Tom had found her on the track the next day and ran backwards beside her, with an optimistic grin. Normally this might have annoyed her, raised her guard with a reflex of aloofness, but despite taking a different route Eloise had hoped he would find her. It was ludicrous of course, and yet, inexplicably, during this second encounter Tom had persuaded her to meet him again. To her amazement she had agreed to go out on a 'date'.

They chose the night of the summer solstice and the grass-worn mound of Primrose Hill, with its clear city views and its urban legend of ley lines, had attracted all the usual suspects. The any-excuse revellers, the hipsters, the tourists, a handful of 'African' drummers competing with a circle of droning didgeridoos. And of course, the druids.

There was something so bizarre and yet so British to Eloise about a gang of white-robed, middle-aged alternatives resurrecting a romantic past while juggling hampers and handbags and organising their worship over mobile phones. It made her laugh out loud, not cruelly, but with a sudden warmth for the splendid eccentricity of it all. It was the first of many times that Eloise would laugh that night, in a way she had forgotten to, in a way she had foregone for far too long. She might have blamed the surprisingly decent wine that Tom had supplied to wash away the awkwardness, but she knew that this was more than disinhibition. It was rare to find a sense of humour in such perfect harmony with her own and they giggled like teenagers in a frequent chorus of carefree joy.

As they'd picked themselves up from the grass to descend the hill she'd stumbled on the incline. Tom's reflex to steady her soon turned into a whole body hug and it had felt like coming home. It was only as they'd unwound the natural weave of their bodies that her defences had sprung into place again. Eloise thanked him, blaming her clumsiness, but avoided eye contact as she searched in her bag for that extra bottle. Thinking she might find his offering undrinkable, she'd turned back to grab one of her own before leaving to meet him (willing herself not to think twice). Now she was glad – of every decision that had led her to this moment – and for choosing the only screw top to hand. Silencing her inner scold once more, she swigged straight from the bottle before passing it to Tom. Then they had walked away in unison from the solstice celebrations and onwards into the late-coming London night.

When Tom had pulled her into the stairwell and manoeuvred her against the wall, Eloise had felt that for propriety's sake she should resist, initially.

Please, he had said. *Please.*

Now, in the comforting loneliness of the after-hours laboratory, she kept her eyes closed and savoured the memory for a moment longer, breathing in the spiciness of his smell, feeling the rhythm of his hips, before fast-forwarding to another cherished episode in this sequence of recollections.

This time Tom is naked, standing on her Indonesian dining table changing a light bulb that has been dead for months. It is perhaps the most beautiful thing she has ever seen. He turns, smiles, winks at her. Her stomach vaults.

In the weeks that followed the solstice, Eloise could not remember having been kissed so much or so passionately since she was seventeen. They were 'getting to know each other' and she'd chastised herself for many of her assumptions and prejudices. For having been surprised to learn that Tom loved to read (OK, not quite her essential library list, but even so), although she recognised that part of his charm was the fluent (and yes, often colourful) way in which he expressed either an opinion or an emotion. Why had she assumed that a certain accent, attitude or aptitude for the Anglo-Saxon (and such freedom with expressing or acting on his desire for her) would indicate otherwise? For all her travel and education, for all her supposed 'worldliness' Eloise realised how conversely sheltered she had been about her own neighbours and compatriots. And how much pleasure there was in stripping all that away.

The laughter! It came often and easily at the simplest and silliest of things. But their silences were never stilted and he seemed to sense when to leave her alone, never took offence at her fluctuating moods. Eloise found that she could fall asleep easily in his arms, a rare feat for such a light and irritable sleeper, and she would wake to discover that they lay together in mirrored, peaceful poses.

Tom's lack of sophistication unsettled her, nevertheless. Eloise had scoffed at the idea of taking him to one of the Foundation fundraisers, trussed up in a tux. The faces, the whispers. Then the sleeping scorpion awoke to raise its sting in a dusty corner of her soul, and she'd hated herself once more.

This is insane. What am I doing? She had known that it was hopeless, pointless. She was thirteen years older and would soon be old and boring enough to disgust her young lover, as surely as she already disgusted herself.

At twenty-five, Tom had no serious education, no discernible job, no 'prospects.' Yet he was exceptionally skilled in all the ways that mattered between them. No, not just skilled. Intuitive. Utterly in tune. Eloise had been unable to let go of that. Not without good enough reason.

For a while, she had felt there were much better reasons to hold on, to keep exploring. Despite being ostensibly unemployed (beyond sources of income that Eloise was not sure she wanted to know about) Tom was not without ambition, or talent. One morning she'd found a few of his doodles in the notebook she kept by her landline, and while lacking in technique, his drawing had a distinctive style and vision. The doodles were mostly an assortment of abstract circular systems, of 'automatic' patterns of dots and spirals and swirls. Some of his work was more figurative, however, and engaged with the here and now. In particular, Eloise was touched by how well and with how much humour and affection his sketch of Newton had captured her cat's inimitable character. She'd asked him to tear out and sign the portrait, thinking she might frame it one day.

(Oh god, where is that now? I must find it.)

'Have you thought about going to art school?' she asked him at the time, 'or maybe doing a graphic design course?'

Tom had looked at her as though she'd suggested that he apply to NASA, and said, 'Yeah. Right.'

She decided not to push it. But it was clear that Tom had a facility with numbers, too, and he'd picked up backgammon as if he was born to it (soon learning how to beat her, as she'd hoped) which made Eloise wonder if he might be musical. Did he play any instruments?

'No,' he'd claimed (beyond being able to whistle with perfect pitch or memorise a rap) but she imagined this denial was more about a lack of opportunity than a lack of gifts. The way he looked at her when she showed any belief in him, in any such potential, suggested a hunger not only for her admiration but for so much... *more.*

Then (of course, of course, she had been expecting it) the mortal blow. Tom had scraped up the courage one day to tell her that a former, occasional 'girlfriend' was pregnant. He did not want her to be, but she was – and she was swearing that it was his.

Five months pregnant, Eloise had been horrified to learn on further interrogation (if relieved that conception would have been well before they'd met). The discovery had come several weeks into their tryst, after countless frenzied couplings and when it was far, far too late to stop. Or rather, to stop *feeling.* But it was the beginning of the end for Eloise. She could not, would not interfere with fatherhood.

One afternoon they had glanced at each other and it had held. Then it was clear. This fever of unfettered lust, for both of them, had become love. He knew and she knew. Profound, authentic, simple. Nothing like the theatre of war it had been with Darius. *Impossible.* This madness could go no further. She would deny him.

*

She is pleased with her work. Some of the creatures have not been captured so well. This is a difficult thing to achieve, she has learned. The heads are too big, or the legs are too small, and yet they live on in new form across the walls of this cave.

The symbols had come easier. Sun, water, tracks, spear, fire, moon. There had been some sadness as she drew the semi-circles of two men at a fire, or four women sitting together to talk, or to trance. Those marks now inhabit the beginning of her handiwork. Towards the end of this progression, the marks show only one woman. But not quite alone, there is the cup of her own semi-circle and also a smaller cup at her back. Within the curve of her own symbol there sits a cross. Only she can understand what it represents. The promise she has made.

She wonders if it would have been right to also honour the thing that had died here with some kind of mark. It had been here first, after all, and this was its tomb. And it had suffered here, that much she felt. She pulls a charred bone from the base of the fire. She still cannot name this thing. She thinks it is better to leave it in the fire. Let it turn to ash. Something else of it seems barely touched by the fire, but it is not a bone.

There has been little in her life that she has not wished to know more about, to look at, to touch and to learn from. But not this. She feels it is best to leave this thing where it is.

17

Eloise worked a while longer, but sorrow was scratching at her focus and soon she struggled to see through the microscope or take in its magnified images on screen. Leaning, back, closing her eyelids and stretching out the creaks and knots, she selected a memory, the way an old-fashioned jukebox finds and plays a record.

That crooked incisor, revealed whenever he smiled, and he smiled often. The soft husk in his voice, the subtle rasp that grew deeper whenever he was aroused. The way he called her 'Girl'. How he pronounced it in his north London accent so that, somehow, it did not seem absurd.

'Alright, Gell?'

Yes, she *had* been alright, for three short months.

Working late and alone was no longer enough to divert her, to keep the barking hounds of loss at bay or to distract her from all the potential for pain. Eloise decided to shut down for the day and face the dismal journey back to her pet-less home. She knew she couldn't handle the Tube so decided to walk all the way, aware that as the evening lost its length any lingering autumnal warmth would soon recede into the dusk. She was lightly dressed but didn't mind the chill, it meant she could pick up a brisk pace. Even so, by impulse she decided on a short cut through a soulless, if well-lit estate.

Social Housing. This struck her as perhaps a tragic misnomer, as she passed by a tiny apron of grass hemmed in by chipped and bent railings. It bore a forlorn yet ridiculous notice forbidding all ball games or the exercising of dogs. It was beyond her own experience, but she wondered how much fun, how much freedom any creature (human or canine) might have growing up here? But then again, she had seen children come together creatively to make their own joy in even the most deprived of circumstances. It was among the deepest of instincts.

Certainly there had been attempts here to create a community spirit, to take pride. A couple of balconies bore flowering window boxes. A mural of 'permissible' graffiti stretched across some garage doors and tried very hard to be upbeat, resisting the art form's roots in political protest. The only protest here now, Eloise lamented, was to spit back at the privileged by overcharging them for their drugs when they came slumming, or to snatch whatever opportunities might arise to misappropriate from the careless.

No, not fair, Eloise, not fair, she admonished herself. She knew that such dismissive cynicism was part of the problem – and she knew that many here, in this cradle of concrete, would be the first to step up in a crisis. That most here were capable of anything given the right conditions. She knew that the genetic differences between rich and poor were negligible and not the key-holders of the poverty trap that were once theorised. Eloise understood that it was environment – from proper nutrition to the encouragement of a support network and, crucially, the right kind of stimulation as young brains were developing – that mattered most.

It was all about the opportunities for intelligence, innovation and curiosity to be expressed. Whether a cerebral withering or flourishing might condemn you to deprivation or propel you to the realisation of innate potential. A potential that would then run headlong into the web with which the wealthy insulated themselves. Into an austerity economy with two sets of rules and a beautifully spun lie of trickle-down rewards.

Eloise knew of one from such a place who would and could flourish. One who, with the benefit of a mother who had read to him and a father who had been lovingly present, had bloomed amongst those rationed patches of green. Then she immediately regretted thinking about him. But with these memories of Tom also came the recognition of why she'd chosen this seemingly random route (other than getting home any sooner) and of the hidden hopes that had pushed her in this direction. She wasn't sure whether this was Tom's estate, *but it might have been.*

As she came closer to home Eloise doubled back, deciding on a detour via her local shop but noticing the round-shouldered, darkly-clad youth a few metres behind her only once she had turned. She walked back past him without displaying any concern, despite the fact that, unusually, she felt some. But she needed to make that pit stop. No wine left at home. But also, as she realised when she got to the till, no cash in her purse either. Mehmet, the shopkeeper, knew her well and would have put it on a tab but she pulled out her debit card regardless. Eloise did not want to impose, preferred to save any favours for when she might really need them.

'When you gonna go contactless?' Mehmet asked with a smile.

'Whenever I am forced to,' Eloise replied, smiling back, still mistrustful of the supposed safety net of that technology.

She did not like the closeness of the other person behind her as she punched in 1953, but as ever, she allowed the benefit of the doubt. Before she could fully turn and fasten her purse she was shoved into the counter, the bag wrenched along with her shoulder, and he was gone. Mehmet was ashen.

'Hey!!! Hey!!! You bastard! My God, are you OK?'

Ribs bruised but no great harm, she could speak.

'Yes, I'm alright, thank you. Did you get a good look at him?'

'No, no, not really. We were chatting. Oh, Dr Kluft, I am so sorry, are you sure you're OK?'

She had been using this corner shop for so many years, she knew three generations of the family, had looked over his daughter's application for medical school.

'Eloise,' she said, 'Please, Mehmet, how long how have I been asking you to call me Eloise?'

He tried to smile but was mortified.

'CCTV! That should have got the bastard! I'm calling 999…'

'Yes, and then let me use your phone, please, mine's in the bag. I need to cancel the cards. No, actually, forget the police for now, let me do that first. Probably more useful.'

As she waited for an answer from the hotline that Mehmet had looked up, Eloise felt the weight of lifetimes of human absurdity dragging at her feet. Had she somehow manifested this mugging by, however briefly, having unkind or patronising thoughts about her urban neighbours? Those inhabiting a world so near and yet so far. A stupid notion, of course. Even so, she found herself suffering from the persistence of her current misfortunes far too sharply.

What is this? What have I done, she demanded of an unresponsive universe. *Why am I having to wade through knee-high crap right now?*

The police came, surprisingly quickly. Perhaps, Eloise thought, she should have called them first after all. They took a statement, radios stuttering. Mehmet had given her a miniature of brandy but the shakes were coming on regardless. The camera was most likely at too high an angle to have seen under her assailant's cap and hood, but Eloise hoped that they would get him. A fingerprint on a discarded card, a quick lead on where he'd tried to use it, a conveniently passing patrol car. Not to see him punished or processed through the crime academies but because she wanted the opportunity to sit across from him, to look into his eyes (to take a swab from his cheek) to talk to him. To tell him that yes, she was angry (very fucking angry) but that she was not afraid and she did not hate him. That she automatically respected people – or at least tried to – until they gave her a reason not to and would have respected him, too, if he'd have given her a chance. Might even have given him the money if he'd asked for it, if he'd needed it that badly.

And then in a moment of clarity Eloise was forced to ask whether that truly would have been the case. Perhaps this was simply wishful thinking as to her own social merit? *Maybe so*, but hypocrisy or complacency aside, she wanted the chance to tell her young assailant that this was all so unworthy of him, and of all that he *could* be. That whatever bars he already felt caged by might be lifted, with time, help, and a little cognitive will. She had read the studies, seen the transformative effects that an enriched environment, physical, emotional and mental could have, reversing the damage of trauma and neglect. Or at least preventing them from being passed on.

But how willing might she be personally to offer such help, to give of her own time and resources – real action instead of theory and good intent? Or was it all as it ever had been and was the desire of the more advantaged to lift the luckless out of their misfortunes no more than a 'bleeding heart' pipe dream? Even if that were the case, Eloise hoped that she might one day have the opportunity to *at least try* to make a difference, to intervene at the right time. Professionally or personally. Surely it would be worth the effort?

Once home (relieved that her keys had been in her jacket pocket and not her handbag) she knew that she wouldn't be able to sleep. Not without assistance. Eloise poured herself a glass from the bottle she'd bought from Mehmet right before the mugging, and sat down to read. But the lightweight Pinot wasn't up to the job. She broke the wax seal on a 12-year-old port and served herself a healthy tot of that instead. She was about to put on a medley of soothing piano music before realising that her phone was now in the hands of her thief, and with it her playlists. She wondered whether perhaps she could find all that again somewhere in the cloud? But it felt like too much effort for this evening. She'd had enough of screens and blue light and software for one day.

Then she remembered that she'd held on to her father's old portable record player and a few of his best-loved vinyls, still there in a nook in his study in the basement. It occupied the sky-lit end of the old coal cellar, the other end having been boxed in and converted to her mother's darkroom. As she switched on the light, which did nothing to dispel the smell of damp (Eloise did not know why she had expected it to) and walked down into that little shrine, the floorboards creaked with unfamiliar weight.

On flicking through the shelf above the turntable-in-a-suitcase (a collector's item that had been one of her father's prized possessions) Eloise found a dusty old Peggy Lee album, gave it a wipe with her sleeve and put it on. She let it crackle and hiss as it played 'Is that all there is' and let it soothe her. Yes, 'vintage' seemed to be absolutely the right prescription for tonight. She sat at her father's roll-top oak desk, which itself had been left behind by its former owner when her parents had bought the house. It bore a brass plaque inscribed to Father Mortimer from his grateful parish. No children to leave it too, clearly, and too bulky to bother moving.

Knowing where to look, Eloise pulled out a yellow foolscap pad from a reluctant drawer. She found her father's old Parker pen in there too. (A gift from her, one Christmas, a tradition acknowledged by her family as a necessary celebration to brighten up the cold, dark northern winter) She scribbled a while to get the ink rolling and then let her scrawling longhand flow.

So, are we really mere algorithms, Charles? To paraphrase my father's favourite songstress, is this really all that there is? Perhaps it's perfectly fine to be something as wonderful as an algorithm. After all, wasn't it Ada Lovelace, the 'Enchantress of Numbers' (and daughter of an infamous Romantic) who conceived the first recognised algorithm, the precursor of computer programming?

In fact, was she not your contemporary... maybe you attended the same scientific salons chez Charles Babbage, perhaps she was even your friend? Perhaps, one can only hope, she would have, in time, 'evolved' your own unfortunate perception of women as morally superior but not quite the intellectual equals of men. A view I can choose only to forgive you for, as being a product of the times and the result of centuries of insidious propaganda and restriction. Or perhaps your brilliant niece Julia, bound though she was to a caring rather than professional role, would have eventually dissuaded you of this error?

But back to my point, such as it is. I wonder if I resist this notion of being 'just an algorithm' not because of its perceived lack of poetry, but because I could hardly bear the mockery of being enslaved to something I've struggled to get my head around for my entire academic career. I shudder at the memory of calculus classes, Charles, I shudder. Oh, the curse of being a scientist with an aversion to arithmetic, of being someone who can barely balance her accounts without resorting to an electronic calculator. (How fortunate, then, that my interviewers for medical school had the charity to ignore my mathematics grades and were wise enough to look for the passion and not at the paperwork.)

In any case, I find the idea of life being inescapably pre-determined by bytes of programming only marginally less disturbing than the paranoia of believing in gods and monsters, conspiracies and cabals, heaven and hell. Although at least being an organic machine seems preferable to the embrace of nihilism, to the enveloping nothingness – or rather to utter *pointlessness*, and the supposed 'error' of sentience. (Or are those anti-natalists on to something?) At least programming seems, by necessity, to have some kind of purpose... and possibly some form of programmer?

Perhaps this world, this human experience, really is some devilishly clever bit of software, an illusion, a contemporary variation on the Hindu theme of Maya. Maybe we really do exist in a holographic universe as pixelated pawns, without even the power of avatars, playing out some unfathomable cosmic game. I mean, we can see evolution unfolding electronically, of its own volition, in generations of 'bits and bots' once the primary conditions are in place. Is our sole purpose, therefore, to inherit, acquire, develop and pass on *information*? Nothing that we know of yet seems better suited to that purpose than DNA after all. Though perhaps the prophets of doom are on to something and AI will replace us all in time, once it can do everything that we do – and more?

Alternatively (and I am rather attracted to this notion, Charles, I must admit) maybe this is some sort of top-down 'non-duality' consciousness in which we become briefly separate units of the whole experience, as it rises to meet itself from the bottom up. The path of evolution follows the upward direction of greater intelligence, after all. As above, so below? What's more, the neural networks of our own brains look uncannily like the cosmos itself when viewed from a distant perspective. There's also the suggestion that consciousness may, in fact, be an emergent property of chaos itself, a natural consequence within our universe, and therefore in us.

Oh, forgive all this existential angst, Charles – perhaps an inevitable consequence of evolution too? The evening's events have shaken everything up. Though I must wonder whether any of these musings really matter. As ever, it seems that all that we can do is seek and wait for more 'information'.

We can wrap ourselves up in all kinds of philosophical knots, in question, conjecture, theory and belief, but whether we subscribe to one viewpoint or another, does it make any difference? I mean, whether we are some form of fundamental, eternal entity, inhabiting bodies created for us over epochs through 'divine' causation, or whether we are merely puppets of programming, or the inexorable result of meaningless mathematics, surely all that matters (indeed, all that we are able to *manage*) is how we live? What we do, the choices that we *appear* to have the freedom to make, moment by moment?

Oh, who knows.

Perhaps Peggy Lee was on to something. And if that really is all there is, my dear Charles, then maybe the wisest move, as the song suggests, is to break out some booze and have ourselves a ball...

Eloise washed down another mouthful of port and went back into the kitchen for a top-up. Anxiety was still gnawing at her inner peace like a rat in a shoe box. She found herself in the mood for further hunting through drawers and cupboards in search of any other treasures those that she had loved had left behind. Somewhere, she knew, in an old round tin of the kind that once held boiled sweets, somewhere at the back of a high kitchen cupboard was something that Tom had left her. A lump of Moroccan resin and the pipe to smoke it with. She wasn't sure why she had kept it all this time, it went against her ingrained, law-abiding caution, but it was surely the right kind of medicine right now.

*

The walls of the cave are closing in on her. She half hopes they will crumble and finish it quickly. The child is sick, will not feed. Had she been near familiar ground, before the nullifying freeze, she would have known what to do. Which leaf, which seed, which flower. As her grandmother had shown her. Few suffered long from sickness in their clan and she herself had known barely a day of it. Until the changes, until the hunger, the swelling limbs, the blood in her mouth, the loosening teeth.

The limp, half-living soul in her arms seems barely aware of her. And now she too has started to feel hot, cold, dizzy, with twisting pains in her joints. She straps the child more tightly to her breast.

She wonders whether this is punishment for all those times she has resented her, strained against the choking bonds of motherhood, wondered whether she was natural to it after all. Or perhaps this is revenge for her marking of the cave – or feeding from the slithering. Or maybe from too closely examining the creature that had breathed its last here, before she threw it on the fire? She cannot know the hand that wields the whip, or why, but she feels its lash. She has endured so much, but this?

In the gloom she has felt the shadows creeping and knows how effortless it would be to surrender to their call. She shivers, and in the moments that she can breathe she gasps and moans. Sliding into the mouth of the beckoning abyss, she clings to a fingertip of faith and forces herself to look away from its sucking vortex. Then she unwinds the snakeskin from her wrist and throws it into the fire.

The best she can do now is rock herself and the child, gently press chosen points on her tiny hands and feet, murmur words of power. Cast her love over her. Wish.

18

Oh hell, no! What now? Eloise did not need to make a forensic examination to know what had stung her as she'd packed down the recycling (a commandment observed diligently, for if the universe could re-use every aspect of itself then she could certainly rinse out a tin). Even while she squashed it unseen under her shoe, she knew its signature of searing pain. Slow, straggling September wasps – they were the worst. This was the second time in her life she had been stung within days of her birthday. *Holy shoe-shine,* she shouted inwardly, *how much strength does one human need?*

Eloise went inside to look for her adrenalin pen then remembered with a sinking stomach that it was lost with the stolen bag. Where the hell was her prescription pad? Drawers overturned, hunting it out, scribbling the request, she rushed out to the pharmacy.

While the venom had entered only at an extremity, she could not risk the anaphylactic shock that had once nearly finished off her father.

Wasps. She bloody well hated the bastards. Even if their nest-making social structure was such a fine example of complexity rising out of the simple and the creation of a whole that was superior to the sum of its parts. But the wasp hive, for Eloise, was not comparable to the lyrical self-construction of each ephemeral snowflake. It was a den of thugs. Not only the common or garden variety (so fond of her climbing passion flower, so crucial to its fruit, so dangerous to a handful of Klufts) she also resented the vile parasitic mutation that paralysed its victims, laying its larvae within to devour the unfortunate host alive. As it had been so famously noted, this was a ghastly reminder of the barbed wire of cruelty lying in wait throughout nature, ready to ensnare any sentimental notions of a 'wonderful world'.

She made it to the pharmacy in time, or so she thought. Before the epinephrine could be injected she wondered if she might be hallucinating, a rare but not unheard of reaction. Her breathing was beginning to restrict and she felt hot. She thought she was underground, not in a brightly lit facility on the high street. She thought she was sitting across a river of fire opposite another woman, their thoughts bleeding together. There was a lizard? No, a large rat, no…? Something roared in agony behind her, something huge. No, it was something shrivelled. Burnt. No… And then it cleared. So quickly. The miracle of adrenalin. She was breathing deeply again. She was fine, bar the pain in her thumb where she had been stung.

The bulging of her hand, bizarre like an inflated rubber glove, created the space for some buried hatred to spring. This was going to make her late for the Friday morning meeting, restrict her ability to handle the equipment.

Once home again, she tried to make some more coffee but her swollen hand was unequal to the task.

'BASTARD!'

Eloise excused herself for cursing the corner shop thief and wishing him equal evil. She retracted it. Took a breath and chose to switch away from all this useless self-pity, this delusion of persecution, back to the core of who she was and what she believed.

Instead of giving in to the bitterness she rehearsed a homily to her attacker, the one that she so wished she'd been able to deliver. Eloise imagined having the opportunity, in an ideal world, to engage with him. Perhaps through some sort of 'restorative justice'. She wanted to be able to accept his apology, gladly, willingly and to see the light dawn in his eyes as she asked him: 'Don't you know what you are?'

(Would the petty thief be surly and silent? Stare her down? Would he insult her in urban youth patois or hiss through a dismissive, sulky pout? Whatever his reaction, she would continue nonetheless.)

'I wish you could appreciate what an extraordinary achievement you are. To know how billions of years ago you burst from one cell into two, and then after many millions more you learned to see, and then to swim, and were curious and courageous enough to leave the oceans and explore solid ground. How you survived that first brave journey, survived a series of mass extinctions.

'Eventually, you grew limbs, learned to crawl, then climb – and at last to walk upright. You made tools. Learned to speak and make yourself understood, learned to reason and have ideas. You lived through meteor strikes, firestorms, famines, earthquakes, plagues and wars. Marched thousands of miles in search of food, shelter, in search of a mate. Raised and protected new generations with an unquenchable fire of love.

'Then you settled and learned to grow your own food supply. You made art, wrote music. And against incredible odds you kept living, seeking, finding and creating. In time you learned to fight and to cure the diseases that destroyed so many of your brothers and sisters.

'You followed an irresistible urge to unravel all the wonder of the planet that you live on. You learned to defy gravity, to reach the skies and then the moon. Invented a microscope so you could see inside the atom. You put a telescope into space to reveal this spectacular universe in all its glory, the very universe that made you, perhaps that it might in turn explore and experience itself?

'Don't you know how magnificent you are? Please, please, don't waste that. Please don't allow the world we have built to waste that in you.'

If only. If only she might have the chance to speak and if only the words might have any actual power, enough to steer him on a different course. If only he might give a damn.

Eloise wondered whether too much damage had already been inflicted on this boy. A hippocampus shrunk by neglect, a prefrontal cortex thinned by lack of care, all the ravages and perils of his particular ecosystem? But neuroplasticity was a wondrous thing, the brain was capable of rewiring itself under the right conditions, and Eloise could never abandon faith in the power of transformation.

It was unlikely such an opportunity would arise, of course. There was no result in her case. Even if there had been, why on earth would the boy want to sit and listen to her lecture, this clueless woman who might as well come from another planet never mind the cosy, middle-class world next door. She knew nothing about the reality of his life or its struggles. She had never experienced the circling sharks of whatever debts he may owe, the unaffordable costs of maintaining innocence, or the price that he may have already paid.

So what's the bloody point? Of any of it. Of the work, of giving a damn, of any of the loftier goals she was striving for. But then, as she so often did these days, Sarah strayed into her thoughts and Eloise wondered whether her elusive charge may have ever questioned 'the point'. There was no answer to that, of course, but could Sarah's discovery affect anything now? Could the envisioning of an ancestor, her struggles and disadvantages, her solutions and triumphs, her endurance and determination – but most of all her *similarity* to us today – somehow connect with the disenchanted or the disenfranchised? Could it encourage or inspire any other kind of human progress, even this boy's – *especially this boy's* – and make it seem achievable? Indeed, was her own passion for the project of any use beyond her own ambitions?

And with this a new idea began to form. Why not work on persuading KC's backers to make a duplicate reconstruction of Sarah available, one that could tour museums and schools once her remains were settled in their new home in Kenya?

Eloise realised she may never see the fruition of such hopes and yet she felt a fresh commitment to fighting for Sarah's 'truth'. Right now, however, the greater truth for Eloise was a desire to put the mugging behind her, if only she could. She had politely declined the victim counselling, replaced all her documentation, her mobile phone (re-composed all those priceless playlists), made all those life-leaching calls to mechanised phone systems. But the loss of her tooled leather Moroccan handbag was the deepest laceration. It had been one of her mother's. Slung over each woman's shoulders, that bag had been *everywhere.* She hoped, at least, that some other woman was making use of it, that it was not now mouldering in a landfill somewhere.

There was one ray of good news creeping up over the horizon and so Eloise decided to concentrate on that. Darius had worked his charm once again and permission had been granted to drill more deeply into the bones, into *any* of the bones, for uncontaminated leukocytes – those precious white immune cells from the bone marrow which were the best bet for a pure strand of Sarah's DNA. Even if this meant taking the remains apart and whatever damage that might cause.

*

She feels changed. The well of despair has receded with the sickness, but something both damaged and strengthened lives within her now. Within them both, although the child has recovered well, if inclined to sleepiness. She too is tired but not drained of hope. The terrain ahead of them is dipping again but not too steeply. They have come far since the cave though still no clear sight of the coast and they have lost both days and energy. But this place is dry, and perhaps has always been dry. There are a few shrivelled bushes, a few fallen trees, but otherwise endless stretches of barren ground where snow, if it had ever fallen here, has failed to cling. She is thirsty.

The vulture blood has helped but not enough, even though she had offered a grateful prayer, even to this creature as she did to every living thing. It had been so surprisingly easy to catch, confident of its ability to fly from her approach as it tore into some putrid remains and yet so innocent of her arrow.

She has found, too, some mushrooms growing in the shade of a rotten tree trunk, which had somehow offered them sufficient moisture. There is only a handful, but she hoped to find more – and to find something else because where mushrooms grow, sometimes they reach out underground to a wider family of cousins, and more importantly to other plants that may be better to eat than these. She does not recognise the stem or cap and cannot risk eating them (even to seek a healing vision) but maybe they will show her the way to something she might sample safely? She scrabbles in the dirt beneath the mushrooms but they reveal no trace, no trail to richer bounty. These too, then, have been deserted by their fellows.

Empty-handed, she walks on a little longer but soon must stop again. She rests against what appear to be some lonely stones, but these peculiar peaks must be something other than the earth has made. They are strong but do not have the smooth, hard surface of rocks and their outer layers crumble slightly with her weight. And now at her feet she sees them, so many, so tiny and beyond count, following each other along the trails in and out of these stones. No, these are not stones, she sees now that these mounds are hollow, like caves. The tiny ones carry the pieces of this place in and out with them. They live here? No, no, it is more than some convenient shelter, she realises. They have made this. They have formed this out of their own will, out of the will of many. How could that be? No, no, she thinks she must be dreaming.

How could something so small, so weak, so powerless make something so much bigger? How could they shift the world around them in this way? She thinks perhaps they do this because they have learned that they can, and so they must. She wants to laugh but her throat is too dry. Is this new wisdom that comes to her now, or is it the deception of thirst – and following so sweetly behind these lies, the relief at last of death?

Not yet. No. Not yet. She must make the most of this discovery. She recalls once seeing some monkeys enjoy a meal of something similar living in a tree trunk, by using a stick to draw them out. The tiny creatures on the ground will escape her too easily, she must get some sort of tool inside this thing and encourage them to attack that intruder in numbers. She can make something thin and sharp enough with her flint and a section of arrow shaft. Place some thick spittle over it, if she can raise any. It is worth a try?

She makes a hole in the mound and probes into it but catches only a mouthful or two. The taste is foul but they offer some sense of food and moisture as they burst upon her tongue, enough at least to spur her on. She pushes away once more, commanding her feet to find new paths.

There seems little distinction now between ground and air. She is no longer sure of what she is seeing, but this does not seem like the onset of a vision. She must properly drink. She must keep milk flowing for the child as it cannot have another day without it. The little one is able to sip now from a hollow reed within a pierced gourd, but that gourd too must be refilled and with any kind of suitable moisture. If only she can find the right root or tuber to squeeze to a pulp – and the energy to dig it out.

And she must gather new kindling again or there will be no fire. She looks around for anything that might work. Then she thinks she sees a figure following them, moving through the emptiness, through the shrouds of dust at the edge of her vision. Yes, it is her father. Has he been behind them all along?

No. These are only the illusions of thirst and hunger again. It is nothing, another of those living, heaving rocks. She knows now why her father had not come with her. He had understood that his weakness, his grief for all the others, his injuries from that last fight would have held her back.

So can she trust what seems to be green in the distance? No choice. Where anything is growing there surely must be some source of water. She aches for it, not only to drink, but to surround her and support her. In days that seem unreal to her now she would spend too long at the shore and was often scolded for it. Even if those salty depths could not quench a human, she knew that somehow they held the truth of life.

19

Saturday at the Natural History Museum was a pleasure marred only by the weekend crowds. (And the incessant screaming of a newborn, beyond all reasonable capacity for such juvenile lungs.) Keep all the palaces, the abbeys, the bridges and the towers, thought Eloise. Leave the Palladian splendours, the Nash terraces, Pugin's halls of power... she would forfeit even brave St Paul's. This monument to the genius of Waterhouse was the architectural gem that made London worth living in, and not only for what lay within.

It was something about the colours of the stone, she could not explain it. Once inside, on each visit, she would observe a tradition to run her fingers over a skilfully rendered relief in one of the pillars or covings. A shell, a bird or a flower. As a child she had begged to be allowed to stay and set up camp right there under the old blue whale. Eloise had often wondered about whales in the years since. What had made their ancestors decide they'd had enough of the land, to shed their limbs and return to the sea? Had they foreseen the mess that we would make of it?

Now she saw the museum as an elegy to knowledge, a dovetailing of the disciplines from geology to archaeology, biology to conservation (and now genetics too had joined that pantheon!). The public displays had evolved over the years, of course, but how she missed all those glass cabinets filled with jars of pickled embryos and foetal failures, a source of disgust to some, but so fascinating to the young Eloise. Later in life she had understood why. In so many species the embryo appears strikingly similar, almost inseparable, until those molecular signals fire and instruct the tiny blind seahorse to become something other, something unique. To grow fin instead of finger, beak instead of snout, claw instead of opposable thumb.

The museum jaunt was not mere nostalgia, however, not only a diversion. Eloise had arranged the briefest of meetings and a walk around the mezzanine with an old palaeontologist friend of her father's, still curating the massed collections both seen and unseen, and here on a Saturday out of nothing more than devotion (and widowerhood?). She had an important question for him. Where, apart from the teeth or the femur, both of which had proven uncooperative in Sarah so far, might the cells they need be hiding? It was not a wasted trip.

'Try the skull,' said her grizzled godfather, as he nodded towards the cabinet that held the Qafzeh skull and then dusted it with a frayed and yellowed sleeve.

'The skull?'

'Yes. The petrous bone, that little pyramid at its base, the casing for the inner ear. I am quite sure it must be an undiscovered treasure house.'

'Oh god, yes, I see, yes. Of course. I think there's enough of that still intact in Sarah, though it could be tricky to get to it. But we have carte blanche now to try anywhere, so why not give it a go?'

'Trust me, my dear. Give it the best of British. What do you have to lose?'

'Nothing. Nothing at all. Thanks! Time for a coffee?'

'Oh, no. No, thank you, too much to do, and, honestly, I can't tolerate anything but a nice warm Horlicks these days.'

He looked so old. As ancient as his cherished collections. Is that how her father would seem to her now? Eloise adored her godfather, he was something of a 'high-functioning' introvert, rather like her. Perhaps that was why they got along so well, why they silently understood each other. But Eloise also understood that her ten minutes with him was up and that she would continue her sojourn here alone. Perhaps she reminded him too much of those missing from both their lives, as painfully as he did her.

'Alright then. I'll get on and leave you to it. But not before giving you your birthday present.'

Eloise rummaged in her bag. The book-shaped parcel she handed to him would offer only the surprise of its title.

'Oh, you shouldn't have!'

'Yes, yes, I should.'

It didn't matter that he'd forgotten that their birthdays were only a day apart. She expected nothing, but she very much needed to give.

'It was so good to see you, Uncle Martin. Now you look after yourself, won't you? Go steady on the Horlicks! And *thank you*.'

'Lovely to see you. Thank you for the gift, Eloise, so thoughtful. So like your mother. I shall open it up on the big day. Good luck, my girl. Good luck.'

They kissed cheeks and parted with a smile of sadness.

It wasn't long, however, before that sense of what was missing in her life was replaced with a ripple of thrill and encouragement... the skull! She must tell KC! She had abandoned all crazy misgivings once again. (Aided by the chance discovery of a friend in common, one she'd since received discreet assurances from that, yes, she was being paranoid, but that, yes, her lab partner really was a 'good guy'.) Eloise texted KC about the skull, excited about the week to come, but not quite ready to leave the museum yet. As habit dictated, she needed to complete a circuit of the ground floor before stopping to enjoy a cup of fair trade coffee and the indulgence of a brownie.

It was far too busy for her liking in the open plan café, but she would not be deterred. The queue at the service counter soon grew uncomfortable, however, and not only from the crush of chattering and elbowing tourists with no concept of personal space. She became aware of that unnerving sense of being stared at. Glancing around a few times along the queue, Eloise eventually caught the flinty eyes of a woman in a scarlet beret an instant before she could look away in a failed attempt to deny her surveillance.

The woman was unremarkable apart from the woollen beret, which Eloise thought must be far too hot for this Indian summer weather, but perhaps her 'watcher' was having a bad hair day? She considered her own appearance and couldn't imagine why it would invite such persistent interest, but then wondered if she might, in fact, know her spectator? Eloise looked back again (had she seen her somewhere before?) but the lady had too quickly turned, anticipating her subject's attempt to catch her out. Clearly, if this creature was somehow familiar with the object of her interest then she was not inclined to renew their acquaintance. Eloise felt an irritation filtering in to replace the awkwardness – and then became resentful that this unwelcome observation was disturbing her weekend peace.

After she was at last served at the counter, Eloise was able to secure a seat as the family with the wailing newborn were vacating theirs. She smiled and cooed at the child and disguised her relief at their departure, then scanned her surroundings before sitting down. Happily, she could no longer spy the red beret. She allowed herself to relax, let the caffeine and sugar rush kick in and then gazed pensively into the middle distance.

Good Lord! Mid-sip of coffee, Eloise was suddenly forced to double-take as a pair of heavy-hipped, middle-aged women waddled towards her, waving and smiling. The twins! Judy and Gina, from that fascinating study all those years ago in the States. But how bizarre to see them here!

As Eloise watched them approach and prepared to greet them in spluttering surprise, she couldn't help wondering whether this encounter was in some way meaningful. (The notion was tempting, as she had thought about the twin study in general, and these two in particular, only the other day.) As a scientist versed in probability she knew the acceptable answer to coincidence but there had been so many chance occurrences in her life, often leading to either significant opportunities or the deepening of connections, so Eloise sometimes excused herself for imagining other possibilities.

An old school friend met on a distant city street halfway around the world – why that street, that moment, what sequence of small decisions had they each made to bring them, staggeringly, face-to-face on a crowded New York sidewalk? Or had they somehow been aware of each other, energetically bonded through a unified field and drawn along the lines of that matrix without will or awareness?

Eloise had often asked herself whether prescience was a cryptic part of the pliability of space and time, or the connective strings of which some theorised the universe was composed, and of their extra, as yet unseen dimensions. Would such mysteries be debunked and explained at the far frontiers of physics or could there really be some kind of integrated 'energy' behind it all? *Heresy*, she could hear many of her peers proclaim in chorus with her own inner voice, as it too heckled with derision.

Of course, she knew very well that an important function of the human brain had been the emergence of pattern recognition, the ability to find and remember signs and landmarks that helped us navigate and optimise our environments in advantageous ways. Eloise understood how this talent might fall prey to more fanciful interpretation, to seeing more than was there and to connecting the dots in ever more credulous ways.

Nevertheless, she was now confronted with the surprising presence of the Ragnursson twins. All the way over from Ohio. Eloise realised that she'd expected these two to come back into her life, one way or another. It felt extraordinary, even so, that it should be here, today. Then again, why would they not choose to visit London at this time of year? Wasn't the city on many an American bucket list? And of course the museum would (should) be on any sensible soul's itinerary for a tour of its treasures. She may even have mentioned this place to them sometime.

But then there was no more time to ponder the mysteries of synchronicity, for having waded through the café crowds, here they were right in front of her, right now.

'Oh, wow! Dr Kluft! How wonderful to see you, how are you?'

Identical sopranos in unison, not even the distinctions found in a harmony, just straightforward stereo.

'Oh, my goodness, how amazing. Oh, wow… how are you both?'

She submitted without flinching to an enveloping two-sided hug. The twins held on longer than would be comfortable for Eloise under normal circumstances, but the cocoon they had created around her seemed to be soothing away her earlier unrest. Judy and Gina had formed the perfect force field against any strange, staring, red-bereted stalkers.

'Please, won't you join me for coffee, do sit down. Oh, wait… Excuse me,' Eloise asked of the table next to her, 'might we steal one of those chairs, please? Thank you, thank you very much.'

Once she had settled in her unexpected guests, she went to re-join the ever growing queue at the service counter in search of three more coffees, insisting above the sisters' protests, 'No, no, please, let me treat you. You're in "my manor" now, so to speak,' (borrowing a phrase from one no longer in her life, if not without a twinge of pain). This time around, Eloise found herself smiling at the others in the queue and not minding the waste of valuable time as so often she might do when forced to wait for anything. The curse of impatience set aside, she was delighted by the sudden company and a chance to share all that she loved about this place with her unexpected guests.

The Ragnursson twins had been an integral part of a study that had proved pivotal in her career, and despite an attempt to keep a clinical distance, Eloise had warmed to the pair immediately. Or rather, she'd succumbed to the warmth that they seemed to have for her and indeed for everybody. Not all the sets of twins had been so open. Many were so tightly wrapped up in each other and in the worlds of their own private making that they were unwilling to expand the circle of their communion to easily include strangers (especially all those peering and prodding doctors).

Eloise had felt her only child status all too keenly at the time and had been envious of the effortless compatibility that twins were able to enjoy. No need for all that 'getting to know you' nonsense, not even much in the way of sibling rivalry, but in its place the constant trust that someone in the world knew you as well as you knew yourself – and would always have your back.

There was so much to learn from nature's own control group of clones, this enduring riddle of a single fertilised egg that for whatever reason, decides to become two (or more). The resulting similarities were not only physical, not restricted to inherited immune responses, but also evident in tastes, inclinations and behaviour. The crucial differences, meanwhile, pointed to precisely how and where external influences played their part, and not only in those rare, poignant, yet incredibly important cases of separation at birth.

So many curious and surprising differences. Eloise had been intrigued by the revelation that political affiliation was less about class or education and more closely influenced by a reflexive response to fear or disgust: greater in conservatives, lesser in liberals. There was also an interesting disparity in sexuality and gender identification between certain pairs of twins, suggesting the effects of very early neurological chemistry rather than genetic factors.

Of course, similarity had been the dominant observation and there had been so many startling affinities. The Ragnurssons had been that bit special, however, and in more ways than academic to Eloise, who'd also discovered a likely ancestral link with the girls going back to Scandinavia. With Judy and Gina the symmetries had exceeded the obvious and the explicable, such as sharing each other's childhood ailments, finishing each other's sentences or meeting up as adults to find they were wearing the same new outfit. If there *was* such a thing as telepathy, then these two were prime candidates.

As Eloise waited to be served (returning the twins' enthusiastic waves with a modest reply) she recalled that Judy and Gina had gone to separate universities, but on the same nights of the year had met boys and started dating. Their respective suitors were eighteen months apart in age, studying different majors, one was a jock the other a musician. One thing the boys had in common, however (as the girls would later discover) was hailing from the same hometown. But then, not just the same town... the same father.

Of course, the fact that the girls had been attracted to half-brothers could be attributed to some shared social conditioning. Maybe even pheromones with similar compositions or the subtle scent of beneficial immune adaptations? But after marrying the boys and moving to different states the girls became pregnant around the same time, both having sons within hours of each other. Years later, Judy felt a sudden pain in her neck while driving from the school run, and once home learned that Gina had been in a car accident, not seriously injured but suffering from whiplash.

The study had attempted to pin down such anecdotal phenomena with polygraphs and other controlled tests. The rigour of the criteria had since been questioned but seven out of ten pairs had shown evidence of a link that went below, above and seemingly well beyond the surface.

Walking back towards the table, juggling hot paper cups with ill-fitting lids, Eloise indulged a whimsy, wondering if this connection might be compared to mycelium, the white web of communicating root systems in forests that had been seen to stretch for many miles while emerging from a single fungal life form.

As she caught up with the sisters and enjoyed their infectious good humour, she imagined quantum theory written in esoteric equations like halos around their matching blonde bobs. The non-locality of particles, forever connected to and affected by each other, no matter how far apart.

*

She walks on in wonder.

Why is there no one else here, in this blessed place? This pocket of somehow flourishing life could support not only her and the child, but it could become home to an entire tribe. Did no other know of it or had they left? Why?

She unstraps the child from her back to carry her on her hip, so she may better see and experience all this. There is new growth on living palms, fruit that is sweet and small, the child's eyes widen with the happy surprise of its unknown taste. There are thriving families of all kinds of four-legged life, not shy, not scattering, but curious and apparently unafraid. She need feel no shame for picking off the easy catch, although she will choose only the slow and old.

There are more riches. Everywhere, fallen to the ground, nuts, still in their shells, handfuls that would last long if carried away. And water. Fresh and flowing from streams that spring out of the ground. Have they somehow left the old world, left their bodies, without her even noticing? Will she find her grandmother, her family here? She takes out her flint and draws it across her arm. She bleeds, hurts and knows she is not in spirit yet.

There, over there, she sees something of such value that she can hardly believe it and thinks it must be something else. Yet on drawing closer it is clear, this is a honey hive after all, the first she has seen since the ash fall, perhaps the last in the world. Beautiful bees come and go with little care and no alarm at her presence. She knows how much she needs the sweet sustenance within, its magic, its power. She needs the wax too, its stickiness and its ability to bond and mend, how it burns to help fuel a fire, the way it can seal a wound.

But how can she get to it without risk? Not only to herself or the child, but to the hive itself. This is a rarity that must survive. She ponders the problem, then looks around and searches. There is a leaf, yes, she remembers now. One whose smoke will make the little creatures sleepy and docile, perhaps long enough for her to reach in with a forked twig and pull out what she needs. Only a little. There is also enough water here to make a mud paste to smother over her body for protection.

Tomorrow. She will attempt the task for sure, but not now. They are both so tired. Tomorrow, after food, after water, after rest.

She follows the path of those wild running freshwater streams and there – yes she had caught the scent, she knew it was so – long reaches of sand open out to a wide shallow sea. It is so long since she has stared at such a vast and unbroken stretch of living water. Its colours are dull but it is gloriously clear.

Leaving the child on the shore she removes the wrappings from her feet and tests the gentle waves. Cold but so delicious. All her coverings are cast back to the beach now and she wades forward until her stomach clenches with shock. Beautiful shock. Further, until she can dip her head and still stand. It is safe here to lift her feet and to close her eyes. To float.

Eventually, the young one's cries call her back to reality, to responsibility and the need to find or make shelter. The wisest choice may be to weave leafy branches together high up in the older trees and bind themselves in. She has not yet seen what walks here come nightfall. She wonders if she will be able to stay awake long enough to see anything at all.

By morning, after the first undisturbed sleep she can remember since the child was born, she is convinced that they should stay. Claim this new home for their own. This is good. This place has seen little dust, although the sky overhead still hides its full light. Yet if they stay she knows (she has felt it) they will be alone. It might be enough for her, perhaps. But for the child?

And if others come, after all, if others find what she has found, would they be welcome? She decides that they will stay for a few days or more to rest and recover a while here. But her heart knows that they have not yet come to safety.

20

Each movement is fluid, unhesitant. The mistrust that Eloise so often felt in her ability to manipulate the physical world – the sense of being at odds with inanimate objects and that each day threw up an obstacle course of hidden hazards – had melted into the suspension achieved only about two miles into a ten mile run. When that frustrating tilting of the world, as she walked through a door and it would malevolently shift its dimensions to move in and bump her shoulder, would dissipate into the grace and lightness she'd always thought should have been hers.

Her lab staff, loyal to her patient support, protected her and compensated for her notorious clumsiness, preparing a path so all she had to do was follow the course of inspiration. Eloise knew that she would have made a terrible surgeon and had suffered horribly as a medical student, dreading any encounter between herself, sensitive equipment and a patient with a pulse. Today felt very different.

'Would you like me to operate the drill, Dr Kluft?'

'No thanks, Rory, I'm fine. I want to do this.'

Eloise understood it was irrational to imagine that Sarah should not be handled by any of the others, by anyone not as *connected* – but if anybody was going to press that probing dentistry drill into the pristine bone then it had to be her. KC had offered no objection. She had chosen her spot in the complex arrangement of bone behind what would have been Sarah's ear, to reach in for the marrow that, surely this time, *must* be waiting there for them. A capsule of uncorrupted time.

Time in captivity. 'In stone, bone, genome' as she had once heard it elegantly put in a documentary. It was all coming together. The visit to the museum had not only settled Eloise, it had given her an idea. A new project, one that would have to wait and would need substantial funding, but something that connected both the study of Sarah and a long-held idea of her father's, for which he had never found the supporting evidence.

Eloise had made friends again with that old skull from Qafzeh in the museum, a cast of which Professor Kluft had kept in his study at the university. After her godfather had left her, she'd taken her time to walk around the original as it sat casually on the mezzanine level, ingloriously discreet in a simple glass box and free from fanfare or fuss.

What had happened to the *sapiens* populations at Qafzeh, 15,000 years before Sarah? Had they completely died out when the Sinai was singed back to desert or did anything of them, their culture, their courage survive? And if so, where?

It seemed unlikely they could have made it back across the Sahara in another long cycle of dry but it may have been possible by hugging the often treacherous route of the Nile. Or perhaps they had attempted to survive somewhere in the refuge of the delta and along the North African coast, once home to much earlier populations of *Homo sapiens*. An arduous trek across to the Euphrates and Tigris valleys and down to the Gulf coast may have been possible. Certainly some other human-like populations had made it as far as Siberia in the north and also to what is now India and southern Asia, whether leaving Africa through Sinai – or from across the Horn and through the coastal oases of the Arabian peninsula at that time. But might there have been other options for the climate-change refugees from Qafzeh?

Her father had wondered if they'd gone north along the Med to the green belts of what was now southern Turkey, to the lands that tens of thousands of years later would offer the ideal conditions for some of our earliest and most persistent attempts at agriculture. But there were no indications that these humans of 90,000 years ago may have gone in that direction (as yet). No tools, no bones to be found elsewhere from the Qafzeh era, only a glaring gap in the archaeological record.

There were teasing hints appearing, however, that survival *of some form* may have been possible. There was evidence of very early plant cultivation from about 23,000 years ago (much earlier than first presumed) near what is now Haifa. These 'farmers' were likely from a much later wave of migration out of Africa, but perhaps they had encountered remnants of an older population along the way? At the very least, such finds implied a more complex and non-linear picture of cultural evolution.

Then, about 9,000 years before present, there appeared the fascinating Göbekli Tepe settlement in Turkey, apparently pre-agricultural but with its curious art and surprising temples. Most intriguing to Eloise were the uncanny similarities between petroglyphs found here and much further afield in places such as Australia, suggesting that various ancient migrating peoples could have been both more enduring and more symbolically and culturally related than previously assumed.

The potential proof to connect these disparate dots remained elusive – without the rare blessing of lasting ice or the preservative of, say, an ancient lake bed. Eloise's own work on the genome project had suggested that, *unless they had gone back to Africa*, it was unlikely the Qafzeh populations had played any significant part in the final selection of our 'founding fathers'. (And Eloise had been a little disappointed at the time, on behalf of her own father.)

But she could not write off the possibility. New theories, new indications both archaeological and genetic, were emerging with frequency to confirm historic admixture between wide-ranging early peoples. Indeed, her father had maintained that despite the inevitable decay of organic remains, meaningful evidence for so much human history *must exist* but had been lost as sea levels rose – or drowned under modern dams – especially as key habitation would have been along coasts, rivers and lakes. *Some such evidence might be right under our noses*, thought Eloise. With improved dating or sequencing methods, a number of fossils now languishing in museums (and about which other assumptions had been made) might warrant new examination? Survival against all climatic and geophysical odds was evident throughout the humanoid saga, perhaps kick-starting certain evolutionary changes.

Event after event, until we were the last men standing. If not quite as 'special' as we once believed.

'Come here LoLo. I know that you must have grown since your last visit. Come stand here against the chart and let me make your mark.'

As she'd drilled into Sarah's skull, Eloise had imagined her father's calm, strong hands guiding her own. Imagined him watching with pride over her shoulder as she'd safely transferred the new bone powder samples from Sarah's skull into a series of waiting sterile receptacles. Now, with the memory of those words, she was drawn back to the life-size chart that had taken up one wall of his study in the university (always a more fascinating environment than her own childish playroom, despite the new worlds opened up by the microscope requested for her twelfth birthday).

That magnificent mural in which the stages and branches of 'man's ascent' were illustrated, emerging from knuckle-dragging ape to Lucy, the *Australopithecus*, then stretching fully upright into *Homo erectus*, at each stage with ever-growing skulls, and onwards to *heidelbergensis* who walked further into the world than any of her forebears. It was believed she had bequeathed two competing branches that would both keep evolving and eventually make their own marks outside of Africa: Neanderthal and *Homo sapiens*, a sibling rivalry with so much in common apart from destiny. The Cain and Abel of pre-history?

Eloise remembered positioning herself at the place between two figures on the wall where her father had asked her to stand. Professor Kluft had found it amusing to mark out the inches of his daughter's own 'evolution' in red pen along the various stages of the life-size mural. Until she had finally caught up with and then surpassed (in his eyes) the Vitruvian perfection of the final figure on the wall. Yes, Nils Kluft knew about bones – and he knew about *beauty*, in all its forms. He saw it everywhere in everything. He had taught his daughter to look closely, so very closely, while always maintaining a wide-angle perspective. And how closely she was looking now, in more enthralling detail than he ever might have imagined.

Her father had not lived long enough to see how enlightening the microscopic record of mitochondria would prove to be, the uncanny paradox that living cells would ultimately reveal the most remarkable evidence for a history he'd spent years seeking in lifeless sand and sediment. And how things had come full circle. Choosing the bright, vital future of medicine and all its possibilities rather than her parents' investigative footsteps, Eloise had not expected to become a detective of the past herself.

Now she wanted to revisit her father's ideas and hopes, to move them forward with all the new tools and tests at their disposal. In later life he had resisted the prevailing culture-historical theory in archaeology, and then the popular but disappointing systems theory. He suspected the effects *not only* of ecology, but also the agency of the *individual*. Diffusion and migration, yes, he accepted those as the key drivers of lasting change, but he'd suspected various significant episodes of localised evolution in both culture and biology, whether it had survived to be passed on or had arisen and then died away.

Eloise decided she would put these thoughts before Darius, but only once Sarah had been fully sequenced. The fragile peace between them these days had teased open the possibility of collaborating with him again. Apart from the support he'd given so willingly in terms of the Sarah project, he was now sending her the odd, overly friendly email that reached beyond their obligatory conversations about the progress of the work. How had the last one gone?

'LoLo, how the devil are you, my love? Devoted greetings from the slopes of Mount Kenya! You really must come out here soon, you know, if you can. I would love to show you Sarah's site. It gives me no end of pleasure to visualise your delightful face lighting up when walking in her footsteps. It would be like old times, LoLo, wouldn't it? All those long holidays from uni that you spent at digs with your father and me. Then perhaps a tour of the rather wonderful watering holes that I have now discovered in Nairobi? Bring your safari gear! I recall how fetching you always looked in khaki...'

Eloise had found this particular invitation a little too tempting for comfort, which gave her some cause for concern as to her fortitude when it came to Darius. Were these conciliatory epistles merely the tentative steps towards a renewed friendship, or were they something more? They *had* been friends once. Very dear old family friends, before becoming lovers. But how could such a friendship be possible now, wouldn't that require much deeper levels of unadulterated trust?

Perhaps this was *something more* after all – and Eloise could not help feeling flattered and vindicated if so. Was Darius experiencing a new and unfamiliar kind of loneliness, were the vulnerabilities of impending age creating a rheumy nostalgia about all they had once built together (all they had torn down since in bitterness and anger)?

Even if she were right about any ulterior motives, Eloise hoped that she would not be weakened by her own (much more familiar) loneliness into looking backwards as Darius seemed to be doing. There were too many fresh and varied possibilities in all the virgin territory ahead.

*

And so, there it is. She had not been wrong to push forward. By following this coastline and its remarkable gift of freshwater streams, by carefully using their hoard (the fallen nuts, the honey from the tiny section of comb that she'd been able to break away, the bounty of shell-flesh at low tide) they have grown strong again. Now the strip of the silty channel that she has sought for so long sparkles with reflected light.

Yes, there is definitely more light now, it's real not imagined. The haunting haze is thinning. Here, from this small inland hilltop (careful not to send any more loose stones skidding down, careful) she can see so much. Beyond the narrow waters, the beginnings of a wide and beckoning new world. A land of opening skies and rising hope.

They rest and wait. The little one needs to move, to keep trying out her weight on her hands and knees, to know that she is in her own body and not merely a part of her mother's. For her own sake, standing tall and lying free of her load is necessary before attempting the crossing.

Over two days, well-disguised by the rocky cover of the hilltop, she watches the tide cycles and knows when it will be low enough to walk at ankle deep, perhaps waist level at most. But before she can get to the vast shallows – so exposed – she will have to avoid the campfire she has seen on this side. The smoke, the movement, does not suggest a clan, more likely a couple of marauders. It's possible, she realises, these are the same men who slaughtered that unfortunate family of Others – the ones she had tried to honour where they had fallen. It is so long since she has encountered the living but she senses these two are not worth the risk of discovery. She cannot tell what is roasting on their spit – and feels it is better not to find out.

Even before all of this, she had known. She had known that there was darkness in the world. Not the blackness in the beauty of a night with no moon. Something else. She understood that everything lived because something else had died, but beyond the natural ripples and circles, beyond the waves that broke upon one shore and then returned to another, there were deeper places. And in these deep places angry, vengeful fractures might occur and through these fractures something might slip and fall and become lost. What had fallen would sicken, but before it died it would drag other things to death, and it would enjoy the death that it delivered.

It would seek power. Not in the natural way, to stay alive and to ensure that anything it loved would also survive and thrive, but rather it would seek the power of fear and of pain. Its fury would feed on what it did not even need. Did not really want. She had always known this despite most of her childhood seeing only peace, bar a few forgivable and fleeting acts of anger or desperation and that one unforgettable battle. She had understood that shadow existed in the world, no matter how well her father and mother protected her. Most days as a child she would choose to forget this knowledge, but in dreams she had seen it and had recognised it. She would know its smell when it came.

It is clear that they cannot hide from whatever waits for much longer. The burrow that she has dug into the denser sand provides some warmth, and the cold here has diminished, but a fire is too great a risk. Their rations are beginning to run out and the shallows may contain vital nourishment – but she must not be seen. And yet she cannot go around them, there is no better place to cross. They must travel by night. Soon.

*

Why did it have to be raining? It was all too prosaic, a graveyard in the wet, a dislocated umbrella, soggy grass staining her new suede boots. Not even proper rain, more that sorry, misty excuse for precipitation so beloved of the British climate. Dripping marble that should have shone, weathered tombstones nursing damp moss in their craters. Lilies wilting towards mulch. No, she did not want to be sad. There was too much to be hopeful for, her mood was rebounding and she wanted to share it.

Eloise had taken the morning off to visit her father's grave, as she did three times a year. Their birthdays. His last day. Her mother had been cremated after every organ, tissue or cell that might have been useful for study (whether cancer-ravaged or not) had been donated as instructed, but Eloise had needed something else for her father.

She had needed somewhere to go and to 'be' – and she'd always loved graveyards. Not in any morbid, romantic or gothic way but more for the simple fact of so much prime and carefully tended real estate that was dedicated purely to the memory of love. Eloise found such places moving, but also strangely life-affirming, despite the mournful stone angels and the inevitable sense of loss. So she had endured a formal service, a eulogy from Darius and the agony of a long, slow interment process, if only to have a standing stone somewhere. Her father had deserved a memorial, something that would last. He deserved an epitaph.

Professor Emeritus. Benevolent genius. Quiet protector. Inspiration. Family man. Haemophiliac.

The stalking flaw. She had denied him any other kind of weakness for so long, refusing to see even a toe-print of clay. Any Freudian amateur would recognise why no other man had come close, it was so dishearteningly obvious (even if too late to change?). She had felt stung to fury when Darius had suggested that he'd known her father better than her. The professor's star pupil, the dashing rake of the Archaeology department, the one who would take up the torch, rude and robust enough to risk any site (no need for coagulant or a chiller packed ready for an emergency transfusion). But they could not have been more different men and Eloise had never resented Darius more than in that moment. Although now, she realised with relief, she felt only the vestiges of that rage.

F8. The guilty gene. Such a small name for such a despised culprit. How long had she stared down at it? Knowing what they had known, her parents probably should not have risked having her, but they could not bring themselves to abort. In spite of all their rational convictions, Nils and Frances Kluft had thanked a fortuitous roll of nature's dice when they were delivered of a healthily clotting girl. Even if they were acutely aware of the legacy she might leave if she ever had sons.

Eloise placed some fresh flowers at her father's headstone. It seemed he had been unable to live without her mother. After a bad fall alone at his last dig he had chosen not to call for help on the fully charged phone that remained in his pocket, not to struggle for the emergency kit that was only metres away, but had allowed himself to bleed out slowly and fade away.

I miss you. I miss you. I miss you.

*

No moon, a chance. In the last long shadows of dusk she eases her way down the hillside but is betrayed by an unsteady rock that sends a pebble shower scattering. Keep moving.

She makes the shore line, its handful of spiky shrubs. The bear claws are bound between the knuckles of her right hand with finely twisted gut, the thigh bone is loose in her left. Her skin is blackened with burnt wood. She realises it will take more strides than she had hoped to make the point of the shortest crossing. Tar pit dark now, but her night vision has always been acute.

No, no please, hush, hush. What has wakened her? Usually the little one sleeps so soundly when bound to her back and with a steady motion. The cry cannot be from hunger, she had fed her well enough. A dream? A nightmare, all too real perhaps, all too soon. Understanding, it seems, the child is silent again.

She presses on through the dark on legs as light as she can make them. But then she knows. There is no sight of them yet but she knows the sounds. They are moving behind her. Still some distance away... but closing in on her trail. Can she silence the drumming of her heart? She must. She must be still and quiet, she must listen.

Yes. They are running now. Now they have split to fork. One has found her tracks.

With what courage she can muster she melts into the scrub and squats, controlling her breath like the lynx.

Now she sees the swing and sway of his flaming torch. As he runs it illuminates a face so carved by rage and hunger that there can be no doubt of his intention. She has seen the death-lust in such vacant eyes before.

Now she hears his heaving exhalations. He moves closer, moves past her, then comes to a sharp and turning stop when he smells her and she readies herself, but he loses his grip of the torch and it rolls towards the shore. He turns back to chase it before the ripples can reach it. He scrambles for the light but the fall has extinguished it. And now her eyes are better in the blackness than his. He must be aware that she cannot be far but he has no idea how close, and where.

Behind him.

One move, one leap, the bear claws rip in and out of his throat and the warm wetness flows. Another move and he is eviscerated. He splutters but can sound no alarm. There is no need for the club. (Later she regrets this lack of mercy, even if these two would have shown them none, shown them only horror.) No need to wait for the other one, who has circled too wide into the scrub. When he finds this one he will not follow.

She runs again, splashing out into the cold water of the mud flats, faster than she will ever know. Into the night, sure of her direction.

21

Driving through a deluge, running late, Eloise had been on the reserve list for the Bach recital for weeks, but the call about a pair of returned tickets had come only late that afternoon. After checking that Anna could get a last-minute babysitter, she had dashed home from the cemetery in a taxi without returning to the lab. (She excused herself for the unusual truancy, but there was no pressing need for her to be there, not until the very special delivery that was due the next day.)

She'd already lost a few moments trying to remember where she'd parked when she was stopped by Mrs Templeton returning fully laden from a shopping trip.

Oh dear, not now? There really wasn't the time. But she couldn't have ignored her.

'Oh, hello, Mrs T. How are you?'

'Fine, dear. Thank you. And you?'

'Yes, fine, thanks. In a bit of a dash really…'

Eloise hated being impolite. A moment or two wouldn't matter? Then while juggling umbrella and bag, she'd dropped her keys into an oily puddle and had to bend awkwardly to retrieve them.

'Oh no… excuse me. But I'm so glad to see you, Mrs T. I've been meaning to ask, how's George?'

'George? Oh yes, he's been shot!'

Eloise wondered if she had somehow misheard. Surely Mrs T had said that with far too much glee?

'Oh no! Oh dear. I'm so sorry!'

'No, no, dear, don't worry. It's marvellous news, really!'

Eloise was dumbfounded.

'Only a flesh wound you see, in and out! In all likelihood he'll make a complete recovery. But not quite yet thank you very much! We're all rather hoping this will keep him out of the thick of it for the duration. Don't you see? It looks as though the old curse has finally been beaten into submission. I mean, he's done his bit now, hasn't he?'

'Yes, I see, yes. Well, absolutely, I suppose that is good news. Do give him my best, won't you. I mean, I don't know him, of course, but whatever we may think of the politics we're all behind our boys...'

Oh god, Eloise cringed (as Mrs T nodded and smiled and thanked her) did she really just say 'our boys'?

Now finally on the road and due to scoop up Anna on the way, she was trying not to speed, trying not to swear at the other drivers. (One of her new resolutions among many, her reflexes of profanity were getting out of hand.) But the day's earlier drizzle was taking torrential revenge for her dismissal of its potency and the traffic was setting stickily. No great fan of popular radio and its trite invasion of her thought processes, Eloise needed to track the travel updates, nevertheless, so she turned up the dial. As her wipers whimpered under the strain the FM scanner came across Candi Staton singing 'Young Hearts Run Free' and complaining about her man. Unable to help herself, Eloise stayed with the song as the lyrics questioned the wisdom of wasting this one and only life on love.

That soulful old melody again. It seemed to punctuate her existence. Eloise recalled dancing to it as a teenager, the sweaty all-nighters, the abandonment of A-level anxiety and crushing self-consciousness into a swirling mass of revellers.

Then another image insisted on replaying itself, another interlude of that same old song – in spite of a recent commitment not to fixate on what was lost. The memory surged through nonetheless, as Candi counted up all those years filled with all those tears.

Tom.

At home with her. Investigating all the cherished curiosities from her family's explorations, the fertility icons causing particular amusement. So many digs, so many expeditions. Such a restless, wonderful childhood.

Such inevitable disappointment in the harsh realities of adulthood? Ha! So much for youthful hearts, running free.

Neither she nor Tom (for different reasons) had been quite so blessed. Eloise had tried to hold back from asking him at the time, but she could not.

'Are you sure the baby is yours?'

Pride pinched, but Tom had thought about it.

'Probably, yeah.'

'Do you want to be sure?'

His eyes had narrowed, the arch of one brow pulled up quizzically.

'I can help you find out, if you want.'

Eloise had shocked herself at the thought of making real for this girl the song's warning about getting the babies but not getting the man.

And in that moment she had almost envied her – Tom's 'mistake' – wondering if she shouldn't have listened so well to Candi's advice all those years ago (or to Germaine). Perhaps she should have bred, unthinking, like Tom's silly girl. And then she regretted taking this sidetrack into her past because thoughts of childlessness usually led to thoughts of Darius, and with them a whirlpool of resentment.

Why was it that whenever he came to mind she immediately smelled his pungent, overpriced aftershave? For a few years after the split if she'd ever caught a whiff of it on anyone else the wrath had risen involuntarily. Fortunately such occasions were now rare (rather like Darius's expensive tastes) and Eloise was not often in that kind of 'elevated' company these days.

Darius, and all the unspoken power of his family money, accrued in ways he'd never liked to talk about. *No doubt squirrelled out of investments in some corrupt foreign regime before the fall of a dictatorship?* Alright, so her ex did have a sense of subtlety about displaying his good fortune (and often used the safety net of his mother's maiden name when travelling to North Africa or the Middle East) but he knew how to wield his privilege whenever it served him. Eloise had never liked the taste of all that entitlement, suspecting that much of this leverage had been gained at the expense of those left behind whenever such regimes or schemes had failed.

She remembered an evening with him in one of those awful Mayfair nightclubs, where the sheaths of respectability were handed in at the cloakroom and the reptiles came out to play. To be fair, Darius was no great fan of such places either but a cousin of his was visiting from the States for an air show and the right kind of entertaining had to be done. Eloise had gone along willingly (and with some hypocrisy, she conceded) knowing that the same cousin kept a yacht in Fort Lauderdale. Eloise loved little more than to sail but rarely had the chance in her land-locked adult life. She knew of few sensations to match the moment when the engine cut and the canvas unfurled and all one could hear were wind and water, all one could feel was life pushing forward through the waves.

Now she recalled the conversation in that dark private booth at a table strewn with champagne flutes, little effort made by their guest to hide the wrap or the silver straw to snort it with. Darius did not partake (he was surprisingly conservative when it came to narcotics – and brutally dismissive of those who lived or died by them) but he was prepared to overlook their recreational abuse when it suited him. He must have forgotten that Eloise was with him for a moment (it would not have been the first time) as he teased his guest about his penchant for poor investments in expensive playthings. Darius thought it madness that his cousin was now in the market to buy a jet to complement 'that hole in the water you pour money into,' and he had gone on to joke, 'Well, you know what they say, don't you, Cyrus? If it flies, floats or fucks, rent it!'

This was not the only indignity of the night levelled at the woman he professed to love and yet always wriggled out of marrying. At one point both men had stared openly at a passing redhead and Darius had tried to persuade Eloise that she would suit her hair that way, asking of her, 'Why don't *we* think about cutting it and going strawberry blonde?'

It was in that moment that she'd seen the writing on the wall. Excusing herself to go to the ladies, she'd texted Anna and asked her to call the club and have 'Dr Eloise Kluft' paged urgently over the PA. If only to remind Darius who it was that he had come here with. Who it was that he was sacrificing. When the DJ called out her name, she took out a pen and scribbled 'For Rent' on a napkin, then put a cross through it and handed it to Darius as she left.

Not long after that he had left her for a woman from these elite, loftier worlds where the air was too thin for Eloise. Worlds in which people were consumed in the same way as luxury goods. In which souls were commodities. He'd said he was leaving because he wanted to have children but that was only half the truth. Clearly his new bride was not a letting option. Darius straddled the twin spheres of academia and affluence and could happily break bread with anyone that interested him, but he was always going to seek his true pleasures at the trough of the latter.

Now Eloise felt the tears seeping up behind the anger. It was a familiar response but she quickly stifled any self-pity. It was not that she'd never wanted to be a mother (but so what if she hadn't? It was a perfectly reasonable choice for so many who declined the role). It was not that she'd been some 'selfish' career woman, or that she was 'having too much fun'. Ha! As if! If anything she erred towards the philosophy that sentient existence was far too weighted to suffering to justify imposing it on another.

Oh, but the silly, smug things that people say to the childless, the thoughtless questions they ask.

Eloise often backed out of events that were centred around families, not merely to evade such interrogation, not only out of a growing introversion, but in case she found herself enjoying the company of children a little too much.

It wasn't that the urge for children had been absent, nor that she hadn't wanted any with Darius. She would have considered trying again after their little 'accident' – and its accidental loss – *if* he had stayed. No. It was the pain, or rather the fear of the pain. Of coming too close again – or not close enough. And what if they *had* been successful before she or any other had found the cure, what if a beloved little boy had borne the burden of a life-threatening condition or if a cherished little girl had been another carrier, how would she have lived with the guilt? Even so, Eloise was forced to concede, that may have been preferable to all this creeping and unforeseen regret, no matter how much it had been resisted or rationalised.

She turned up the radio. Swayed along with the next soul tune. That was quite enough self-punishment for now. And enough of hating Darius. (Enough for several lifetimes.) Eloise was relieved that the age-old rancour was beginning to recede, whatever the outcome of any rapprochement. She realised that if Darius hadn't left her when he did, sooner or later she would have asked him to go. So perhaps he'd done the courageous thing after all? Perhaps it was time to recognise all that they had been to each other, for better or worse, and to reconcile with all of that.

In the rain and in her reverie, Eloise almost missed the turning into her best friend's street but thoughts of Darius germinated still, pushing up into their conversation once they were underway again.

'So… you know I've had a lot more to do with Darius since Sarah came into my life?'

'Oh, bloody hell, we're not going to talk about bloody men are we?' asked Anna, finger-combing through the long, damp, wavy hair that she had allowed to go grey, and which looked so striking against the canary yellow of her trench coat. Was this refusal to dye a form of rebellion, wondered Eloise, or more a lack of time and concern for expensive grooming now that she was single mother to a young child?

'What about our pact,' Anna complained in her Edinburgh burr, 'What about failing that bloody Bechdel test?'

Eloise was embarrassed. Since discovering the criteria for judging a movie by whether or not two women engage in at least one conversation that is not about men, the two had re-affirmed a commitment to more fulfilling discourse rather than any moaning about relationships (or the lack of them). Indeed, there were many more important things to discuss, but Eloise needed to talk about all the ancient history that was suddenly adding new wrinkles to her romantic life, such as it was. She knew better than to bring up KC, however. Anna had been married, been cheated on, been left. Eloise could predict her friend's opinion on that near-miss.

'Oh, I know, I know. But we've done the weather and even a bit of politics with the underfunding of nursery facilities and all, and I do want to hear more about May-Lyn and tell you more about Sarah – but the trouble is, Anna, she and Darius are now so impossibly linked!'

'Of course, darling, I know. Don't worry, I'm only teasing! But please tell me you're not having any silly thoughts about that old bastard, are you?'

'No. God no, of course not. Oh, but I don't know… Maybe at last here's a chance for what our Americans friends would call "closure"?'

Anna shrugged and smiled. 'Well, I suppose that would be no bad thing. As long as you don't indulge in any of that "conscious uncoupling" business! Darius deserves every bloody poison dart you've ever thrown at him, my love. Never doubt that. Mind you, maybe a bit of *unconscious* coupling might not go amiss for you? I mean, when *was* the last time you got laid?'

Eloise was affronted, but with affection.

'Ha! You can bloody talk!'

'Well, I've got a bloody excuse. Morality has nothing on a toddler when it comes to abstinence, let me tell you.'

'Maybe we should stop saying bloody now, Dr McAdams?'

'Oh, alright then. Yes, we ought to do better really, ought we not, Dr Kluft? But anyway, speaking of Darius, you do know that I never understood what you saw in him? I mean, yes OK, he has a certain… magnetism, I suppose. And then there's all your family stuff, I get that. But he was sooo wrong for you. And as much as your father loved the both of you, even he knew that.'

'Did he?'

Eloise looked sharply at Anna, took her eyes off the car bumper in front, nearly caressing it with her own.

'Oh god. You can be so bloody blind sometimes, Eloise. Sorry, no, just blind. Anyway. I liked that *other* one.' Anna's soft tones grew deeper, taking on a knowing growl.

'Which one?'

'Oh, come on! The cute one, the young one, the one that looked at you like you were a goddess. The one that made you happy?'

Eloise had forgotten that her friend had made an unexpected visit one morning when Tom had been there. Anna had said nothing at the time (observing their oft-broken pact, Eloise had presumed) but while taking in more than she'd let on at the time, clearly. And could Anna see her cheeks reddening now?

'Oh, him! That? That was just a silly fling.'

'Was it? You know, I don't know whether I believe in unconditional love as such, sometimes not even between parent and child if I'm honest, but if it does exist then I saw it in the way that he looked at you, my love, and the way he was around you. The way you were together. Fling? My beautiful great arse, Dr *Bloody* Kluft.'

'Well, whatever. It doesn't matter now. It couldn't have lasted.'

'Couldn't it? Why? Have any of the men your own age, or your own class, or education, or profession been any better for you? All those cleverly rationalised and well-funded excuses to behave like a complete and utter shit?'

Eloise was glad there was a good reason not to look at Anna, not to let her see the moisture in her eyes, but to keep them focused on the wet road ahead.

'No. Perhaps not. And, yes, OK, I will admit that it was love. Oh god, it really was. But it wasn't as simple as it may have looked, Anna. There were… complications. Anyway, never mind, we're here now. Why don't you jump out and pick up the tickets while I try to park…'

*

They have finally turned south again. It is a relief, although she recognises that these new shores bring fresh fears. Further back along the trail and many days behind them now, at the ragged and rising edge of their westward path, she had noticed what seemed to be steam rising and had hoped for another hot spring, but what flowed within this chasm had whipped her back to childhood visions of a world in flame.

It was a well like no other, turning and climbing, folding thickly upon itself. Bubbling and burning with crimson rage. Was this an open vein of the earth itself, with blood made of fire? Where and when might this wound purge, bringing its now familiar death and dust? Not again, she prayed, not again. Such heat was beyond appeasing, beyond dousing. She wondered whether the First Spirit might live here? Or something else, something made of shadow? It was no place for her, she understood that much. She had wrenched herself away from its transfixing hold and turned back into the black-stoned valley.

Now, with the channel crossing and the river of fire far behind them, the ground is quiet and healed. The chill has retreated and the land is greener. She has seen – and tasted, tested – animals and plants that are completely new to her. Several she would never try again. But the greatest wonder had come at another strange new place, perhaps the strangest she has ever seen. There was unfamiliar liquid of so many kinds here, some so thick with salt that it was unyielding to the living and she has learned to drink with caution. Other crystal pools in the midst of the great dry stretches beckoned with their clarity, the water seeming so fresh, so pure, but it stung the fingers and released a rotten aroma just in time to prevent her from drinking in its death.

And yet one spellbinding creature survived this bitterness and in numbers beyond imagining. She had seen it a few days back. As they'd travelled along the crusting shore of a still and shallow lake, she'd noticed a flowering tide in the distance, a pink pool of blooms swelling on the surface. Closer and she'd realised that this colourful mass was made of many things that moved together. Closer still and she'd thought she was in a dream.

They danced. These moving, feathered 'flowers'. Turning together this way and that. On legs so long and slender it was unthinkable they did not snap with every step. Their limbs were matched by stretching necks that rose to curving heads and into beaks of a shape that she did not understand. And then... they flew. Her breath had fallen short as she watched them flock and rise into a cloud of shocking, streaming colour overhead. She'd wakened the child, shaken her and pointed to the sky. This sign was so clear, so special, surely it could mean only good for them. Yes, it must be so. Even in pools of poison, such life, such unbearably beautiful life, could not only survive but thrive.

Luckily, she has found other kinds of water here too. The right kind for her and the child to drink – and for a few careless others too. Yes, there is just enough water, or rather enough *lack* of water in a few receding drinking holes that it forces those high-jumping little deer to take chances. They crowd together thirstily to drink and make themselves such easy targets for spear, sling or arrow. Not since the oasis before the channel crossing has she enjoyed such abundance in choosing which animal to take, no matter how big or small, fast or slow, close enough for a confident aim or far enough away to demand a very lucky shot. But she will take no nursing mothers, no, never again, not if she can help it. And never any healthy young.

Because with every waking morning she thanks the watchful

mother moon, as she slides towards her rest, for the gift of healthy young. For this precious, lively child who is beginning to take her first shaky steps. These efforts have slowed their progress but she cannot refuse her these stumbles towards freedom. She will be strong. Growing fast now, her daughter eats well from the ruminated morsels she feeds her along with the milk that still flows.

The little one is curious too. She will not let go of something that she has found, and her mother has indulged her in this. Although she watches her ferociously, reflexing to any small movement or noise around them, she knows that the tiny walking shell the child has found, blessed with its own protection, presents no risk. And it has a kind of charm. Four fat legs and an odd little face that emerge from safety given any opportunity to escape, though what the spirits had granted in shelter, they had denied the poor animal in speed.

At first she had considered trying to make a meal of it but food is bountiful here – and the ripples of honeyed laughter the little creature encourages from her daughter make every hardship worthwhile. The sound of this giggling, although light and lilting, is familiar. Then she realises that the shape of the mouth that makes this music is that of her own grandmother's, a recognition that carries with it a deep sense of calm.

The next morning, a rip begins to open up in the pelt of grey overhead and she sees the colour blue for the first time in what feels like a lifetime.

22

The rain was pounding still, rattling the skylight in the attic, drowning out the sweet memories of Bach. Eloise could hear it from the comfort of her bed, though she was not yet ready to sleep, her smartphone keeping her awake. Her plan had been nothing more than a quick check of the forecast to discover how long this gale would last, but then before switching off she had made the fatal error of opening up her email. Amidst the logjam of international spam there was one new message from KC. She knew what to expect at this hour, their own particular and innocent form of 'billet-doux'. Nothing more than a 'Check this out...' accompanied by a link to click, a smiley face, and a 'U OK?'

Eloise had taken a chance and confided in KC about the mugging. She was learning to/wanting to have confidence in him and she'd needed to tell someone else who might care, someone other than her reliable coterie of female friends, as distracted and dispersed as they all were. Before the impromptu evening with Anna, she'd needed to tell somebody *in person* – and the two hands that KC had placed firmly on her upper arms, the look of sincere empathy in his eyes, had indeed comforted her.

Ideally she would have preferred complete surrender to the kind of swaddling hold that Tom had mastered, an embrace that told her silently and soothingly that everything was OK. Although Eloise was forced to admit that this natural protective reflex soon might have been followed by chest-beating threats to gather up 'the boys' and go seek out her assailant. But even this would have been preferable to a cold reprimand from Darius about her having too much trust or taking too many risks. At least KC's apparently genuine concern and his appreciation of all her mixed feelings about the incident had made her feel less exposed and confused, if only by letting her talk about it for an hour.

The link he'd shared was in reference to that discussion and to where it had led them, the ongoing debate about inheritance versus environment, about the nature of 'character' and the effects of stress. Eloise clicked through to read a paragraph or two so that she might politely reply, but the article's content called to mind another form of correspondence that was waiting to be finished. She could not resist. She opened up her notepad app and pressed the microphone button. (This was a new discovery that delighted her beyond description, as her fumbling fingers had never been able to keep up with the pace of her thoughts, and the tragicomedy of predictive text only made matters worse.) Eloise picked up where she'd left off at breakfast that morning and dictated into her phone.

So, where were we, Charles? Ah yes, I had been telling you about non-coding RNA and its role in gene expression, and its effects on its big brother, DNA. Oh, Charles, the pace we are moving at now is breathtaking. The things we're learning about DNA, not only what it does in terms of protein building but everything else that it might be able to do and, more to the point, what *we* might be able to do with it! From medical applications to 'fishing' for particles or even data storage, the potential is astounding.

From a physician's point of view we have begun to understand more about epigenetics now, or the changes to the ways in which genes behave depending on environmental factors. Not only 'external' stimuli but 'internal' too – and the role that chronic stress plays is particularly interesting. We have discovered that 'memories' about altered gene behaviour can be inherited, affecting the next generation without necessarily altering the genes themselves, only how they operate (or fail to).

There's still so much we don't know yet but the clinical hope of such research is exhilarating, from treatments with fewer side effects to earlier interventions with far less collateral damage. As for the social implications, we're reminded of the importance of optimised environments and not only in terms of air, food and water quality but also in terms of quality of life – and, yes, even the quality of 'love'. Or at least parental care. The effects of either its presence or lack thereof are measurable, Charles, whether that be in mice in the laboratory or in our own children, and whether they live in the poorest or the richest places on earth.

It should really come as no surprise but well-loved, cared for, properly stimulated and *safe* offspring do so much better – not only socially but also in the expression of their genes – when positive, nurturing conditions are in place. And this tendency can be transferred! (Consider how one person's laughter can make a whole room start laughing, or how one angry person can make the whole room, or village, or tribe angry?) So it seems that not only the gene but also the way in which its blueprint is activated has the ability to be passed on... and I haven't even started on the relationship between epigenetics and neuroplasticity yet because, well, we would be here all night.

There's so much more I want to tell you, Charles. For example, what we are learning about your beloved nature (how I wish I could have joined you and little Flora on any one of those daily constitutionals!) and what we're learning *from* nature offers such practical potential to improve life and not for the privileged alone. Indeed, as much as technology has helped us to understand biology the reverse is now equally true. We can see, on a microscopic scale, exactly how nature has already solved many of the problems we are juggling with today, but with maximum efficiency and minimum waste. (Albeit having taken millennia to do so.)

And soon we may have at our disposal, Charles, tiny, tailored 'time-bombs' of directed medicine that can *boldly go* where none have gone before! (Forgive the split infinitive, but you would have loved Gene Roddenberry, I'm quite sure of it. Although this is yet another tangent that sadly, we don't have time for tonight.)

It's all so thrilling, my dear, dear Mr Darwin, but also rather terrifying at times – and so dependent on trusting in the better part of human nature. Which we must, mustn't we? I mean 'goodness' is essential to the equilibrium, as seems to be understood throughout the natural world, and apparent altruism has been observed even in colonies of microbes where some seem to sacrifice themselves when necessary for the good of the 'guild!' But what of us? I mean, what is human nature, after all, other than what *we* make of it? We are not reduced to its helpless slaves, we all have choices however limited they may first appear.

And what of our precious Sarah, Charles? Was she what might have been considered a *good* person and would we find her so today? Would such judgements have existed, or mattered? Yes, yes, I do believe they would. It's been observed that even our monkey cousins have a well-developed sense of justice and fair play, throwing back slices of cucumber when they should have had a grape, with other monkeys 'striking' and refusing the grapes that their companions should have been given.

But what sort of choices might Sarah have had to make, Charles? Indeed, what choices might have been made *for her*? Might she have had to do terrible things and if so, would she have suffered any guilt? How might she have survived any of the terrible things that may have been done to her, or even the most basic yet relentless trauma of staying alive? Did her experiences change her as a person... more to the point, *did they affect her genetic material, or her children's?*

We are getting close now, Charles. Did I tell you? So close. We think we might have the right set of cells now, finally.

Eloise could have carried on for hours, but it was getting late and she had a big day coming up. She knew that she must try (at least try) to sleep. She replied briefly to KC (a suitable interval having passed) with a 'Thanks! And I'm fine, really, but thanks for asking,' then switched off her phone. The blue glare that had been the only source of light in the room gave way to the orange facsimile of darkness that was the best the overcast urban night could offer and the white-on-white tones of her bedroom did nothing but enhance this half-life effect. She closed her eyes and curled up on her habitual left then immediately changed sides, wincing at the tenderness in her ribs from the mugging, and in turn thinking about (then trying very hard not to think about) either Darius, Tom, or KC.

*

She expects the skies to darken again, for the precious light to be stolen back from the earth, but instead it grows brighter by the day. There is colour in the world again. She thinks she may have forgotten how to see it because it keeps surprising her. One of the many amazing things about this land is how the brightness belongs not only to the plants but to all things, to animals, to insects, to birds – and, oh, the birds! It's as if these creatures have no need to fade into sand or bush or forest. They shout their beauty out loud.

And they are clever, these flying rainbows. In the shelter of the thick forest they have now passed through, she had watched them as they built or played, or as they fished for food in bark or lake, with beak and claw, as they stole from their fellows and then hid their hoards, as they chose to fool or fight or flirt with their friends. As they called out in such complicated songs.

One, who kept his colour under his tail to show it only when it suited him, seemed also to talk. They had rested for a few days in a good, strong and shady tree, sharing it with a few of these watchful new friends – and she was sure she'd heard one of them say sshhh to the child, exactly as she herself had done when the little one cried out in her sleep. She was sure they shouted out the name she used for her daughter as they had left. Understanding that these creatures had wisdom to offer, she'd watched what they had chosen to eat, and had been right to trust their lessons. The brightness in those berries might have been a warning as much as a lure, and may have as easily poisoned them as nourished them.

All this fearless colour thrills her but also frightens her. Will any men or women they find also be made in startling shades of red and yellow and purple and blue? She is aware now that other colours are possible, she had seen it in the eyes and the hair of her child's father, although his skin and features were much like her own. What will they make of her here, how could they become a part of this new world? Her instincts tell her to hide, to blend into the trees, the long grass, the rich soil when needed. But what if they might want to be seen? And what if they seem ugly and frightful to any others?

She begins to gather any bright, discarded feathers that she finds, binds them to her necklace, weaves them into the little one's hair. She puts aside her fears. They will find a way to fit, if they are lucky enough to meet any others. They will find the way to belong to their bold new world.

23

The anticipation was fizzing, as if it were a first date. Eloise left for work early, relishing the quiet streets and bright skies of the post-storm calm. The reconstruction arrived by secure courier shortly after ten (too many coffees later) and the team had gathered directly outside the tempered glass box of the Clean Room, removing their protective gear. They could not risk contamination by taking the reconstruction inside the room, but it seemed only right to unveil the bust as near as possible to what remained of Sarah.

It had been premature perhaps to complete the visualisation of Sarah before all of the DNA evidence was in, but any unlikely minor adjustments such as colouring should be simple enough to add – especially before going public. For many reasons, from motivating both the team and the money men, they had needed move things along. They had needed to put a face to the name, at last.

The bust that emerged from the packaging was a brilliant, painstaking and inspired realisation, although surprising in so many ways. Eloise looked at KC to gauge his response. It was typically enthusiastic.

'Hey, Sarah, wow, good to meet you!' he exclaimed. 'So, Eloise, is she what you were expecting?'

'Well, based on the skull I would have to say, yes, I suppose so but, oh, I don't know...'

'I gotta say she's kind of a shock to me. I mean, considering where she was found I was expecting something more like the Bushmen, the Khoi-San?'

Yes, that was it. Eloise realised that she too had envisioned an echo of those living archives of human genealogy, a remarkable hunter–gatherer people who had changed little over tens of millennia. It was now believed that they had once stretched from Southern Africa to the Rift Valley, some eventually diverging into variant tribes and a remainder resorting (or rather being pushed) to an almost mythical tradition of desert survival in the parching west. Ancient faces that she knew, personally. Eloise had spent some time with what was left of one branch in the Kalahari (so nearly the victims of an insidious genocide by white and black alike) while taking samples for the genome project. She felt privileged to call some among them friends.

'Well, yes, that certainly would have been a fair assumption, taking into account Sarah's location, age and mtDNA indications for that area and time. And they do call themselves the 'First Humans' after all,' Eloise replied, a little disappointed that Sarah was not more like her friends.

'But, hey,' KC added, 'I guess we can't be influenced by expectations, or by folklore?'

That subtle, lopsided smile of his. It still worked on her. Eloise looked back at the reconstruction, cleared her throat.

'No, quite. But I think we really do have to trust the Dutch team on this one, those guys are the best when it comes to anthropology and anatomy. And they do seem to have referenced the current morphology of the Khoi-San to some extent, with the golden brown skin colour and full lips. But you're right. Her jawline is stronger and more masculine than I had visualised, I must admit. It's her nose too… it's longer, narrower. Still flared, but the bridge is much more pronounced. That must have been suggested by the skull? And the epicanthic fold of the eyes, it's far more subtle.'

Eloise looked to KC again.

'Yes, exactly,' he agreed, 'I was anticipating similar eyelids to the Bushmen too, though not as developed, obviously, as in modern East Asians. It's there but her eyes are less almond-shaped than I thought they'd be.'

Yes, thought Eloise. The eyes again, leaving such clues to selective or random mutations. Changes over time to colour and shape probably affected by adaptations to shorter, darker northern days, or a narrowing protection from the glare of Siberian snow fields.

In the more detailed digital version of Sarah's reanimation, which had come on a flash drive along with the clay 3D model, Sarah's eyes were a deep dark brown. This was an appropriate supposition to the team, as the agreed wisdom was that no lasting variation in eye colour had appeared in the gene pool earlier than around 10,000 years before present. However, instead of the low hairline and tight peppercorn curls of the Khoi-San Bushmen, Sarah had been given a higher forehead and slightly looser, longer, almost dreadlocked hair – and a surprisingly powerful, muscular build. Eloise wondered if this was an excess of artistic license or interpretation.

Or... could Sarah have come from another heterogeneous *Homo sapiens* line of the time, one that had either died out or perhaps spread north or west into other parts of Africa from the Rift in the following millennia? Sarah's height might corroborate a connection to other present day African ethnicities. Had the Rift Valley highlands always been her home, or was she more nomadic than previously considered? Could she have travelled there *from* northern Africa, or even further away? Perhaps to worship on the mountain in some way... or was she trying to escape from something up there?

Eloise thought about the 90,000 year old Qafzeh skull again, which although at least 15,000 senior to Sarah, was anatomically modern human and may have shared a branch of not-too-distant ancestry. She returned to her recent idea about reviving her father's hypothesis that the Qafzeh group of early pioneers out of Africa had not completely disappeared but may have left something living behind, something inherited by modern humans.

Neanderthals had occupied those Levantine lands as well, though it was unclear if the populations had been concurrent. But having worked in that region, having stood in one of the very caves these people had called home, having envisioned their lives, their joys, their struggles, a sense of continuation had been something that her father had enjoyed imagining. Eloise now hoped to link up with other projects tracing contemporary genomes back along all the key African, Middle Eastern and Asian migration routes.

And, like her father, she had often wondered which of these plucky migrants may have then survived the cataclysm of the Toba supervolcano, the massive and devastating eruption exploding out of Sumatra 74,000 ago. Father and daughter had been in good company in gnawing on this particular bone of contention. There had been persistent doubts that only a few hundred souls leaving via the Nile or the Horn 60,000 years ago (well after the supervolcano) were the sole source for all present-day populations outside Africa. Even before the proof of tiny percentages of archaic interspecies gene flow, evidence found along the Asian coastal route and as far as Australia, in terms of artefacts, symbols, anatomy, and even language, had fed these schools of thought.

Most intriguingly, tools found both below and above the Toban ash deposits in hard-hit India suggested that some hominin groups had indeed prevailed, despite the choking falls and inevitable drought and famine that must have followed – and were able to re-establish in the same locations. What's more, curious species such as the 'hobbit-like' *Homo floresiensis* had survived in an isolated pocket of the Indonesian archipelago with the explosion on their very doorstep. Any humans or distant relatives much further north may have suffered less from the heaviest ash falls and more from the volcanic winter, but some could have found ways to survive there, or to migrate south again?

It seemed that where there was a will – or rather a need – the various branches of humanity had found a way, and with extraordinary adaptability, pragmatism and ingenuity.

Now Eloise asked herself whether Sarah, who had been carbon-dated to a similar period for Toba, could have been one of its original 'refugees' – and perhaps a part of the population bottleneck it may have caused? Did any of her descendants also survive and if so, had her dynasty remained in Africa or could some have joined the most effective expeditions outward again? More to the point, might Sarah's legacy live on in anyone walking the planet today?

She shared nothing of these thoughts for the time being, she would wait for further clues from Sarah. The full isotope analysis was due back soon. Yet for all the surprises, all the new questions, now gazing at Sarah fully fleshed once more, she looked to Eloise so... familiar. Almost as if she had met a close relative of hers quite recently.

Of course she looks familiar, Eloise chastised herself, you have lost your objectivity, become too involved. Step back. Get some bloody detachment.

*

The stars. So many now under these clear skies, so, so many. So different, somehow, from the way she remembered them. Hypnotic, soothing, stirring. She has fallen in love with the night.

They have been following the shore of a massive inland lake (at first fearing they had somehow doubled back and reached a calm sea coast by mistake, but the star shapes have reassured her). They rest often as the little one grows heavier by the day and her back has begun to suffer. This lakeside route is probably longer in steps than by wing line, but it is easier to manage than the challenging terrain she has encountered so far. And here, they are also more likely to find life. For good or bad.

They camp by night and she manages some long spells of sleep inside the tight circle of spikes that she cuts down and drives into the ground around them, each a hand width apart and strung with shell and pebble. The cut branches are a long-learned habit in the lack of any safer, higher shelter, or when she feels the fire may not be sufficient deterrent... or worse, may attract those unafraid of it. But the rattling shells are a new idea, along with the sharp thorns and crushed leaves from a plant with an unpleasant sting (discovered the hard way) that are sprinkled around the boundary with a pouch-wrapped hand. Any noise, any movement and she will raise the flint hand axe curled in her palm, or her spear, or both.

First light. So much light now and blinding when it reflects off the lake. It feels wrong to wish for shade again. She pulls up the spikes before the child awakes, some she will re-use as arrows. They pack up and set off again, augurs of discovery under her skin but she cannot tell whether these bode well or ill.

Before long she sees tracks leading inward to some thick growth. The marks are old, it has not rained for a while, but these are the footprints of men. Perhaps made by a pair of hunters of the lake-life? She has seen one scaly creature with long snapping jaws and learned how to avoid it, and she keeps the child away from the water's edge – but on land it is slow and she thinks it might make good meat if you could get a spear to its underbelly. Now she notices that the older tracks of the men she has been following are pursued by fresher paw prints.

At a distance on the plains, she has seen the kind of huge, fierce and beautiful predator that stalks this new land, and has studied its ways. But even if they had caught sight or scent of her and the child, they seemed too well fed, or too lazy in the heat of day to show any special interest. Perhaps unsure if the meal would be worth the effort? If the child were not with her, if she had a band of companions, she would get closer, take the time to watch them and draw on their essence. These tracks are smaller, she realises, not made by those great yellow beasts but not to be ignored. Something more like a wolf perhaps, but she has seen no wolves in this new land.

There are only two of the creatures, so far, from what she can tell. But the marks belong to something with sharp teeth – of that she is sure. Even so she follows them through the dense green bush, in the same way as these paw prints seem to be shadowing the unmistakable steps of her own, rare kind. At last the thorny growth begins to clear, a relief in so many ways, as her anger has begun to spike with each stinging scratch to her impatient arms and legs.

There – ahead, she sees it now, a camp!

But then it becomes clear that she is too late and her heart drops. Whoever was here has now gone. Were they forced to leave quickly? No, the multiple imprints leading away from the camp appear calm and steady. Men, women and young. There are no signs of violence. Then why had they left the camp like this? Discarded. Wasteful. Soiled with scale, skin, bone, ash and scat. Half a carcass, they have taken only the haunches, not buried or burned the fly-blown entrails, not used the bone. The head stares, the horns and the rest of the striped hide are unharvested. This is not wise.

Worse is to come. It seems not everyone has moved on from this place, something shifts and groans under a pile of unwanted skins. A grey head struggles to lift. It is an old woman, half-travelled to the world beyond and helpless. She will not approach her yet, conscious of the sleeping child, her soft breath so close on her neck – and the handful of small stones within reach of this withered heap, the sharpened stick beside her (which surely she has no strength to wield?).

They have left her. Her people. To the makers of the paw prints waiting nearby. She feels them now, hears them growling and realises what they are. She has seen them once before, snarling and cackling and squabbling over carrion. Ugly. As though some angry spirit had punished a wayward wolf by flattening its face, hunching its back and raising its spiky hair. Cowardly, thieves, but capable in numbers of killing a child – or her. While she respects that every living thing has its place, its worth, she feels no special kinship with these.

She must go now. She cannot wait, she must follow the roaming clan, must catch up with them, needs them. As she turns away the old woman cries out, grasping at some wisp of desperate breath. Those half-living eyes are seeking her out now and she looks back into them.

No. She cannot leave her like this. But she cannot carry her with them. Cannot kill the lurking scavengers, not all of them, though they will begin their ripping and feeding well before the old woman is still or cold.

Is this her people's tradition? Will she somehow curse her by interfering? The eyes of the one they have left behind give a different answer. Eyes that once were young, that once had found food for her children, that once had seen beauty and been of use to her kind.

She will not abandon her to the waiting ones, not like this. She knows that they are near, even if in hearing her approach they have chosen to hide. As she moves close to the old woman she allows herself to grasp a bony outstretched hand. The grip that comes in return tells her all she needs to know. Released from this pleading hold, it takes only one deep tensing breath and one swift movement at the neck, and it is done. She closes the now silent eyes. No time for anything more, she must go forward from the dead, away from the ravening and after the living.

She stops. It begins to rain so suddenly as it does here, dancing drops of clear fresh water. Good, this place needs cleansing. The torrent seems to wash something within her as well. She is unwilling now to follow the tracks but does not know which way to go. When the rain begins to peter, she looks up and through the soft separation of colours in the watery air she sees a single hawk, determined in its direction. She closes her own eyes and lifts her inner vision to share the eyes of this bird, to imagine and to see what it sees. When she comes back to full awareness of her own body she steps forward to follow a different path, without looking back.

24

The South Downs sunset was sublime. A symphony of dust and vapour, scattering the spectrum, stretching out into layers of sky fire. It had been far too long since Eloise had allowed such loveliness to soak long and deep into her psyche. It was good to be out of London.

Eloise had treated herself to a folding Brompton bike. She needed to escape the metropolis more often, get off the Tube and out of her car and this was the ideal solution for adventures beyond any chosen railway stop. She needed more exercise, more fresh air but could not risk pounding her knees in any more mini-marathons.

And what a bike! This smart bit of engineering was testament to the kind of genuinely 'intelligent design' that got things so right (rather than those frustrating imperfections in the protracted trial-and-error of natural selection). The free-wheeling took her mind off everything for a while.

If she was honest with herself, it took her mind off KC, although they had now established the nature of their relationship, its allowable possibilities and its unspoken borders. Another time, another place, different choices, different paths perhaps, but this was the tack they both had taken and accepted. Eloise was comforted, however, in the new conviction that this could become a life-long friendship or working partnership, and she looked forward to shared discoveries with a sense of optimism she had not felt for some time.

They had discussed a potential collaboration on retroviruses, a form of medical archaeology to genetically retrace the evolution of HIV in particular, a project that would call for a return to Africa. (How she longed to go back! And a chance perhaps to walk in Sarah's footsteps, independent of Darius and whatever his agenda.)

Eloise had told KC about her time on that fascinating continent for the sampling project, how she had been moved by its beauty and vitality, its wisdom and warmth, devastated by its problems, its colonial legacies, its looted wealth, its crushing health crises, the ethnic conflicts exacerbated by competition for misappropriated land, power and resources. The genome project had shown how meaningless such imposed divisions were upon the human family and had once seemed to point the way to so much hope, but Eloise could not deny the daily disappointments since those halcyon days.

She had agreed with KC that for any fresh collaborations they would seek the kind of funding that would allow any results to be posted online as open source. (No more paranoia, no more suspicion, no more commercially driven backing.) It was clear to her now that whoever may have been trying to interfere with or sabotage the Sarah project, it can't have been KC. She felt guilty, even a little foolish for having considered it. Although he was largely unaware of the extent of her suspicions, she wanted to make it up to him somehow and felt that a joint project such as this would bring them both the considerable satisfactions of a sense of purpose and contribution. (Eloise felt that the exploration of any other form of satisfaction between them was no longer either a risk or an insistent desire.)

There were other enticements back to Africa. While any new microbial detective work they might undertake there would be concentrated in the cities, typical hotbeds for vector-borne viral fermentation, in truth Eloise hoped to find an excuse for a return to the Kalahari. To the Bushmen, the Khwe, the Basarwa. Probably among the most examined indigenous peoples on the earth, likely among the most endangered, definitely among the most genetically preserved. She often felt that these were the best and most playful, generous, egalitarian and relaxed people she had ever known – the indulgence of romanticism aside. (And all the guilt of imperialism acknowledged.)

They had much to teach. Also much to be angry or despairing about, yet for the most part, it seemed they had resisted this course. Yes, OK, they practised what many might see as superstitious ritual – and Eloise had witnessed the shrieking of a shaman who had 'inhaled' an unnamed evil from a sufferer in order to spew it back to its source. But she had also seen the calm after that storm, the renewed unity of the group after what evidently had been an important bonding experience.

Admittedly, she had not stayed long enough to see how the shaman's 'patient' (who had seemed to be more sad than sick) had fared in the aftermath, but even while respecting their traditions, Eloise could not help but worry about their reliance on this kind of 'healing' and how dangerous any encounter with a ruthless new pathogen might be. As it had been for other communities, rural and urban, persuaded by wild rumour that modern medicine (or even basic infection control) was a conspiracy to rob them of their identity at best, or murder them at worst. Eloise tried hard to be neither sentimental, nor to condescend about a system of living that, against all odds, had kept this genetic line alive and well for so many millennia. She knew they had no need of the 'white saviour' but she also knew it would be impossible to bear if some unthinkable tragedy ever befell the Bushmen.

Her subscription to an advocacy group for the survival of tribal peoples seemed like a band-aid against the inexorable forces of land grab and cultural decimation. But what else could be done? Was it the fault of economic pressures alone, she wondered, or were their oppressors also somehow afraid of them, envious of them – these people who held up a cracked mirror to what humanity might have been, and to what it had become?

Or maybe they would have the last laugh? Eloise believed that it was indigenous peoples of such a robust and ancient nature who would likely outlive the rest of humanity if the worst of the Armageddon scenarios ever played out, especially if they were able to isolate themselves.

She drew in the sweet Sussex air and gazed upwards, away from earthbound worries, to seek some elusive peace in place of all this moral rage, and was happy she had done so when she noticed a flock of swallows heading home.

'Does the hawk fly by thy wisdom and stretch her wings toward the south?' Job 39:26

It was the only biblical verse that she knew verbatim but it came to mind every time she saw a starling murmuration, or the ecstatic mating dance of the grebes, or a drag-efficient V-formation of geese riding the generosity of an updraft. Now, as she watched the darkening violet of the skies above, the swallows migrating overhead had triggered a grammar school memory about an assignment to address Job's biblical rhetoric.

What indeed made a young bird take its first brave flight southwards, home to Africa, with no concept of how long the journey would take or what it might encounter? With only innate programming directing it to follow the magnetic lines and navigate via the solar compass? Instinct, yes, necessity, of course, but what of subtler guidance, perhaps even at a quantum level? At eighteen she'd concluded firmly on the side of adaptation and on the inescapable engine driving the need to reproduce, achieving the grade she'd aimed for in the process. But here, in this enchanted moment, with everything seeming at once in flux and yet fully present, might there be a window opening to some other form of 'emergence'? Were these sudden tears of rapture telling her so?

Eloise had experienced another such surprising yet uplifting moment recently after her visit to the Natural History Museum. Realising that she was long overdue in paying her respects to the tomb of Charles Darwin, she'd decided to go into Westminster Abbey for the first time and had wondered, naturally, how he might have felt about the irony of his burial there.

There had been other 'tourists' visiting, like she, but as she'd relaxed into the calm cradle of all that cool stone, so lovingly laid by working hands in honour of something greater – as she'd observed those church-goers who'd come here to pray or to contemplate or to revere their god, Eloise had felt profoundly moved. Oddly 'at one'. Not with any narrative, or ritual, or dogma, or any subjugation to a club and its rulebook, but with the vulnerability of her fellows and their humble yet exquisitely bonded humanity in the face of *all that is*.

No, this was no more than what some might describe as a 'peak' experience, she decided. A lull in the roiling seas that had surrounded the Sarah project and which had spilled over into her personal life. Eloise forgave her distracted mind.

Surely this was nothing more than the mischievous stimulus of the sunset over an excitable party of neurons.

*

Warm, like it once was in the summers of home, with a moistness that caresses her flesh. The rolled bear fur has become a dead weight, not needed, especially on this uphill climb, but she will not discard it. Now at last they breach a ridge and she sees the lush, sheltered valley below. Yes, yes, this is the site that she somehow *remembers*. Water cascades and flows through it, alive with energy. This is the place, it must be.

No sign of people. For a moment she doubts. Could her dreaming have been wrong? She decides she will wait for the night and watch for any fires.

She takes this time to let the little one play, devising a game designed to tire her out, gently rolling and wrestling her while mimicking the monkeys and their noises, their grooming, their fearless affection. Letting her daughter find and forge her own strength until she is breathless and sleepy.

Before dusk she rigs the sling she has devised, an idea inspired by the tree-dwellers that have amused them so, howling to each other as they swung and hung above. Between two strong branches she fixes a nest of safety for the child, binds her in gently so that she cannot roll out in her slumber. Then she climbs to the highest vantage point that will take her weight and lashes herself to the trunk, so that she too will not be deceived by the sleep that comes more easily these days.

The moon, whole and huge, throws ghost light over the treetops and shines the river into writhing lizard-skin. How could something that allows the spirit to soar in such ways bring harm? Still, she is vigilant.

25

The irregular assembly on the steps up to the Institute seemed unusual, but didn't register as anything threatening until Eloise came closer and could see a group of people handing out leaflets with a body language that was verging on belligerent. There were no placards, no loud-hailer, no shouting, but then she saw the silver gaffer tape that was fixed over their mouths. The quiet insistence as their pamphlets were thrust at passers-by and the glazed-yet-gleaming look in the eyes of these activists suggested neither the old nor new brand of revolutionary. Despite their silence, every stifled breath they took screamed 'cult'.

Oh, bloody hell, Eloise moaned inwardly, what manner of misinformed loony now?

She tried to avoid them, swatted away a leaflet pressed upon her by a determined middle-aged woman in an oversized burgundy sweatshirt which may well have been borrowed from her teenage son, and she resisted any kind of eye contact. Whoever they were, this targeting of the Institute was an unwelcome new development. Eloise briefly registered a vague, if easily dismissed, déjà vu about the group. This was not a sensation she willing to indulge.

Once she was inside, she could see that one of her colleagues was already having a word with security, and she noticed a couple of flyers abandoned to the marble floor. On a curious impulse she picked one up and read it when alone in the lift.

'WE SPEAK FOR THOSE WHO CANNOT!' It claimed. 'STOP EMBRYONIC STEM CELL RESEARCH! LIFE IS LIFE! MURDER IS MURDER! SCIENCE IS NOT ABOVE GOD'S LAWS!'

Misinformed indeed. No embryos here. Possibly very soon, synthetic DNA, yes, but no donations from tragic miscarriages, despite how those who had lost a little hope might want that loss to mean something or for something else to be gained. (Just as she had done.) Even those who had chosen to donate after abortion, or following successful IVF, had chosen. *Chosen.* Eloise was a big believer in personal responsibility (and felt that many humans of both genders could certainly apply a little more) and she was passionate about prevention over cure, but she blamed no one, judged no one – and would fight to ensure safe access to healthy procedures, if necessary.

Perhaps, she asked herself, she should have stopped to talk to them, whoever they were and whichever version of vengeful deity they subscribed to (and to whose wrath they might gleefully dispatch the rest of creation). Or maybe this lot were not so quick to condemn, after all? Maybe their action was driven by a kind of love? Compassion for all life, in all its forms was an aspiration that Eloise could appreciate, despite the way that modern lifestyles led to a constant wrestling match with one's own hypocrisy.

The possibility of some kind of original or unifying intelligence was not something she could dismiss outright, not without clear evidence either way. Indeed the very notion of *possibility* itself was her guiding light. But she knew from those searchlight stares outside that in this case, any discussion would be futile. She tossed the leaflet into the nearest recycling box. Waste nothing, she thought, for nothing in life or death is wasted. Besides, there were many more enlightening things on the agenda today.

The much-delayed mineral analysis was due that afternoon, finally the backlog at the specialist lab had cleared and Eloise was hoping it would form another corner piece of the puzzle, shedding light on Sarah's diet and lifestyle. She kept herself busy until lunchtime then popped in briefly at the farewell do in the canteen for the retiring caretaker. Eloise was sorry to see old Mr Morrin go, but he had done in his time in overalls.

She was introduced to his now fully-trained replacement, a tall and pale man called Calumn who possessed a cold-fish handshake and what appeared to be a crippling shyness, and Eloise felt rude about an immediate desire to leave as soon as was polite. But she attempted to engage him in the briefest of exchanges, nevertheless.

'Hello, Calumn, welcome! I'm sure you will do a fine job of replacing our irreplaceable Mr Morrin!'

'Hello. Yes. God-willing I will do my best.'

'Indeed. Indeed.'

Mr Morrin piped up to close the painful gap in what could hardly qualify as a conversation.

'He'll be grand, I've no doubt! And I'll tell you this much, Dr Kluft, Calumn's your man if you were ever wanting or needing any kind of tape. And I mean *any* kind. What a collection he keeps! String, too, and cable-ties, super-glue, whatever kind of packaging or fixing sundries a body might ever need.'

'Wonderful! I shall certainly bear that in mind. Thank you. But I'm afraid I can't stop, I'm needed back at the lab. Well, all the very best, Mr Morrin, I hope you enjoy every moment of your new-found freedom. Though try not to drive your dear wife up the wall with all your spare time!'

Eloise slipped away without staying to enjoy the finger food buffet that some kind soul had laid on, a choice that for the sake of her stomach she regretted soon after.

To fill the dead time in the remaining lunch hour (while KC skyped his family) and to compensate for an appalling sandwich from the corner shop, Eloise cruised the travel sites. It was time to plan another voyage, she felt ready to explore again and would need something to look forward to once Sarah had told her story (and KC had gone home). It would be a while before their Africa idea came together, if it came together at all, and they would both want and need to work closely with local specialists. It would take time to make those key contacts.

So how about that long-postponed holiday in Iceland? No, not on her own. Besides, she hoped there might be a better and properly funded excuse to visit if one of several recent proposals to the foundation was accepted. The population of this historically isolated isle boasted one of the purest pools of genetic information to be found in the modern world. Eloise had the same reason for postponing her longed-for excursion to Nepal, where the mountain air – and a likely inheritance from archaic hominin encounters – had given rise to remarkable adaptations to altitude in the blood of its natives. Such scenes, such people, she would want to share all that with a companion, whether academic or romantic.

Then Italy again, perhaps? Or the Greek Islands? A few years earlier, between assignments, Eloise had embarked on her own version of the Grand Tour, minus the Byronic debaucheries and solo, apart from a passing encounter in Venice. (She had absolved herself the morning after with the excuse that it would have been churlish, somehow, not to partake of all that was on the menu in this delicious country.)

Italy had caught her off guard. In the quiet moments she had found herself contemplating faith, in this place so dedicated to it and yet so paradoxically carefree of its constriction. No ascetic self-denial here. Love, beauty, food all to be celebrated and enjoyed. The art, the music, the architecture.

Why, Eloise asked herself, did these seem to flourish so much more satisfyingly under the patronage of church rather than state? And why were we so often at our best – and worst – in the name of god? When did we first seek him out? Was this longing for the divine, for an afterlife, for belonging and meaning always within us or simply a cynical way to scare the herd, a lazy relinquishing of responsibility to a greater authority? Eloise was learning to dance with the dichotomy. There was the empirical evidence (and the lack of it) and then there were her *feelings*, for want of a better word. She found that she could not consign these intuitions and sensations solely to her personal or isolated neurochemistry, not quite yet.

At last, her inbox chimed and even before the printer could churn into action she was scouring the results on screen. The isotopes told an intriguing tale and also brought KC back to her workstation, leaning over her shoulder, just close enough for comfort.

'So what you got, Eloise?'

Without the chance to fully digest the information, her response was more of a running commentary.

'OK, so… Indications of a varied diet, but predominantly protein-based, as we'd expect. But here's something, a suggestion of significant marine sources in the diet. And more, they're saying these seem common to people living around the eastern Mediterranean or the Black Sea – but Christ, that can't be right, can it? Even if the marine diet was more local, it's quite a hike from Mount Kenya to any kind of sea coast for a spot of fishing? Maybe her tribe started out near the Indian Ocean or the Red Sea coast of Africa, or made seasonal forays? Now here's something else. Evidence of higher than normal levels of fluoride over a period, though not enough to cause skeletal or dental deformities, clearly.'

KC's expression was as quizzical as her own.

'So what does that tell us?'

'Could be a number of explanations – but isn't there a high content of fluoride in volcanic ash, KC? And yes look, look!' Eloise's pulse was quickening, her voice rising. 'Here it is – notable sulphur levels too!'

KC did not seem to find this as exciting as she.

'Well, Mount Kenya where she was found is volcanic, and Kilimanjaro...' he shrugged. 'Heck, that whole valley straddles an active thermal seam. The lava is exposed in open wells in some places.'

'Yes, but it's *ash* that I'm talking about, KC – and Kenya's extinct, the plug is over 2 million years old, despite the odd recorded rumbling or venting. Kilimanjaro's been inactive for major eruptions for over 100,000 years, though there are some gas emissions from the crater. I'm not aware of any other significant activity for Sarah's time and location.'

'So, how about Toba? Did that eruption spill as far west as the Rift?'

Toba was definitely on Eloise's mind, but not in the way that KC had made the connection.

'It's possible, depending on monsoon winds, but the ash fall went mostly north-west from Sumatra. It's unlikely it fell in anything like the devastating degree that it did in Southeast Asia and India, or even the lighter but still dangerous fall in the Middle East and Europe. And while we know there was a very light and clearly survivable fall in South Africa, as far as I'm aware there's no evidence of ash layers in east Africa to suggest a meaningful deposit from the supervolcano. They certainly escaped the worst of the global six-year winter from the stratospheric sulphur that followed, and the ensuing thousand-year ice cycle that it may have kicked off.'

'Well, you've been doing your homework... So what are you saying?'

KC searched into her eyes. She was at ease enough with such

familiarity now to look right back, though not enough to raise the shield of her reading glasses.

'I'm not sure,' she replied, 'but maybe Sarah wasn't originally a local chick? Maybe she came from much further away? We have to factor in the morphology too, although there could be many reasons for that. I mean, we can only guess what any of the native populations looked like at that time. But water levels between the Horn and the Arabian Peninsula might have been low enough at that time to cross back into Africa? Or back along the Nile? Maybe some of them got out of the devastation, or survived the volcanic winter, made it 'home' to the motherland?'

'Well, I guess it's not impossible. I mean, we know that some pockets of early human types survived much nearer that mess, but it's still stretching the hypothesis pretty wildly in terms of Sarah. That's one hell of a journey in only a single generation, or even a few years? And hey, you know that the simplest and most obvious explanations usually turn out to be the right ones, Eloise. We need to source more geographical evidence and check on other volcanic activity in the Rift. We need to pin down her environmental exposures more specifically – and we should be looking at other hypotheses too.'

*

The mark of their location came well before the deep darkness, as she had prayed, the unmistakable smoke signals from a camp in the distance. By morning, with the music of the birds, the fires had not yet been dampened and she knew which way to walk. Quietly, carefully. She would not give away their presence until she had watched them for a while. Made sure. Saw what they did, how they were with each other, how they lived. What they fed on. Made sure that these were not the same tribe that had discarded that poor old woman to her fate.

Before the open expanse of the riverbank clearing at the top of a gentle rise, she finds a leafy place and waits. The campmates, several families at least, go about their day calmly, taking time to work, rest, gather and eat. Food that seems plentiful, enough to share equally. They laugh often and the children play freely. There are also elders here, she watches as one is assisted to some shade as the shadows grow shorter. But it is only the men who go and return from a hunt.

Will she be accepted? Will they recognise the markings on her spear, the record of her skill? There is no way to tell. But she realises now that she has seen none among them carrying a bow, none making arrows. Perhaps she can offer them something of value, after all.

Her daughter wakes and grows impatient while strapped to her back, wriggling and pulling at her mother's hair, though she has learned well the necessity of silence and obedience. She moves away from her vantage point now, does not want her child to see what she has seen, not yet. Or to alert those she is watching should her restless young daughter decide to make any noise. She takes this time to distract her, devising a game for her, one that her own mother had taught her. She finds as many pebbles as they both have fingers and sorts them into the most similar pairs. She hides each stone separately under a leaf and the child must turn over one leaf at a time and then replace it, trying to remember where each pebble is hidden. When she finds a matching pair within two turns of a leaf, they are taken out of the game until at last, she matches them all.

The triumph on that tiny face when the task is complete is enough to assure her mother that the little one must be given the chance to live with others, to play, to learn, to grow. But not yet, not as the dusk draws in and she can hold the child closely while she sleeps, hers alone for at least one more night. Whatever may come.

They return to hide and rest high up in the trees, and as the child sleeps she keeps her watch to the dawn. In the darkness, she is reassured that the risk must be taken, for while she can see nothing of the new clan now, she can hear them. These people know music. Their voices lift and fall and fade and surge together, in chants she does not recognise and yet somehow understands. The voices of men and women, young and old. The meaning of the music is unknown but undeniable, she feels it in her heart. These are chants of joy, of gratitude. And the sound is more beautiful to her now than any other she remembers.

In the morning the hunger begins to gnaw, in spite of the single egg she had emptied, one of a speckled pair taken with some sadness from the nest of the bird with feathers like the rising sun.

They must go towards the camp. Yes, they must take their chance. As the day flows upwards to its fullest height, she is ready.

Now. She leaves the basket behind and walks out from her hide, the child on her hip. They do not see her until it is far too late to turn and run should they meet with reactions of fear or hate. She stops, and slowly, one by one, without sound, so do they. They are smaller than her, their eyes, even as they widen with shock have the look of one who has just awoken, but they are people, people like her.

She lets the child slip down from her hip so she can stand on her own sturdy feet. Drops of liquid begin to pool in her eyes and to blur her sight. She is still now and lifts her head high, though she feels that her legs may not hold faith. She abandons her spear, unstraps the bow and the bear bone from her back and lets them fall in front of her. She stands.

Then one of their young approaches, too late to be pulled back by its mother. He runs towards her daughter, who has never seen another child before but is unafraid. The boy reaches out, touches her cheek, her mane of hair, then takes the little shell-walker from her hand as it is held out in offering. The smile that has kept her mother alive for so long comes easily, followed by curious laughter from the little boy. Some of the adults walk so near now, almost within an arm's reach. Her legs fail her, the world grows white and then black, and she falls. Falls into the willing embrace of the tall, waving grass.

26

It was a day of introductions – and goodbyes. KC had brought his luggage to the Institute as he was flying home that night, immediately after their joint interview with the documentary team. The lab was busy, a gathering in honour of Sarah, and the producers had brought Max Michaelson back to film a sequence of him meeting her reconstruction face-to-face. Eloise had feared this might come across a little cheesy and was about to go and get a coffee, but was drawn back to watch as the moment played out in a surprisingly poignant way. Max became visibly moved, and even Marcy the ever time-conscious director grew misty-eyed and lingered over the scene.

Today, Max had been accompanied by his wife, Jessica, who was not quite as Eloise had imagined her (not at all, if she was honest). There was none of the glamour that she might have expected, in its place was more of a discreet English rose. She told Eloise that she was a nurse and was very interested in the research that was going on in the lab, but Eloise had no time to continue the conversation as she and KC were then summoned to take their places in front of the camera. She watched the couple for a moment longer, as the film crew set up their angles, and saw the way that Jessica nestled under her husband's arm as if she had been designed to fit there. They were clearly very close and this was an experience that Max was keen to share.

Eloise was pleased to have met Jessica, who seemed to be a lovely young woman, if quiet and inconspicuous – apart from the startling glint of sunset in her otherwise hazel eyes when they caught the right light. She had never seen eye colouring like it. She watched the couple say their mutual, carefree farewells to the crew and felt happy about their happiness, glad that such contentment existed in the world.

As microphones were clipped on and tested, Eloise found herself throwing regular glances over at KC's minimal luggage, stacked casually in a corner. It seemed inadequate. She had nothing against packing light but the sum total of his baggage was insufficient somehow. Surely he must have needed more, or have acquired more while he had been here. What else might he be casting aside to leave behind?

KC's was not the only impending departure. Soon Sarah, too, would be packed up and ready for her own journey home. She had earned it, given them enough, a priceless bequest. A full and complete double helix. Sequenced, mapped and compared for variation against layers of controls from various present-day human genotypes in the GenBank, as well as ancestral patterns from ancient hominins and also, for good measure, the chimpanzee genome.

Before Eloise could gather her thoughts the cameras were rolling and the questions were being fired.

'So, you two look happy?' asked/instructed Marcy.

Eloise paused to breathe and to make sure that this time her hands were clasped together so they could not fidget and spoil the shot. KC answered first, as nervous as she from the unusual quiver in his voice, but gallant enough to step into the breach.

'Hell, yeah, we look happy! I mean, we have so much more to investigate, but our first readings have told us that Sarah, as expected, is a daughter of our own Mitochondrial 'Eve' – so essentially an Anatomically Modern Human who would have looked not so different to many people around today. We weren't so surprised either to find a miniscule percentage of Neanderthal DNA, although this would have become blended into her *Homo sapiens* ancestry millennia earlier, but it's fascinating to wonder where and when and how? And we've had some other expectations confirmed.

'For example, being a hunter-gatherer Sarah would have been lactose intolerant in adulthood. She also lacks the post-agricultural adaptation for increased amylase in the saliva to enhance the digestion of starches. We see no resistance to the kind of diseases that have plagued us since we began living in towns and cities, nor the sickle cell protection against malaria that's common in modern African populations. Although, in general, she seems to have been remarkably robust, right, Eloise?'

'Yes, that's right – and we plan to look much more closely for genes associated with immune responses – it's a key area of interest for us. You might wonder at the contemporary relevance of this as pathogens constantly evolve, but with climate change and the melting of the permafrost, or deep mining in the Arctic, or exploration of other areas that have been sealed off geologically for millennia, we may encounter archaic bacteria and viruses to which we ourselves have no immunity – and for which we are entirely unprepared.'

Before Eloise could continue along this gloomy trajectory the director intercepted, 'But you've found some other interesting things too, haven't you, to do with behaviour?' Marcy had now defaulted to her habitual impatience after that brief interval of mellowing with Max. (Eloise wondered if Marcy too had developed a soft spot for the young Aussie, with his crown of golden curls that glowed so angelically on screen. This notion surprised her as she'd assumed Marcy to be gay, certain sartorial choices suggesting preferences of another kind.) At last, however, Eloise had found some on-camera confidence. Not quite in the same league as Max perhaps, but now she jumped back into the interview to respond.

'Yes, that's right, we've also found startling suggestions of what we'd once thought of as 'modern' differentiations appearing much earlier than expected. Certain aspects of the *Homo sapiens* genome, in what's called the Human Accelerated Region, have been around for a very long time so no surprise to see those. They distinguish us from other primates and affect things such as anatomy, metabolism, sweating, cognitive capacity and even language mutations, courtesy of the famous FOXP2 gene. These differences would have been present in all early humans, even before the split from a common ancestor with the Neanderthals and others. However, a few extra adaptations have been identified in the present day genome which were presumed to have arisen only much later, relatively speaking, and in response to more recent stimuli.'

Eloise paused, familiar now with the need to leave gaps to assist the editing process and not sure whether or not she was rambling, but Marcy nodded that she should continue.

'These have become fixed variations in today's humans, encoding proteins for skin pigmentation, aspects of morphology, sperm motility, etcetera. However, research into families of particular social interest suggests that some genetic changes are related more to behaviour, and until Sarah, we saw them as adaptations to greater population density and social organisation.'

At this point, KC raised a hand and interjected. 'Actually, as I said earlier, we still have so much more investigation to do, especially into immunity, but I ought to say now that it was one of Dr Kluft's priorities to look for the particular variation on the gene we're talking about, the 'warrior gene' as it's sometimes misleadingly known. Call it a hunch, I guess – but what she's discovered has really rocked the boat.'

Eloise was still unsure why one of the first places she went hunting along Sarah's DNA was for the notorious MAOA allele and its two distinct versions but she'd been both flabbergasted and elated, even vindicated, by what she'd found. She smiled at KC as she accepted the generous baton of credit that he'd handed her and continued.

'Yes, you see, everyone has at least one copy of the MAOA gene, as it's properly known, which is responsible for the activity of key neurotransmitters affecting mood, stress-response, risk-taking etcetera. But remarkably, Sarah has what we'd previously believed was the more recent adaptation, known as MAOA-H. This is a high-frequency variation that's common to the greater proportion of people today, but which we'd assumed had emerged only in response to civilisation. We see it as a version better suited to living in proximity and learning to get along in greater numbers, and in situations where instinctive, reactive or unorganised violence is no longer beneficial to survival.'

Eloise took a breath, cleared her throat, and KC in his enthusiasm jumped back in.

'Yeah, you see the modern high-frequency variation codes for higher activity of some crucial brain chemicals and so, we believe, allows for calmer or more considered responses to potentially violent situations. It doesn't mean that Sarah or anyone who carries the so-called 'good' version of MAOA-H is incapable of violence, more that it's less likely to be an uncontrollable response or a dangerous tendency. A carrier of the modern version may be more inclined to avoid a heated situation – they will still take calculated risks when necessary – but probably in a more measured and possibly empathetic manner. Unless of course circumstances are extreme... or maybe when testosterone or the mob mentality is running high.'

KC was in full flow now and Eloise let him continue.

'But the unlucky few to have the older, lower-frequency copy called MAOA-L are well represented in the world's criminal and mental health institutions... or, hey, maybe even making up the more reckless elements of our governments, armed forces and stock markets. And yes, it has to be said, most of them are men because this riskier low-frequency version is found only on the X chromosome so is more commonly expressed in males. That's because with only one X and one Y there's no chance of the gene's influence being overridden by a copy of the 'better' version. Females have a second helping of the X chromosome, so their odds of suppressing a bad copy are much better.'

Eloise felt it was important to clarify this further and not to cast genetic aspersions on those with the 'wrong' version, so she interrupted. 'Of course, the older version, doesn't have to mean a life sentence of violent or impulsive behaviour and, in fact, most people who carry a copy live normal and decent lives. Willpower and cognitive choices play an important part and neurochemistry or wiring, if you like, can be positively affected in all kinds of ways, whether therapeutic or behavioural, and this can rewrite the risk of expression. However, studies have also shown that an explosive cocktail can emerge when the low-frequency version is compounded by a history of childhood abuse or neglect, or even by prolonged and serious stress. Some susceptible families can have siblings with a high-frequency copy who stay out of danger while those with a double helping of the low can get into all kinds of trouble, despite each sibling being raised in the same if difficult circumstances...'

It seemed that Marcy wanted to avoid this section becoming a sociology lesson so interrupted to steer it back to its primary subject.

'But what does all this mean in terms of Sarah?'

Eloise edged forward, this leg of the relay now very much hers and the excitement still so fresh. Perhaps her imagining of Sarah's distinctiveness had not been a self-indulgent projection? (And perhaps her struggle to stay objective throughout this process might be excused?)

'Well, you see, the single copy of the modern or 'good' version of MAOA-H that we've found in Sarah opens up a thrilling new perspective on our ancestry. It makes everything much more fluid and suggests all kinds of possibilities. And having found this so surprisingly early in *Homo sapiens*, we decided to look for other genes associated with personality. For example, we found a marker in Sarah called DRD4, also known as the 'Novelty Seeking' gene. This acts on dopamine receptivity or the reward transmitter in the brain. It was probably already present in older hominin genomes but it would have been fundamentally important in the last 70,000 years of our history and vital to our drive for adventure, exploration and invention.'

Eloise disguised a wry smile, as DRD4 was also the perfect scapegoat as far as Darius was concerned when it came to his own wander-lust (and his wandering lust). She knew that cause and effect was not so simple, however, and believed the gene expressed itself according to many factors, perhaps resulting in addictions for the unlucky or a more welcome spirit of innovation in others. However, once again she'd been unsurprised to find the short-repeat version of DRD4 in Sarah's DNA. And there was more, so much more...

'We've also found a polymorphism, or variation, connected with greater resilience to stress, which is of particular interest in clinical studies into depression. But all these discoveries have made me wonder,' Eloise continued, risking a little speculation, 'whether Sarah and her kind might have been a crucible of early mutation. Perhaps even an 'ark', if you like, of particular strengths and abilities? Of potentially valuable resistance. I have to ask myself what part she, or rather I should say, what part any of her surviving descendants may have played in the later millennia – both at home in Africa and during the most significant wave of human migration out of Africa and gradually around the globe?'

What Eloise really wanted to ask but knew was too much conjecture at this stage (even with the isotope results) was whether Sarah belonged right where she was found, or whether she really may have escaped the Toban apocalypse and re-migrated to the African

Refugia, that teeming nursery of life... somehow serving there as a repository of particular genetic information and a profound knowledge of viable migration routes? And, if so, from how far had she come? And indeed *how*? Had she been alone (surely she could not have survived alone?) or with some ragtag gang of desperate exiles?

Darius was still excavating at the site, slowly due to the environmental sensitivities, but there had been no further archaeological clues as yet. Perhaps they would never fully decipher the mysteries of Sarah. Nevertheless, Eloise reassured herself, *'Light will be thrown.'* She felt somehow that Sarah's usefulness to humanity was only beginning to unfold.

She became aware that she had paused too long but felt determined to have the last word. She carried on, levelling her comments at KC with a brief moment of direct eye contact, before looking back to camera.

'We can never really know the complete story of Sarah, but she is such an invaluable gift. The comparative study of her genome has implications from understanding our deep ancestry right through to modern medicine. Who knows what else Sarah might teach us, or allow us to achieve?'

'OK,' Marcy decided, 'I think that's a good place to leave it for today.'

*

She has noticed something. She is not sure if it comes from the growing independence of her daughter, or the support of her new friends, or the gradual renewal of the world. Perhaps it is because of the time she can now take to stop, to look without desperation, to listen deeply, to go within. But the days seem to last longer, the nights are less fearful and she is not so quick to anger.

She is able to place a breath in between whatever might vex her, be that the wilfulness of the child or the failure of one of her bows or the breaking of a sling, and the quick desire to break something else. She shouts less at the flint when she drops it, or the hidden stone that she trips on, or the scratch of a branch. She understands the imperfection of her own efforts and of all that is around her. Imperfect, and yet somehow just as it should be. She finds that she can let time travel at its own pace, let the sun draw its semicircle, let the seasons turn, let the child grow up without constant fear.

She has discovered a particular tree that has become a permanent marker, not merely another lost friend or another lost hope along the way. Each new moon, each time they return to this camp, she lays more stones around its trunk. It has become the place where time is her companion, not her pursuer. Like the other trees she has honoured along the way, these stones will stay here long after she has gone. But here around this thick, smooth, round and ancient trunk perhaps it will be remembered who first laid down these stones and began to build them up.

27

It was oddly quiet at the Institute after the commotion of the filming, after her team had gone home for the day and the documentary crew had packed up and left. Eloise strolled back from the cafeteria, having charmed them into giving her one last latte before they shuttered up. Her thoughts turned to KC. That strained farewell, wanting to embrace but settling for a peck on the cheek instead and the firm pressure of a long handshake.

She glanced at her watch. He would be somewhere over the Atlantic by now. She wished him happiness in his homecoming (with only the slightest twitch in her heart as an afterthought). Despite the sense of emptiness, the sense that it was time to go home like everyone else, Eloise decided to stay on late at the lab. There were some notes to type up, some thoughts inspired by the day.

As she walked back to her wing of the building she was still making mental lists. She would, of course, want to take a long hard look at her old nemesis, F8, and other genes involved in wound healing or clotting. She also resolved to search in Sarah's code for 'health' related markers such as the RS2395029G allele, likely to be ancestral but shown to be associated with a reduced viral load in those HIV-positive individuals with long-term non-progression of this modern disease today. Such discoveries might well provide a further spur, a fish-hook for the funding of her 'Back to Africa' project with KC, one she hoped might materialise for many reasons, both personal and professional.

In the stretching, featureless corridor towards the lab, unable to wait until she was settled at her workstation, Eloise teased the lid from her cup (she hated sipping through plastic) and took a swallow of her coffee, trying not to scald either lip or hand. She did so regardless of her caution as soon as she remembered her manners and stopped abruptly to wish a 'good evening' to the new caretaker as he mopped up a spill from the scuffed linoleum floor. He barely acknowledged her, this odd, taciturn fellow, but her gentrified mother had instilled in Eloise a reflexive courtesy and so she smiled at him anyway. It was warm in the building but a shiver took her by surprise. Oh please, not now, she thought, no time to get sick.

Back at her desk, she decanted the coffee into her favourite mug. A gift from Rory, printed with a chocolate-box photo of an eager-looking beagle. A little tacky, yes, but it was more pleasant to drink from than cardboard. Rory was fond of the ironic, the obscure reference, the kitsch. Each day his T-shirts revealed his mood, always a slogan, always odd, always interesting. From 'My Body is my Spacesuit, Man' to 'Stop Dark Energy!' Eloise liked Rory.

Once her latest thoughts had been captured digitally and before finally logging off and heading home she climbed into a white Tyvek jumpsuit, diligently applied her mask and gloves and went into the clean room to be with Sarah one last time (before it would mean an eight-hour flight to her new home in the museum in Nairobi). She did not fully register that Calumn, the new caretaker, had come in with his cart until he had sealed the door behind him.

'Oh, hello,' she said, lifting up her visor as she turned around with a prickle of apprehension, 'give me a minute, and I'll let you get on… although, wait… surely that cart shouldn't have come in here, have you not been trained on the protocols for this room?'

There was something glacial in the way that he was staring at her and the surface of her skin responded in kind. At last, he spoke.

'Sorceress'

'I'm sorry?'

'You call it science but it's simply a more sophisticated kind of spell.'

'I'm sorry, what?'

*

The mountain is awakening. She senses their unease, though they say nothing. Slowly, she has learned the meanings in their strange noises (a sound as if something swallowed had stuck, their clicks and grunts and bird-like chirps) but it remains difficult to mimic them. She can barely repeat the gentle nickname they have given her, after the small, sharp-faced creature that ran in packs above and below the ground, always watching together in little groups, standing comically upright to survey the landscape for any threat.

She understands why the clan tease her in this affectionate way, for even after all this time, after so many years of safety among them she is unable to abandon the vigilance learned by necessity during those long travels alone. Even now and knowing a much greater peace, there are shivering moments when she is summoned back to those dangers while both waking and sleeping.

Her daughter has been gifted with a far less humorous name, after the clicked and hummed sound by which their new family calls the colour of the late-afternoon sun, inspired by the shards of golden light that shone within those beloved eyes. In her own quieter moments alone with the girl she still uses the old words and calls her after the precious glowing stone which seemed to trap that same sunlight (and other tiny living things) within its mysterious, clear-yet-stony form. This treasure had been shown to her by her grandmother, a precious thing that sometimes was found in the ground, or sometimes washed up along a shoreline, and which was known for its ability to heal.

It is true that she has found none of those stones here but she has learned about so much more. New plants, new poultices, new ways to make something well again, and her daughter seems to have an even greater talent for this work than her. The girl chooses to forage and to tend rather than to hunt. She seeks out anything that suffers. Her child has too much softness perhaps, but at least here with their new family it is safe for her to be so. And they seem to recognise this in her. They come to her daughter when their pain is unseen, hoping for the lightest touch to lift an inner darkening. Like her mother, however, the girl is often overly vigilant, too quick in her reflexes, even when they are not needed.

As for herself, the tribe allows her to live as she pleases, and it often pleases her to wander away alone. She always brings back gifts for her friends (for they give freely here rather than trade) be that an antelope or some other boon, such as the crawling or hopping little creatures that they love to eat. She tends to decline when they are offered to her on stick straight from the fire, for while she happily swallowed whatever would not kill her on the way towards these people, when she has a choice she prefers to refuse those six-legged morsels with their unappealing crunch.

She has learned of one particular crawler, however, that is deadly if eaten, but whose poison she thinks might be borrowed and used to enhance the work of her arrows. She has an idea about how to safely make this work and has shared it with a young huntsman in whom she sees great promise, one of the few not to treat her with puzzlement.

She knows that she is often a source of both mystery and mirth to her new tribe but she does not mind. Even though they respect and accept her valuable talents, she remains different and apart and has never taken a mate. She has felt no need or desire, rather she enjoys the sense of her own fullness that has come with time. Yes, perhaps the tribe do not understand her so fully in return but she has watched and listened closely and has come to understand her adopted people very well. And as she thinks of the smoking mountain peak in the distance, she understands their present fear. They ask nothing, but they look to her now – and for all that they have given her all these many seasons, there is nothing she would refuse.

The mountain's significance has become clear, it is their protector, the source of their strength, its permanent snow caps so pure, so potent. Though reverent, she herself would care nothing if she never saw such whiteness again nor felt its bite.

The snake of smoke began to puff and twist from its top only days before, after the strange burning torch had appeared in the southern night sky as though dragged by an invisible eagle. She has heard a distant whisper of danger in her dreams, though not for the clan, or for her daughter, who is now as much a part of them as of herself. As the girl emerges from the cocoon of childhood, her nascent gifts unfolding, the signs speak to her mother only of clear bright skies. It is her own path that now grows disturbingly dim.

Yet she cannot deny them. When the sacred is torn away from the living it leaves only empty walking skin. That way she has witnessed and it is unthinkable. So she finds what is left of the old bear fur, half-rotten with unfamiliar humidity, rolls it and ties it to her back. She gathers up something else both beloved and essential, something that has been given to her in gratitude by her new family. The engraved egg from that large and laughable bird that walks taller than a man.

The shell has long since been emptied of its original purpose and is now pierced at the top to take water, then plugged with hardened beeswax and cradled in a sling woven from the tall grass. The egg bears the swirls and three-armed spirals that she had once drawn in the sand after trancing, thinking she had left them there to fade in the wind, not realising that the tribe's most skilled carver had found and reproduced them here. This gift had touched her deeply.

Now she walks around the camp under the silence of starlight, trailing her fingertips along a hide that is slowly drying, strung between two huts of grass and reeds. There is no shortage of tall grass here to make easy shelter, no shortage of life. She feels every beat of it. But now it is time. She returns to her own hut for a moment to see if the child might be awake, half-hoping that she might be. She does not know what she will do if this is so, as her daughter may well guess what she is planning and may try to prevent her. This would cause a pain she could not bear. Fortunately, she finds that her beloved still belongs to her own private world of dreams.

She gazes long at her sleeping heart (unties and leaves her necklace of shell and ochre near her curled hands, soon to become the hands of a woman, soon to open up and learn of all that they must carry). Then she tears herself away with a torment that she knows she must withstand, and sets off before dawn to walk the slow, breath-sapping ascent.

*

He said nothing, took a bottle of cleaning fluid from his cart, began to pour it around the door and floor. But it did not smell of bleach. It smelled of kerosene.

'What the hell are you doing?'

Calumn looked at Eloise, pulled out a lighter, and then the fear reflex triggered in full. A sudden weakness in her limbs and abdomen, tiny hairs rising wherever they might rise. Her heart (that four-chambered triumph of evolution) thundering into readiness.

She looked outside the clean room, searching, hoping for help, but what she saw looking back at her from the other side of the glass only deepened the chill in her veins. She *knew* that face, she knew those stony eyes? Oh god, YES, the woman from the museum, the woman in the red beret! Eloise looked back to Calumn, were these two connected? How? Was she his friend, his accomplice, his puppet master? Oh god. Of course. The group on the Heath, the cult protesting on the steps, the hacking of her email, it all merged into a sickening thunderclap of realisation.

The woman walked closer to the glass, her breath leaving the lightest kiss of steam on its cool surface. She pressed a red-gloved hand against it and nodded her encouragement, her silent commands to Calumn. Then she smiled in triumph at Eloise, turned and walked away.

Eloise returned her startled attention to Calumn. He looked back at her as he flipped open the lid of the Zippo lighter and spoke at last, broken bottles in his voice.

"'Thou shalt not suffer a witch to live.' Exodus 22:18. The only way to deal with a witch is to burn it.'

Oh god. Calm now, Eloise, calm. Think, think.

28

The summit is evading her. It is unveiled of its clouds only in the first and last light of day, but she knows how many paces it will take. Although these years have seen little hunger, she does not have the stamina that she used to. Her knees are swollen, like some of the more unfortunate elders, though she is not yet old. Long-standing stresses in her back, from immeasurable travels with a growing child, have returned and the feet that carried her so far are now gnarled and crooked and have begun to crucify with every step, despite the deep padding of the bear-skin wraps. The urge to empty her stomach has come and gone but the chill brings on a cough, stealing breath she cannot spare. That old suffocation that came first with grey dust and has never fully left her.

But she will not stop to camp again until she reaches the sharp black spine ahead rising out from the first long fingers of snow. How long has she avoided this climb? Even though the scaling of open heights has always brought an expansion in her heart, a lightening that thrills to new vitality. Even now, despite the pain.

The prey that she took from the trap as she left the encampment is bound, laid across her shoulders, its eyes gently wrapped and quiet now, breathing slow. The last of the figs is eaten but the animal is not for her, it is for the mountain. She can no longer see the fires of her tribe but other sights of endless horizons, for which she can only be thankful, unroll around her. Such silence. Such peace.

On again, despite the resistance in her thighs. The animal is too heavy now, she leaves it, will come back to it. And the bear-skin cloak is too hot, it has become too restrictive around her neck, she loosens it. The climb is much harder here, the staff is useless, it only hinders her and she lays it down. She lets go of everything. She needs both hands now.

Nearer to the peak and she can smell the smoke, a bitterness she has encountered three times in her life. In the dreaming that first warned her and changed everything so long ago, then again when that promised ash came, and one more time at the lake of fire on the journey of days without count. While she understands that the old nightmare will not happen again, not here, not now, she accepts the necessity of this sacrifice.

Will it be fire or ice? Surely it will be no other human, not this high. A predator? Well below her position now, she has seen old marks, probably made by a leopard. (The bear claws are bound and ready, although she is no longer sure she has the heart for a fight.)

This ridge was the wrong choice, it has become impassable. She will have to climb down on to the fresh snow, walk it slowly to the next outcrop. Ah yes, the old enemy, the old companion, crunching beneath her blackening toes. Hard as her own resolve.

But no. Not hard at all, it seems, not solid. It splinters under her weight with a whip-crack of long-held malice and she is tumbling until her shattering calf bone breaks the fall. A further creaking above and the sheet that she has loosened now falls and lays itself over her, almost lovingly.

Darkness, though still some air. She moves, and then knows that she will never move again. Mercifully, the cold begins to numb the pain and her struggle subsides to stillness. If this is what the mountain asks, she will not resist it.

So.

She smiles.

It will be ice. So be it.

Death will claim her whenever it desires, but she is captive now in its tender hold, this much is beyond doubt. She welcomes her passage through the deep and beckoning cavern, at last. Each moment becomes lighter, easier.

Is that her grandmother now, smiling and waiting for her with such patience beyond the gloom? Perhaps she will meet another old friend here, if she is worthy of this long, slow walk towards the whiteness. Perhaps that giant and hungry old bear waits for her too, with equal patience? She hopes so. There is something that she must return to him.

*

How long had they been locked in this room together? How long had the cable ties cut into her wrists at her front? Eloise had no idea.

Pavel, the Polish security guard had raised the alarm on his last round. Outside the glass, he had been joined by a gathering of uniforms and plain clothes. Fire and ambulance crews on standby. And Eugene Vanterpool, suited and booted (pulled from the opera, perhaps?) wide-eyed, pacing and hand wringing.

The extension in the clean room kept ringing, but Calumn Berryman (his full name read from his ID badge, why had she not remembered it from their first meeting?) would not answer it, not again. He had stated his case and his intentions in the first, curt conversation with the young red-haired officer who seemed to be in charge.

'Do not try to break in, or she burns. She, and the fake bones,' he had said. 'Do not try to negotiate or everyone and everything in here will burn.'

He had pulled out a note from one of the pockets in his overalls and read it aloud, stumbling over some of the words: 'You will issue a statement confirming that the discovery of these remains is an elab… elaborate lie, and that all false work to prove otherwise will cease. That all your lies will cease. And that all work on embryonic cells at this or any affil… affiliated laboratory will stop.'

Then he had rolled his thumb over the flint and sparked the flame. 'This lighter is full. I have many others, I have replacement fluid. I can wait.'

Now Calumn was standing near the door, matching its height, and holding the lit Zippo aloft. He looked at and spoke only to Eloise now, but she'd had some time to regain composure, to run through all her options, to hold on to some faith in the help that had arrived outside.

'So God created man in His own image, in the image of God He created him; male and female He created them. Genesis 1:27….'

Eloise now understood what was meant by the paralysis of terror, but also knew that she must *try* to respond. How could she answer this in any way that he would listen to? How could she confront the cognitive dissonance within his citadel of belief? How could she explain that maybe, yes, maybe, certain aspects of his supposedly infallible Bible had been drawn from a 'well' of greater wisdom (cellular or ethereal) but that it was written down then translated, compiled and edited by the cultural limitations and personal or political impositions of men? A few well-intentioned men maybe, seeking to explain and guide and give shape to deeper insights, but without the language or understanding to extrapolate beyond accessible metaphor. That these men had been followed by several less well-intentioned editors looking to exploit the dogma in order to enhance their own ambitions or empires. How could she argue, without incurring his wrath, that those words had been taken down when we still believed the earth was flat, for heaven's sake – and who now could deny the circling of the spheres?

'I am not descended from an ape or a monkey,' proclaimed her captor. 'I am descended directly from Adam. Made in the image of God.'

Yes, thought Eloise, from Y chromosome Adam, the last shared male ancestor, mathematically traced back to about 190,000 years according to the molecular clock. But she decided to try to reach him in a different way, not to argue but to try to re-align his views, however risky it might be.

'Yes, Calumn, in his image, from the stardust created during the first explosions into being. And no, Calumn, you are not descended from an ape, neither am I. But all primates are descended from a common ancestor.'

'And where is that ancestor? This missing link? It never has, nor ever will be found.'

'Well, it's still possible that it might be, Calumn, we have found so many transitional species, humanoid or otherwise… a fish with a neck and the beginnings of digits, dinosaurs with feathers. And we can see evolution at work in a single generation of microbes, or insects becoming resistant to pesticides. Yes, the fossil record does have some glaring gaps, but despite the very real difficulties in finding fossils, we are finding them all the time and we will continue to…'

'All fossils are relics from the Flood.' Calumn was so sure, standing to attention as if trying to please a drill sergeant, or resist a torturous inquisitor. Eloise wondered how long she might be allowed to keep talking, how long before he pulled out that roll of silver gaffer tape from his pocket and threatened to gag her once again. Before he told her to be silent while the 'silenced' spoke through him. Right now however, it seemed that he wanted some kind of verbal response from her, if only to acknowledge that she was listening.

'No, Calumn,' she corrected gently, aware she should maintain a soothing, non-combative tone, 'fossils have been found in many layers of slow and gradual sedimentation, they've been found in bogs and tar lakes. The earth is four and a half billion years old. Some bacteria have been around for three billion years. And life exploded into diversity during the Cambrian era, over five hundred million years ago.'

'Lies! Clever confusions. You have been led astray by deliberate temptations planted to test our commitment.'

Then it dawned. 'Oh, wait... Calumn... Was it you who was coming in here and handling Sarah's bones? Before we put in the CCTV? Calumn, did you not feel then how real they are, how very old, how very precious? I am sure you must have had some sense of that?'

'All lies. All bedevilment. And to name her after one so precious in The Book, such blasphemy!'

'Well, that's just a coincidence, Calumn, I'm sure no insult was intended. But I promise you, those bones are 74,000 years old.'

'No. The world is no more than 6,000 years old. It was made by God in six days. As he has told us. Let there be light, He said, and there was light.'

'But how could there have been light, Calumn, as we know it, before the sun or the stars ignited? The sun was there before the earth, so how was there even a 'day' as we call it, before the earth turned on its axis? Or a year before it went around the sun? Can't you see that these terms are just poetic figures of speech? Symbols, maybe, to be better understood once we had the evidence? I mean, if we ourselves have learned to use such expressions as a short cut to meaning, why would God not have done the same to speak through the prophets?'

She knew she could not diminish his god, but perhaps she could try to help him interpret the verses less literally?

Then Calumn moved, but only a few inches from the spot in front of the door to which he had been rooted, a foot soldier refusing to leave his post. It seemed his legs were beginning to cramp (hers too, she took the opportunity to shift positions subtly at the same time). Was he tiring? And would that be a good or a bad thing?

'The Almighty has no need of the ways of men. His light is beyond our understanding. He can do anything that pleases Him.'

'And does hatred please him, Calumn?'

'He has smote His enemies, and so will I, in His name.'

'Calumn, you will kill us both if you drop that lighter.'

'I am prepared to die for Him. For all mankind, as did our Lord.'

Eloise clung to something, to certain words of pacifist wisdom she'd always admired in the scriptures of Calumn's 'Saviour' – this figure who seemed to embody the potential for the best in humanity, in spite of how it all had been twisted or enlisted since.

'Oh, Calumn, yes, but as I understand it Jesus died out of *love* for of all us. For forgiveness. And he did not kill?'

He stopped to think, as if he was searching for an answer that would not be beyond her understanding of his truth. Eloise looked closely at her captor, trying to establish some connection. In less adrenalin-charged circumstances Eloise might have looked more kindly upon Calumn, perhaps even found him sadly appealing, regardless of a nose that strayed too long over narrow lips, a chin cut too short. If his hair was washed, his skin clear, his teeth attended too. If his eyes had showed her anything other than aggression.

She pitied him. Who has done this to him, she wondered, what has made him this way? Could it be a genetic predisposition, or a prefrontal cortex damaged by indoctrination? What had created the void that allowed all this nonsense to rush in and give him such a warped sense of purpose or belonging? And who had exploited all this fear and anger so cruelly to their own ends? That woman so fond of her scarlet insignia must have played her part, for sure, but not she alone.

Then, above the settling pools of kerosene, Eloise caught an unusual aroma and she was a child again in her grandfather's old Rover, searching through the glove compartment for the bag of pear drops that he always kept there. One for her and one for him. *Why am I smelling pear drops?* She shook off this perplexing flashback and looked back at Calumn. She noticed how he scratched at his skin where he could reach it under a white jumpsuit that was at once too small and yet too loose for his emaciated height, the friction rendering his neck and forearm livid and raw. He seemed to have trouble focusing on her, rubbed his angry eyelids.

Then Calumn found something else to parry with, something that might well have been spoon-fed from a pseudo-scientific sermon.

'The Second Law of Thermodynamics! It means your EVIL-ution was never possible!'

Yes, here it comes, she thought. That old creationist chestnut. That all closed systems have constant amounts of energy and matter and are subject to inevitable entropy, disorder and decay, rather than the upwardly mobile order and irreducible complexity found in biology, and the argument that therefore natural selection could not have occurred spontaneously, if at all.

Eloise also knew the standard evolutionist rebuttals: that the earth cannot be considered a closed system due to the energy of the sun (and eons of celestial impacts) or that *life* is somehow not subject to this otherwise irrefutable law, seen everywhere except in the animation of organic matter. That entropy may in itself lead to consciousness, as some experiments had suggested, and so perhaps even to life itself? Yet, inwardly she had to admit that she remained intrigued by aspects of the argument, for *how*, indeed, despite the algorithmic patterns that arose out of apparently nothing, had that first self-replicating molecule found the information, the instruction, *the cause*, to do what it did? To build itself into a cell, and then to divide onward into all of the dazzling diversity that had ever lived? Could she use this somehow, explore it with Calumn, engage him?

No. There was neither the time nor the available level of reason to address these issues with him, it was likely only to further enrage. She decided to try a different tack, to personalise herself. After all, was not the process of dehumanising the enemy the way that every sick death cult in history had brainwashed its followers into massacre without remorse... by making whoever was in the way of what they wanted seem less worthy of life? Eloise knew that she must try to reconnect

Calumn with his sense of empathy. She thought of what John had said about love being the greatest message of the gospels.

'I have a friend, Calumn, a man of god... yes, I know that might surprise you, but when he talks of his Lord, his Saviour, he talks only of love and compassion and forgiveness. He says that these were his greatest messages, his deepest truth, and that these commandments supersede all others. That above all we must do no harm.'

She heard him clear his throat, noticed that he swallowed often and with difficulty, as if his mouth was dry. Was this the climate-controlled air of the clean room? Eloise decided to turn this observation to her advantage.

'Are you alright, Calumn, are you thirsty? I'm sorry, I can't offer you anything to drink I'm afraid, no food or beverage is allowed in here, but I could ask for some...'

'I need nothing from you, I am sustained by the strength of the Lord...' but his voice was disintegrating.

His breath became shallow, gasping. He seemed to wobble and had to steady himself against the examination table with the hand that was holding the naked flame, still burning, as he had promised, since he had first flicked the flint. Time stalled. But then he was still again – and still gripping the lighter. Eloise caught that fruity pear drop smell once more and at last recognised it as the sickly sweet aroma of ketosis, of a body breaking down. The symptomatic clues came together sufficiently now for her to grasp at a notion.

'Calumn, are you diabetic? Do you need insulin? I have access to a range of medicines here, or I could ask the paramedics?'

Eloise could hardly bear the absurdity. Before Sarah – and in those lulls when her progress had stalled – she'd been working on a project to replace faulty pancreatic cells. Calumn might have been a prime candidate for the ultimate clinical trials. On a different collision course, she might have been able to help him.

'I said I need nothing but the grace of God! He will heal me in His mercy if He sees fit.'

'Calumn, I am so sorry if I have offended you. You know, I don't presume to have sole possession of the truth and I respect your love for God, I really do. I'm only a doctor, Calumn, trying to do the best that I can, trying to help people…'

'By your disgusting vivisection of babies?'

'What? Calumn, I have never vivisected a baby!'

'Oh yes, you would rip them from the womb and use them to harvest these cells you speak of!'

'No, no, Calumn, I promise you, I am not doing that, nor do I want to! Yes, some research elsewhere does use spare human embryos donated from IVF, but that's not what we do here. The stem cells we can get from the umbilical cord after birth, or indeed in some truly amazing new processes, are helping us to acquire the knowledge we need.'

'Knowledge!? Trickery. Wasn't it someone exactly like you who exiled us from Eden? With your filthy, greedy hunger for knowledge?'

Eloise exhaled. She had no answer for biblically sanctioned misogyny or wilful ignorance. She was running out of ideas.

And then a miracle. The phone began to ring again and as she looked out through the glass she could not believe what she was seeing, had to whisper it silently to herself to make sure.

Oh my life… it's John.

Eloise thought she might be hallucinating for a moment. How could he be here? Then she remembered the breadth of his ministry, remembered that he attended the cells of police stations on request, so why would he not be known to the force and on their books for persuasions of a more pastoral nature? John looked at her, right into her startled eyes through the toughened glass and she wanted to cry.

It's alright, everything will be alright.

Calumn looked out through the glass too and appeared taken aback at the sight of a crisp white dog collar. John smiled at Calumn and motioned politely for him to pick up the phone.

The ringing began to hurt her ears. Eventually, Calumn answered the call. Eloise could not hear what John was saying but she could imagine. He would not argue or accuse or patronise or dismiss but he would find a way, through his unshakeable love, to reach him. Was she still breathing? She wasn't sure. Then Calumn responded, at last, to John.

'Yes, of course I remember the testing of Abraham. Yes… yes…'

He kept listening. His posture softened, his eyes seemed to moisten, he looked at John as though he had found something, something he had not known he was looking for. Something important had changed and Calumn was allowing that rigid arm holding the lighter to relax a little, to ease down to his side.

'Yes, yes. Alright. I will pray with you.'

He closed his eyes. He listened to John, he nodded, he breathed deeply. Eloise inched closer to him, close enough to see the sweat that now slicked his sallow skin despite the chilly air. His eyes rolled back. Was this some kind of spiritual ecstasy?

Then he convulsed – and then it became clear. Calumn was slipping into a hyperglycaemic fit. As his knees buckled, one hand dropped the receiver and the other jerked up in reflex, arcing the lighter across the room. Eloise tracked its endless flight, willing it away from the pools of kerosene. But then a face flashed into her mind, a face that she wanted to keep seeing, keep looking at, clearer to her now than ever. A face that she needed to live for, to see again.

It was no longer enough to will or to hope – she must act, now. She dived forward with hands still bound together, crashed hard to the floor too soon, but then slid through a slick of kerosene and somehow… somehow, caught and extinguished the lighter.

A fire officer in full protective gear rushed to ram the door but it would not give. Pavel finally came to some clarity and pulled out his all-access pass card.

As he fought to keep his hand steady enough to open the door, Eloise pushed herself to her knees and pressed the closed lighter deep into her pocket. Her eyes raked the room for a makeshift weapon in case Calumn recovered too soon. Briefly, she considered opening the chiller drawer to grab Sarah's thigh bone, but then as she glanced through the glass at John she felt something change. Eloise smiled back at him through rising tears. Then she mouthed the word 'Diabetic' to the waiting paramedics and ignoring the pain in her elbows and knees, shuffled over to sit behind Calumn. With cable-tied hands she lifted up his thrashing head and cradled it gently above the cold and pitiless floor.

*

She knows that her mother will not return but she waits, even so. Each sunrise, each sunset by one of her beloved trees. She lays a new stone or pebble there each time. Soon, one or two of her friends begin to come. Then one day they all come, each to lay one stone.

After every season has turned she decides that she does not need to do this every day. She goes only once, at each new moon. It is enough.

*

My Dear Charles

Yesterday, I nearly died for my work. For my ideals. I write this now at home, alone (by choice) and more at ease with that condition than ever, and yet also feeling more open to *whatever* may come. My work has been everything, my hope that we can keep evolving, keep getting better at being human. Not only fitter, but wiser. And *kinder*. (A vain hope, perhaps, witnessing the world that we have made – even if the world has also made us. But can each yet re-make the other?)

And is that it for me now... my work, my observations, my wish to contribute?

You waited so long to publish, for various reasons it seems, from needing to present the most detailed supporting work, to health problems and a variety of other conflicting demands? Until Wallace spurred you to action. But you must also have understood the shockwaves it would produce, and what effect that might have upon your family. And they brought you such comfort, Charles, did they not, they were not only a distraction? But I'm forced to wonder, can love really nestle comfortably within the life committed to discovery or will it always wheedle away at the dedication, particularly if it demands a greedier share of time and care? Must one or the other always suffer in some way from neglect?

Family. What now defines our fitness to breed, Charles? (Or indeed, to parent?) To have a line of surviving offspring. And now that our 'information' can be carried by other means than competitive sexual reproduction, does it matter anymore?

We may never know for sure whether Sarah's descendants survived, or if she remains a part of us now, but I find that I *want* to believe they did, and that she does. I want to believe that she mattered and that she matters still. (That *I* matter?) We do so want to believe, in something, don't we? Even in the face of any evidence against.

Well. I may not write again for a while. I think it really is high time I took a holiday. I love my work, of course, but I am feeling a deeper and more forgiving love for so much more lately, for nature, for people, for *life* – but what use is any of that if I don't live it as fully as I can, in the here and now?

I've been thinking about taking up something more adventurous, climbing perhaps. Maybe I should join young Max, that fine fellow who found Sarah, on his next expedition? No, perhaps not. Sailing is more my style. I must find a way to get down to the coast more often. I must make that happen somehow, find my own weekend 'Beagle'. And perhaps I should take up painting, do something purely creative? Oh dear, no. It's not likely I'll be any good at that (unlike your own talented children). How about pottery? Yes, that would be better. Get my hands dirty, shape something new out of this glorious earth.

I need not have given birth in order to create something *meaningful*, even if only to me? Or to love completely and without condition. (To die for that love, if need be.) Because now, having stared at death in its half-blind eye, I am not afraid anymore, Charles.

I am not afraid.

Later

It's him. There he is, yes, it's him. Eloise feels the palpitation, tripping behind her ribs. There, on the corner outside the pub, smoking, talking with some friends, or perhaps some nicotine-bonded strangers. It's only his back, his profile fleetingly, but she knows. Will she walk there? How can she not. It was his face she saw in that moment of choosing to act, to leap for that lighter, to live.

Will he be happy to see her? He had fought for her when she'd ended it. No one had ever had the courage or commitment to fight for her before, or since. But she'd resisted at the time, stone-set (paternity proved). Eventually he had given up. Or perhaps he had thrown himself into his new role for her sake, to prove something?

She approaches, perhaps in his peripheral vision, perhaps not.

'Tom?'

'Jesus. Eloise.'

His eyes widen, and he attempts to smile but then he also takes a step back, away from her.

'Oh my god. Tom. It's so good to see you. Gosh, how are you?'

He looks at her. It hurts. She walks away a few steps from his friends, beckons him to join her with a tilt of her head and the subtlest of smiles. He draws a lungful of smoke, exhales, then stubs out his roll-up, wipes his hands on his sweatshirt and follows. She smiles more openly now.

He speaks first, hands thrust low into his jeans' pockets. 'I saw you on the news. Christ, Gell, are you alright?'

'I'm fine, absolutely fine. Never better really. How are you?'

But this is a stupid question, she realises. He does not *look* good. Pale, thin, tired. He has a purple horseshoe scar over his left eyebrow.

'Yeah... not bad, considering.'

'Considering what?'

'Oh, you know. Had a bit of trouble. Had to get out of London for a while.'

Eloise wants to have heard him wrongly, wants him to rewind, wants all to be well for him. She wants him to be happy, even if this is without her.

'Oh god. I'm so sorry, Tom. What kind of "trouble"?'

'Long story. No big deal, I'm getting it sorted.'

'Oh. OK, that's good.'

'Yeah. Trying to, anyway…'

'And your son? I'm sorry, I don't know his name… What did you choose in the end?'

'Josh.'

'That's nice.'

Tom's eyes grow moist but his soul seems too parched to weep. She begins to worry now.

'Is he OK?'

'As much as he can be. He's in foster care.'

'Oh! I see. Do you mind if I ask why?'

'His mother… We tried, you know, for a few years, but we couldn't make it work. I still saw him every day, picked him up from nursery. But then she started getting into some right nasty shit. Dealing, you know, and not just weed, the heavy stuff. Eventually she bunked up with a proper dodgy geezer, really bad news. Yeah, the lovely fella who gave me this, in fact. Though, he offered worse.'

He indicates his scar, scratches it lightly, half smiles and shrugs.

'Oh no! Oh, Tom.'

'Yeah, I tried to get Josh out of there but his mum wasn't havin' any of it. And then *he* got stuck in. God knows why, neither of them could give a toss about the kid really. Some kind of power thing, I suppose. Respect, as some like to call it.'

Eloise is horrified now, but also confused.

'So, why is Josh in foster care?'

'Well, that bastard eventually went down, didn't he, for some other piece of serious violence. And then she lost it. Got a bit too friendly with the needle. Overdosed.'

'Bloody hell! Is she…'

'Yeah, she's alright. Alive anyway. But then the council stepped in and took my kid. No one knew where I was, see, which obviously was the whole idea up until that point. Mum wanted to have Josh, of course, but she's not well. Emphysema. And it's all my dad can do to look after her.'

'Oh god, I'm so sorry.'

She wants no more pain for him now. She wants to be able to stop frowning, not to feel her stomach clench at each new piece of his news. She wants to see him smile again, to hear that irresistible laugh.

'Yeah, but it's OK. Or it's gonna be. I mean, I get to see him twice a week. But now I'm home I've got to get settled again, get sorted. Then I can get him back. And I'm really getting my shit together, you know. You'd be proud of me, darlin'. I took your advice, you know, I studied art. Well, in a way. I'm a tattoo artist now. Doing alright, making some decent dosh, building up a clientele. So now I just need to move out of my parents' tiny gaff and get my own place again.'

'Great! Of course, yes. Oh, Tom, that's really good. Good for you.'

She can think of nothing else to say.

He moves closer. 'I think about you every day, you know. Apart from getting Josh back it's what keeps me going, remembering you. Thinking about what's possible... about everything it's possible to feel. And to do.'

Her pulse responds. 'Really? That's good. That's really good to hear, Tom.'

She needs to change the subject while she takes this in.

'So, how is Josh? How's he coping with everything? What is he now, seven?'

'Yeah, he's doing alright considering. He's a good kid. You'd like him. Bright, sweet. Loves his music.'

'Oh, Tom. I'm so sorry that all this has happened to you. To Josh.'

'Yeah, it's all a bit shit. All fucked up. But I'm working on it, and we'll be alright.'

She still doesn't know what to say. She wants to tell him that she thinks about him too, all the time, but she can't. So she reaches out to touch his face. He bends into it.

She wants to hold him but doesn't know if that would be right. If it would be welcome. She wants it all to be OK, to *make* it OK for him, she wants to go back to that sense of possibility that he talked about, to a love that could be anything it wanted to be. Is any of that still possible? Now?

She cannot know, not yet. But she also cannot stand back from him any longer, so she moves in to hold him.

The holding in return comes slowly, but then feels as though it will never end.

'Don't hurt me again. Please,' he asks. 'I couldn't handle it if you hurt me again.'

She holds him, and hopes that she never will.

*

As she looks into the faces of her own children, she remembers the first time she set eyes on another child. The memory is unsurprising as her offspring are now so like that other child. That wondrous new being first encountered in the tall grass, after the long walk. Now fully grown, now her mate. Her children live within the comfort of his skin, and with his kin. They have the shape of his limbs, his hair, his face, his eyes. Although the colour is her own, so she is told.

But their smiles... their smiles belong to another, to one long gone. So long now since the sacrifice on the mountain that ensured all their survival. She knows that this is where her mother would have gone. And now there comes another sharp pang, the stabbing knowledge that her brave, strong mother has never seen these faces, never seen her own living echo within these fearless little souls, and never will. Not with eyes that belong to the body, anyway. Perhaps in other ways? Yes, perhaps.

Sometimes she imagines that her mother walks besides her, or maybe it is something else, something made of light. She cannot know, but she feels only this, between all things seen and unseen there is no separation.

Acknowledgements

Thanks to the early readers for their input and encouragement: Michael Carroll, Lucy Allen, Robert Morgan, Kate McLaren, Alan Brooke, Melinda Chandler, Helen Robertson and Linda Garry Bretherton.

For listening to some very strange questions and giving some very useful answers: Professor Mark Thomas of University College London.

For invaluable editing, mentoring and expertise: Dr Stephen Carver and The Literary Consultancy, Sadie Mayne, Kate Coe, Ruth Redford, Jill Sawyer, Annabel Wright.

For their professional faith in me: Kwaku Afrifa-Osei, Xander Cansell, John Mitchinson, Unbound.

For solidarity (and free therapy): The Unbound Social Club.

Very special and loving thanks (which can't begin to cover it): Simon Stanley.

In loving memory of: Robert, Marjorie and Simon Bretherton.

A word or two on inspiration and sources: There were so many different sources of inspiration and information for this book, I couldn't begin to list them comprehensively. Some were indispensable mines of expertise, some ignited a chain reaction of ideas and many more stretched the limits of comprehension for a simple storyteller. However, with a broad brush stroke, there were several sources that played a consistent part in my research and motivation and these were (with thanks): The New Scientist; thedarwinproject.ac.uk; and with caveats acknowledged – Wikipedia; the BBC, the Discovery Channel (and any 'body' investing in science education, popular or academic); pretty much anything on TV from Lord Attenborough or Professor Alice Roberts and other translators of nature, genetics, deep ancestry etc.; Maria Popova's Brain Pickings; Dr Jon Lieff's Searching for the Mind – and for its very existence – The Natural History Museum in London. Several spiritual teachers, especially those exploring 'the middle way' also informed certain characters and aspects of the book, but the words of Alan Watts perhaps proved the most resonant. Also of great interest in this aspect of the book was the work of the Science and Non-duality Conference. However, the last word of thanks must naturally go to the great man himself, Mr Charles Darwin, who changed *everything*.

So, should anyone other than the fiction lover in search of a distracting tale be reading this book: To the scientists, I apologise. To the philosophers, I send my humble regrets. To the faithful, forgive me for I am riddled with doubt. *Bone Lines* was written as a meditation on evolution (personal and general) and on the power and possibility of synthesis. It began with a series of *What Ifs* but is offered to any others fascinated by the human condition, or nature and survival, or moved by tales of love, hope, ingenuity and the yearning for meaning. Perhaps it may also resonate with any other 'lost souls' juggling the cerebral imperative of the rational with an emotional pull to the 'spiritual'. Whatever your experience of the book, I thank you for the gift of your precious time.

(If you enjoyed Bone Lines, please be so kind as to share a review or recommendation where you purchased the book, and/or on goodreads.com. It's very straightforward and is a great help to authors. Thanks!)

Patrons

Paul Almond
John Atkinson
Sophie Baylis
Harald Bjerke
Mark Bretherton
Holly Bretherton
Keith Brodie
Elaine Chambers
Linda Clayton
John Comerford
Virginia Fassnidge
Miranda Gold
Jackie Griffin-Lea
Catherine Hills
Johari Ismail
Dan Kieran
Sarah Lambert
Joanna Mayers
Katie Mccrum
Paul McDowell
Daisy McEachen-Bramwell
Nadia Mladenova
Carlo Navato
Christopher Neophytou
Mark O'Neill
Annemarie Planck
Vanessa Playford
Justin Pollard
Sandra Sandra Burgess
Larry Tranquillian
Shani Zion

Book 2 in The Children of Sarah series

'Eloise.'

'Darius?' she whispered, 'what is it, why on earth are you calling at this hour?'

She might not have responded to the humming vibration at her bedside, had she not seen his name light up. And if he was addressing her as 'Eloise', it must be serious.

'Is something wrong?'

'Oh no. No, my love. Something is very, very right.'

She was wide awake now. Sitting up, reaching for her glasses, though she was not sure why.

'Hold on.'

Eloise did not want to waken the sleeping soul that now shared her room. She went down to the kitchen and without turning on the light, picked up the glass of wine by the sink that she hadn't had the time to finish. (There were other more compelling distractions in her life these days.)

'What is it, Darius? Where are you?'

'We've found something.'

'What, where?'

'In what's left of the glacier.'

'What?'

'A claw, LoLo. And not just any claw. A *huge* claw. A claw that we really don't think should be there at all. Not by itself, not naturally.'

Eloise drained the Rioja, right down to the sediment. 'Do you think it has something to do with her?'

'We won't know until we age it, but there's more. It has markings, LoLo. It's been *carved*.'

'Christ.'

'Exactly.'